THE STUFF OF MALICE

THE STUFF OF MALICE

AN OLD STUFF MYSTERY

KATHLEEN MARPLE KALB

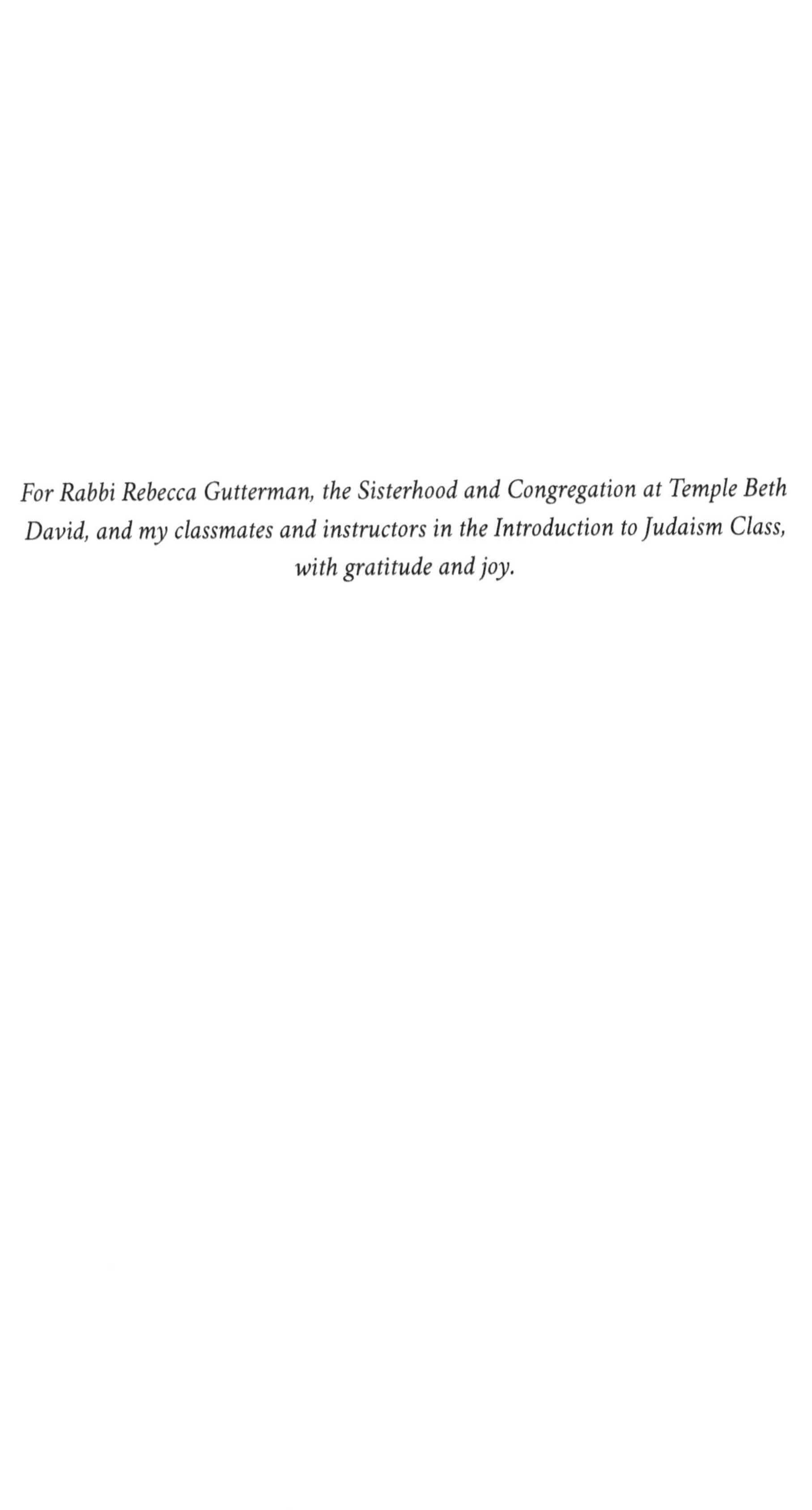

For Rabbi Rebecca Gutterman, the Sisterhood and Congregation at Temple Beth David, and my classmates and instructors in the Introduction to Judaism Class, with gratitude and joy.

Praise for The Stuff of Malice

"A Fun, History-laden Whodunit That Will Blow You Away!

If you're looking for a cozy mystery that will keep you on the edge of your seat, look no further than The Stuff of Mayhem. Book Two in the Old Stuff Mystery series is a real blast, and I mean that quite literally! The explosive death of Rowland Stark sets off a chain of events that will have you turning pages faster than a cannonball.

Historian Christian Shaw and Assistant State's Attorney Joe Poli team up to unravel secrets in the charming New England town of Unity. Their investigation is full of twists, and antique artifacts add to the intrigue. Fans of modern mysteries with a historical twist will undoubtedly enjoy this fun, fresh cozy and be left eager for the next installment!"—**Sarah E. Burr**, award-winning author of the Trending Topic Mysteries and other cozies

"Christian Shaw returns in *The Stuff of Mayhem* and this second outing is every bit as good as the first.

Kathleen Maple Kalb excels in drawing modern small town life, filled with characters who feel authentic, while combining realistic problems and issues with warmth and optimism. It's impossible not to feel invested in Christian, her son Henry and her friends. This series also combines two of my favourite things—history and mystery! Christian's position in the local historical society leads to intriguing situations. In The Stuff of Mayhem, a historical reenactment on July 4th backfires spectacularly when a local is killed, but that's just the start of the chaos. Against a backdrop of seemingly ordinary life, the mystery unfurls at a satisfying rate. Christian is helped by the lovely lawyer, Joe and her perceptive son Henry who is—like my own child—a type 1 diabetic. It's great to see this condition represented and most importantly handled so accurately.

If you like small town life, we'll crafted mysteries and great characters *The Stuff of Mayhem* should be your next read!"—**Nina Hayes**, author of The Old Bat Chronicles, and the Ellie & Lexi Mystery Series

Praise for the Old Stuff Series

From **Aunt Agatha's Mysteries (Robin Agnew):**

"…pretty much top of the heap. Her voice, pacing and storytelling ability are just terrific. I can't recommend her books more highly."

From **T.G. Wolff's** Toe Tag Podcast:

"*The Stuff of Murder* is for you if you like cozy mysteries, charming characters, and everyday old stuff."

Sarah E. Burr, author of the Trending Topic Mysteries, Book Blogger Mysteries, & Glenmyre Whim Mysteries:

"*The Stuff of Murder* checks all the boxes of a great, modern murder mystery. A strong lead with a diverse supporting cast, Kalb's latest is a charming read for mystery fans."

Geraldine Byrne, author of the Irish Music Shop and Caroline Jordan Mystery Series:

"This is a thoroughly enjoyable modern murder mystery with a likeable, diverse cast of characters and a town that has a charming sense of community. An additional plus for me was the addition of a young character with Type 1 diabetes, and as the parent of a 9 yr old with the same, the descriptions of diagnosis and general life with T1D were accurate, positive and at one point, brought tears to my eyes."

Chapter One

Race to the Date

The first surprise of my big date night with Joe was a good one.

The second, not so much.

Murder has a way of ruining the evening.

For weeks, we'd been hoping to sneak off for a real boy-girl night out, with a nice dinner and private couple time. That Friday, with his daughter at band camp, and my son at a family sleepover, was our last chance of the summer.

And we grabbed it.

Well, we intended to, anyhow.

The way it often is when you have big plans for the weekend, the day was one hurdle after another. None especially serious, all annoying.

My day at the Unity, Connecticut Historical Society began with a flurry of texts and emails from people in the *Shakespeare on the Green* production, all convinced they couldn't survive because their coffee machine was malfunctioning. I texted the festival head and volunteered the coffee setup in the Society workroom, then walked over from dropping my son at the day camp bus, to find two docents having a hissy argument. The argument was loud enough to scare the Society cat into hiding, not to mention remarkably stupid: which was worse, an ancestor who was an indentured servant or one who was hanged for witchcraft? The eighty-year-olds were about to start throwing things when I stepped between them with a reminder that it wasn't a competition, and the whole point of history is to do better.

"Right you are, Christian!"

We all turned at the sound of a musical Irish accent.

"Niamh!"

Three of us, three different pronunciations of her lovely name. Niamh ("Neeve" is pretty close) Stanley was used to it by now, having come over during the Celtic Tiger era, starting her own boutique IT business, and marrying an insurance exec. She'd long since traded the cheating exec for a kind and fun middle school teacher, but the business was still ticking along, putting her three charming Black Irish kids through college. A few times a month, she spent an hour or so at the Society working on our computers and updating the website, and I wrote it up so she could take a nice tax deduction.

"I didn't know this was your day," I said. "I'm just getting ready to make fresh coffee."

"Tempting." Niamh had picked up the New Haven County love for Italian dark roast, and we usually enjoyed a cup and a good conversation about Irish folklore after the tech work was done. "But I've a nine o'clock. Just dropping off that cable you needed."

"To download pics from the digital cam?"

"Yes. You can email them, of course, but hooking it up will allow you to send all the images at one throw. Much better."

"Thanks." I took the cable. "I'm going to start putting pics of interesting objects on the website. When I get around to it."

"Terrific idea." Niamh gave me a canny glance. "I'll talk you through it if you have any problem setting up the pages."

"Thanks much."

"Of course." She turned to the spatting docents, who were still glaring at each other like senior division reality stars. "Come along, ladies. If we Irish can mend fences with the damned English, how can anyone refuse to make peace?"

A very valid point, I thought. Not to mention one of the very few times I'd heard Niamh refer to the Troubles.

The ladies had just started a grudging make-up when I heard a melodramatic cry from the entry hall.

"Dr. Shaw! Dr. Shaw! Where are you?"

Niamh gave me a puzzled glance.

"It's the director of the Shakespeare on the Green production. He must be seen to be believed."

She rolled her eyes. "I have to get to work. I suspect I'm well out of it."

"Oh, you are."

Niamh was ahead of me, and I saw her take one look at my latest visitor and freeze for an instant. I didn't blame her. Sir Jeremy Hightower looked like he'd been dropped in from a *Downton Abbey* knockoff, in his bespoke white linen three-piece suit, lavender oxford and heliotrope tie, with matching pocket square. One too-perfectly manicured hand sported a signet ring and clutched a large antique book bound in green leather.

"May I help you?" he asked her in his crystalline aristocratic accent.

"Not even a little," Niamh replied in a cool and scathing tone as she swept past him. The damned English, maybe?

He didn't even notice.

Sir Jeremy, whose self-conscious importance and elegant demeanor made King Charles III look like Paulie Walnuts, had been finding it difficult to deal with the lesser orders—meaning everyone who was not him—since he arrived in Unity earlier in the week.

He had spent most of his time hunched over that big volume, an antique prompt book, like Gollum with his Precious, occasionally raising his head to snap at an actor or demand yet another change in blocking, costume, or scenery. As far as I could tell, he was obsessed with the text, dragging the heavy book everywhere he went and pointing to this line or that as evidence everyone except him was doing it wrong.

Normally, I would have brushed him off with a comment better suited to the Jersey Pike than the Court of Saint James, but he was my client, and I had to be at least civil to him. In addition to running the Historical Society, I have a nice little side hustle consulting on period costumes, housewares, and lifestyle for film, television, and theatre projects.

A friend at the Shoreline Shakespeare Festival had sent Sir Jeremy to me, and I had the dubious honor of ensuring the verisimilitude of his 1848-dress production of *Much Ado About Nothing* on the Green. So far, the play title was proving remarkably appropriate.

Sir Jeremy stroked his salt-and-pepper Van Dyke beard, emphasizing the chunky old-gold signet ring, and tapped his cream-and-tan wing-tip brogue in annoyance as he looked up at me, my height clearly an issue for him. "Dr. Shaw! Have we not discussed Hero's sleeves?"

"We have, Sir Jeremy," I replied. At least four times by my count. I took a breath and reminded myself not to fall into the stereotype of the hot-tempered Celtic redhead. And that it would not be good for business to pick him up and break him like a twig, which might also have been a viable option.

"Then why did she appear in puffed sleeves at our costume trial last night?"

"They are period-appropriate low leg-o'mutton sleeves," I replied, as I had when the costumer replaced the equally period-appropriate double puffs because they looked, according to our fearless leader, 'too Renaissance.' Pronounced, of course, with affected, slippery enunciation: *run-ess-annnnce*.

"They may be period-appropriate, Professor, but they are not appropriate to the message. Have we not discussed this in several emails?"

"Yes."

"And why, pray tell?"

"Because we do not want it to be mistaken for an ordinary Shakespearean production rather than a new critique of attitudes on sexuality," I replied, spooling off the same verbiage he'd used in five different emails.

"Precisely, Professor. I knew we could come to a meeting of the minds."

Much more of this, and it would be a meeting between fist and face. Not a productive thought.

My client, swept away by the wonder of his own genius, continued: "Did women not wear sleeves with fullness closer to the wrist at the time?"

"Yes." I tried not to sigh. "You are correct. Bishop sleeves were also seen."

And actually looked far more like what we think of as Renaissance dress, I thought, but didn't say.

"Good. Then I shall tell the costumer to change that misbegotten mutton to bishop sleeves. Do please bring her by a fashion plate later."

I'll bring her by a drink. "Of course."

Sir Jeremy brightened, giving me an elfin smile. "Many thanks, Professor. It is such a relief to work with someone intelligent enough to understand my vision. It is beyond me why I keep bringing back that dim costumer and her worthless ham of a husband."

"Alannah and Sean are highly skilled professionals," I said. Even if costumer Alannah hadn't been a friend, the pretentious jerk didn't need to run down the hardworking journeymen who were just trying to execute his ever-changing vision.

Vision, my foot. Or some other nether part.

"You are far too kind," Sir Jeremy said, scowling for a moment, but then choosing diplomacy. "In any case, I appreciate your attention to the matter."

"My pleasure." The polite reply came automatically to my lips. If it occurred to me that pleasure and Sir Jeremy Hightower did not belong in the same sentence, I had no need to share the thought. "May I offer you some coffee?"

"No, thank you, my dear. I cannot abide the liquid tar you people drink in the morning. I shall be enjoying my breakfast cup of Darjeeling in my trailer."

Of course, he shall.

Sir Jeremy hefted his book and sailed off for the Green, crossing paths with a few tired theatre types. I directed them to the back workroom, where we had a good-sized coffee urn for board meetings and other events. We were going to be up to our eyeballs in walking zombies all day, thanks to the coffee machine issue. I reminded myself to put out an extra bag of our perfectly good dark-roast everyday coffee, so nobody came looking for the really terrific imported Italian stuff I keep in my office.

Good thing I managed to settle that before the real onslaught.

A dozen rising tenth graders from the town's Summer Enrichment class descended upon us at midday for their "Real Life in the Regency" session, a highlight of their course on Jane Austen and the Brontë sisters. At least, they kept me so busy explaining slippers and reticules and stays and bonnets—not to mention fielding inappropriate comments about *Bridgerton*—that I hardly had time to think until early afternoon.

After the kids finally left, I found a few minutes to run over to the Green and speak to the costumer. Alannah Yard, whom I knew from earlier productions, called Sir Jeremy a few creative names that sounded far more elegant in her New Zealand accent, and picked up her seam ripper as if it were a weapon.

"I'm sorry," I said, holding out the bishop sleeve fashion plates I'd printed. "You may be able to get the effect by putting the earlier ones back on."

She pushed back a curl of her colorful mermaid hair and gave me a cagey smile. "Exactly what I plan to do, Christian. I know how Sir Jeremy works. I never make anything without a plan for alterations."

"Smart."

"Just good survival skills." As she placed the offending bodice on her worktable, she shot me a grin. "Don't worry, it won't get in the way of your evening."

I stared at her, blushing and guilty. "What have you-"

"I'm sorry." Alannah's blush matched mine. "I didn't mean to presume about your religion…I saw you talking to the rabbi the other day and…"

"Oh, jeez." I sighed. "Yes, I'm taking my son to temple. I'm sorry."

"Sorry? I'm the one who offended you, Christian."

"No, you didn't." I leaned in and dropped my voice. "I have a date tonight, and I thought you'd found out somehow."

Alannah beamed. "Well, that's wonderful! That big blond fellow I saw at the Society the other day?"

"None other."

"Good for you. Enjoy your night, and don't give a thought to the Lord High Executioner and his damned sleeves."

"Do my best."

We shared a smile, the way you do when you work through an embarrassing moment with someone and end up with a closer connection, and I scooted out of the tent.

On the way back to the Society, I stuck my nose in the main theatre area and took a moment to watch the scene work, enjoying Shakespeare's timeless words and the energy of the mostly young cast.

In the maelstrom, I didn't check my phone or see Joe's text about running late because of an unusually long motion hearing until I was walking to pick up my son, Henry, at the summer camp bus. Probably gave me more time to pretty up…but it also gave me more time to vex.

Fortunately, it was also "Tot Shabbat" night at Temple Beth Shalom, the monthly early evening service for families with young kids. At eight, Henry was just about aging out, but he enjoyed the informal atmosphere, and on this particular evening, it was a convenient way to get our weekly infusion of Jewish culture and spirituality. The really good news was, Henry was far too excited about the grandbabies' sleepover at Garrett and Ed's to notice my vexing…or he wrote it off to the usual maternal churn about his Type-1 Diabetes, which sometimes troubles me far more than it does him.

Henry also didn't notice the grin and wink I got from Rabbi Dina Aaron, or the "You Go, Girl!" text from my other good friend, EMT Captain Tiffany Medina, as we walked to the sleepover. A few blocks from the temple, my former history department chair from Shoreline State, Garrett, and his husband, retired state trooper Ed Kenney, were just moving into serious outdoor cookery when Henry and I stepped into their garden.

I like to describe Garrett and Ed as the dads I should have had. Garrett, who'd worked his way out of Akron, Ohio, as a bookish misfit back in the day, took me under his wing when I arrived, having worked my way out of Mars, Pennsylvania, as a bookish misfit, too. We were already found family by the time Ed, recently retired from the Staties and ready to live his truth, took the job as security director at Shoreline State. I'm not a meddler, but I admit I shoved Garrett out the door for his first date with Ed. The next summer, there was a big joyful wedding. Ed simply added me and Henry to the brood of kids and grandbabies from his long-ago first marriage to a woman, and that was that.

Henry dashed right off to join the pack of Ed's grandkids playing hide and seek in the hedges. Ed sent me a smile from behind the grill as he tossed a bit of sausage to their big red mutt, Norm. It was as much of an endorsement as I'd get, considering his skepticism over whether Joe, an Assistant State's Attorney, could give Henry and me the kind of time we deserve.

A more enthusiastic Garrett gave me a hug and a playful shove out the gate. "Get outta here and have a good time."

"That's the plan."

Later, I would remember the Jewish saying: "We plan, God laughs."

Chapter Two

Never Mind the Reservations

A short, but brisk, walk later at the snug converted carriage house Henry and I share, I switched my temple outfit of twinset and long floral skirt for a coral-colored fit-and-flare dress with a skirt that barely hit midthigh, added some saucy but light perfume from a beauty-box sample, and did one last check of the overnight bag, peach satin underthings, and personal landscaping.

Yep. If you hadn't figured it out yet, it was *that* big date night.

Joe and I had been together since May, but thanks to a summer of murder, mayhem, competing work schedules, and medium-to-large kids, we hadn't been able to get a real night to ourselves. And honestly, neither of us had been in a rush.

But now, having exchanged I-love-you's and introduced our kids, there was only one big bridge left, and it was more than time. Even for a wary widow and a gun-shy divorcé.

Being us, Joe and I had planned it to death, with that dinner reservation at Due Fiori, the most romantic restaurant in New Haven County, a good bottle of prosecco waiting back at his house, and a big box of farmstand berries to go with the breakfast waffles. Whenever we got to them.

Of course, there'd been plenty of nervous chats with my girlfriends, and a crash *Cosmopolitan* reading course. I really hoped Joe wasn't into things that required diagrams.

I didn't think they'd had diagrams when my late husband and I had *that date*.

Probably better not to think too much about Frank tonight.

Probably better not to think, period.

Tough for me. Overthinking isn't just my job, it's my life.

The sun was just starting to fade when I rang Joe's doorbell.

"*Dottore.*"

His nickname for me, the Italian for my PhD, was adorable anytime, but there was something extra in his silky tone that night. I walked into the high-ceilinged, very beige entryway of his house, decorated by his ex—I'm not the only one with history. I stood there for a moment, in the warm light pouring in through the big front window.

On any day, Joe is worth a second glance, an inch or so taller than me, strong but not chunky, with Northern-Italian blond hair and brown eyes, and a smile that warms me down to my toes. On this day, with everything in play, he was worth far more than a glance.

"Good to see you," I said, leaning in for a greeting kiss.

"Good to be seen." He pulled back to look at me. "Oh, I like that dress. And what's under it."

"You don't know the half of it," I replied.

"I like the sound of that," he said.

"You're looking pretty fine yourself, Counselor," I said, taking an appreciative look at his khakis and navy oxford, with collar open and sleeves rolled up.

"Do my best."

A small scrabbling sound came from the floor, and a minuscule black mop trundled over to us. Cannoli, his tiny dog, has decided to tolerate me, even though I smell like Cookie, our large, scary black tuxedo cat, who likes to menace him when Joe brings the dog to our house.

I held out my hand and gave Cannoli a pet. Joe did the same, then scooped him up and moved him into the living room, where the big TV was on.

"I put it on his favorite channel," Joe said. "He'll be happy for a while."

"Nice." I chuckled at the sight of the little dog eagerly staring at a wildlife documentary. Cookie likes the same channel…they actually do have something in common.

"Now, something for you."

"Oh?"

Joe turned to the small table under the wall mirror.

Flowers would not have surprised me. But he wasn't holding a bouquet. He had two small votive candles.

"I wasn't sure if you'd get a chance to light candles at sunset, and I know that's important to you."

"Oh, my." My eyes were suddenly damp. I've never had the time to go through a formal Jewish conversion, but Henry and I light candles every Friday night, and Joe had been there a few times when we did. "We went to the early service, and of course I wouldn't leave them burning in an empty house."

"So you can light them now." He set the candles down on a metal tray on the table under the foyer mirror.

"Yes. And it's sunset. Perfect."

"Here." He handed me a small box of matches, and our fingers touched.

We hardly needed the matches.

"Thanks." I struck the flame and began the short candle blessing Dina had taught me. Joe watched as I lit the candles, finished the blessing, and shielded my eyes for a moment, as was traditional.

When I brought my hands down, Joe was watching me intensely.

"Wow."

"It's a moment, isn't it?" I asked.

"Yeah." He took my hand. "I've been reading up on Jewish tradition a little."

"Have you, now?"

"I've read that it's considered a blessing to enjoy all kinds of physical pleasures on the Sabbath."

"A good dinner, of course."

"And other things." His fingers twined with mine, and he pulled me closer.

"That too," I said. "With your partner in a committed and loving consensual relationship."

Dina had given me a Reform Jewish version of the ethical line when I was vexing earlier in the week.

"That's me, right?" Wicked little smile.

"Oh, yeah."

Our eyes held.

"How much do you care about that reservation?" I asked.

"How hungry are you?"

"Not that kind of hungry."

"Me either."

He smiled and pulled me close, then scooped me up, romance-novel hero style.

"Wow," I said. "This is new."

"Yeah?"

"I'm six feet tall. Never have I ever."

"Well, we'll have to do something about that…"

Let's just say being carried up the stairs for a night of passion is everything it's cracked up to be.

And so is Joe.

Quite a while later, we were spooned together in his moonlit bedroom, all the big questions answered to mutual satisfaction.

"*Full nakedness, all joys are due to thee…*" Joe said, nuzzling my neck.

"Ah, the good Reverend has arrived," I said. Joe has a fondness for John Donne and can turn up an appropriate line for just about any occasion.

Of course, Donne had a lot to say about moments like this.

"None other." He kissed my shoulder. "I've been saving that one."

"Bet you have." I turned to meet his gaze in the half-light, saw his dark eyes sparkling. Oh, this was good. All the warmth and the feels…

And suddenly I was crying.

"Ah, *cara*, it's okay." Joe pulled me to him without hesitation, rubbing my back and reassuring me. This wasn't hot, it was warm and loving.

Safe.

I burrowed into his embrace, trying to get myself back under control.

After a while, he asked, "Want to tell me about it?"

"I guess just everything. You know, I haven't—since—"

"Your husband."

"Yeah." Pretty much the last person I wanted to talk about at this moment. I wasn't sure it felt like cheating, but it definitely felt like something I shouldn't have enjoyed nearly as much as I just had.

Joe stroked my hair. "I bet I don't have to tell you this is normal."

"Nope. Dina warned me." I hate when she's right. She'd also told me if it happened, to acknowledge it and then just keep moving forward. *The less you look back at that point, the better,* she'd said.

Joe was silent for a moment. Then, "So did my pal."

"What?"

"I have a social worker buddy who does reports for the court. Just asked him if there was anything I needed to keep in mind with us getting serious."

"Wow."

Joe took my hand and laced fingers with mine. "Well, I love you, silly. I don't want to screw this up."

"And I love you." I leaned in and kissed him lightly. "You're pretty wonderful."

He grinned.

"Did your friend tell you that I might climb you like a jungle gym?"

"Why?"

"There's nothing hotter than a man who understands your needs."

"Oh, I'm right here for your needs, *cara.*" Joe kissed me back, and the chemistry between us took over again. I probably wouldn't tell Dina the details, but just then, I was very thankful for good old-fashioned lust.

The evening would have continued according to plan—if his phone hadn't rung.

It was unbelievably loud.

We startled and broke apart, and he grabbed for it, mumbling an apology.

None needed—grownups with kids and jobs can't be completely incommunicado, no matter how important the night.

"What the-" he snapped as he hit the button.

"Poli."

Chief State's Attorney Amelia Porter has a voice that carries.

"Oh, sorry, Boss." Joe sat up and pushed his hair back with his free hand, immediately serious.

"Sorry to bother you, Poli. I know you had a big date."

"All due respect, Boss, somebody better be dead."

An ominous pause.

And then she replied, her cool, deep voice full of gravity, "All due respect, Poli, somebody is."

Chapter Three

Death on the Green

As Joe scrambled back into khakis and oxford—the minimum for a prosecutor on duty—still talking to State's Attorney Porter, my phone went off, too.

My blood went cold when I saw the caller ID: Unity Police Department. I picked up. "Christian Shaw."

"It's Sergeant Ellis from the desk," a cool female voice said. "I'm sorry to bother you, Dr. Shaw, but you're the designated call for the Historical Society."

"No bother," I replied, relief washing over me. Probably the damn alarm again. Happened a few times a year, and why not tonight?

"Well, that's good, because you probably need to come down to the Green. There's been a homicide, and the crews need the private drive near the Society."

"Homicide? That's awful."

Awful…and probably not just an unfortunate coincidence.

"Sure is." A small note of regret crept into her cool, professional voice before she quickly returned to the task at hand. "We really need to make some space for all the trucks."

. "I'll be there as soon as I can." Ellis was right. If they had a major crime, they would need the drive, which went around the back of the building. It was chained off at night, so the Town Hall folks across the street didn't take our staff parking spaces.

"I'm sorry, Doc," she said. "Lousy start to the weekend."

On the other side of the room, Joe was tucking in his shirt and stepping into his shoes.

"No kidding." If we'd been in person, the sergeant and I would have shared a rueful smile. "Thank you for calling. I'm on my way."

"Thank you, Dr. Shaw."

I hit end.

"I've got to get dressed and get down to the Green," I said. "Do you remember what I did with my bag?"

"I think it's downstairs." Sheepish grin. "I think your dress ended up in the hall."

I climbed to the floor, grabbing the beige chenille throw from the end of the bed, then realized there wasn't much point to modesty. "Well, you've seen it all already."

"Seen, appreciated, and hope to see again soon." Sudden puzzled stare. "The Green?"

"The Green. Is your homicide there?"

"Yep. How—"

"Police desk just called me because the crews need our private drive for a homicide."

"I'm guessing no coincidence." His jaw tightened.

"I'm guessing the same."

"Okay." He checked his pockets, came up with a key fob. "I'll drive you."

"Do you know…" I started, and trailed off because I didn't want to ask for anything confidential.

"I don't, *cara*. You know what I know. Homicide on the Green, called in about half-an-hour ago."

"Guess we'd better just get going."

"You probably want to find your dress first."

"And blow out the candles, too, darn it."

Ten minutes later—it would have been five, but Cannoli had somehow taken possession of my right ballet flat and had to be bribed to give it up—Joe pulled up to the Green in his spiffy silver sedan. A relic from his earlier life in a white-shoe firm, with the vanity plate TRUBILL, as in an indictment, speaking to his current line of work, it was an announcement of his presence.

He parked just inside the little road circling the Green and turned to me. "Off to work, *cara*."

"Maybe at least breakfast later," I said, giving his hand a quick squeeze.

"Keep a good thought." He went for a kiss on the cheek and got my ear. Which was okay too. "Love you."

"Love *you*."

Out in the humid night, the Green was ablaze with the light from five or six police cruisers: Unity's goofy mini electric one, joined by SUVs from two larger neighboring towns, and the State Police Crime Scene Unit truck. An ambulance and a fire rig were also there, racks blazing.

Since Tiffany, the EMT captain, was off tonight, I didn't look too closely at the emergency crew. I didn't see the Medical Examiner's van.

Near the State Police truck, Unity Police Chief Tony DiBiasi was surrounded by several troopers, all significantly younger and taller. Joe moved toward them.

I turned for the Society drive, where the town's third officer, rookie Jaden Colby, was standing guard. Colby, who's only barely old enough to legally carry a service weapon, looks like Raggedy Andy and has a sweet personality to match.

"Hi, Dr. Shaw!" He greeted me with a big, bright smile, then quickly pulled back to a serious face. "Um, thanks for coming out tonight."

"Of course." I pulled the big ring of keys out of my purse. "This is an easy fix. Do you know what happened?"

"Well, the deceased was found over there, near the trailer for the play."

"Do you know who he was?" Seemed to be the obvious first question.

"That weird British dude from the show."

"Oh, no!" Even Sir Jeremy didn't deserve to end up dead on the Green. Though there were probably plenty of people who'd have wanted him to.

Colby gave me a grim nod.

"Do they know what happened to him?" I asked.

"Looks like stabbed in the neck. Maybe bashed in the head too."

"Ow," I said. I'd like to say I was surprised Sir Jeremy sparked such fury, but I'd just spent three weeks working with him.

Suddenly, I was very glad I had an ironclad alibi.

Can't beat being in bed with the prosecutor. The thought made me blush, distracting me for a moment.

"Um, Dr. Shaw?"

"Sorry, Colby. It's shocking."

"Definitely." His soft face went bewildered for a second, then returned to cop-serious. "Some guy found him about an hour after the temple let out."

"The temple?" I asked. Temple Beth Shalom, formerly the Congregational Church, dominates the Green, a beautiful white-columned presence with a soaring steeple. In this day and age, unfortunately, it's also a giant target.

"Yeah." Colby tried for a reassuring tone and almost managed it. "It's near the theatre setup and doesn't look like it has anything to do with the temple. Nobody wants to bother Rabbi Aaron until after service tomorrow if we can avoid it."

"That's kind," I said, impressed at his understanding of the basics of Jewish sabbath observance.

"It's Chief DiBiasi. He had me talk to Rabbi Aaron, so I understood about the temple and all. She's pretty cool."

"That she is," I agreed, turning for the door. "I'm going to go in and start a pot of coffee."

"Really?" His smooth, open face lit up. "I could really use some—I'm working a double."

"You got it." I headed into the building.

The society cat, Empress Frederick, gave me a contemptuous glare as she passed through the foyer on her way to the front window. A tiny, regal white kitty with bright blue eyes, she ruled the Society with the imperious charm of her namesake, Queen Victoria's oldest daughter, who happily reminded all comers that she was both an Empress *and* the Princess Royal. Unlike the late Empress, though, our Imperial Majesty had been re-homed and was a very happy fit with us, since she had far more control over when and how to engage with her human staff than she would in a family setting.

The Empress took no further interest in my invasion of her privacy and hopped up into the front window to enjoy all the interesting lights and movement. This might be tragic for humans, but it was good entertainment for the kitty.

In the time it took to start the coffee and rummage out an unopened package of biscotti left from this week's board meeting, the M.E.'s van arrived. Colby was standing guard over it when I walked outside and handed him a paper cup and a cookie.

"Aw, thanks, Dr. Shaw."

As he sipped and crunched, I looked over at the Crime Scene van, where Joe was now in animated conversation with DiBiasi, the troopers, and a tall Black man. Joe waved.

I stared back. Who, me?

"Dr. Shaw!" Joe called.

Yes, me.

It took me only a moment to cross the gravel road and a few yards of grass.

Joe gave me a quick, twinkly glance, which DiBiasi clocked, as did the tall man.

"Chief DiBiasi," Joe said, "I think Dr. Shaw might be able to help you with the questions about why Mr. Jeffries was here. She's involved with the workings of the temple."

"That's right." The chief snapped back to game face as he turned to me. "Do you know if the temple has called in an architect?"

"Well, yeah," I said. "It was time for a ten-year structural inspection. I'm not on the board, but I gave Rabbi Aaron a couple of names of firms that deal with historical buildings. I think she settled on Norton Jeff-"

"Norton Jeffries?" DiBiasi asked, turning to the Black man. "Well, Mr. Jeffries, I'm sorry for the misunderstanding."

A small, entirely appropriate, pause before the architect took DiBiasi's outstretched hand. "Thanks."

After the handshake, Joe stepped in. "Easton, I'd like you to meet Dr. Christian Shaw."

The slight stumble on my first name made me smile. Joe, like most New Haven County natives, swallows his T's, so unless he tries very hard, it comes out "Chris'shun."

Joe continued, "Dr. Shaw, Easton Jeffries."

Our turn to shake, as I appreciated my new acquaintance's good looks and friendly smile. "Nice to meet you."

"Likewise. Joe and I went to UConn and Yale together." Easton shot an eyebrow toward the scene. "Too bad to meet you under these circumstances."

"Absolutely."

As Easton pulled back, his hand went to his midsection in a gesture I recognized.

"Are your numbers okay?" I asked.

Easton blinked. "Oh, that's right…your son has Type-1."

"Yep. I've got some appropriate snacks over at my office if you need them."

"I think I'll take you up on that."

"Better to catch it now," I said, motioning toward the Society building.

"Good idea, Dr. Shaw," DiBiasi cut in, nodding to the M.E.'s van, "we're about to get very busy here. I'll take good care of A.S.A. Poli."

"Thank you, Chief," I said. "There's coffee and cookies at the Society for anyone who needs it."

"We may take you up on that later," DiBiasi said.

"See you later, Joe. Nice to meet you, Chief." Easton nodded to both, adding only a tiny bit of edge onto DiBiasi's title. Just letting him know.

Entirely fair, considering.

As I turned to go, Joe caught my eye for an instant. All we needed.

Chapter Four

Nighttime Snacks

As Easton and I approached the Society, I could see Colby talking to a tall, spare older man with a big dog, whose coat shone reddish in the lone streetlight.

Oh, boy.

Things were about to get really interesting.

"...so the best thing you can do on a night like this, son, is keep your eyes open and learn all that you can."

Colby nodded eagerly. "I will, Sergeant Kenney."

"Hello, Ed," I said. "Norm."

The dog, used to people shouting his name (yes, it's a *Cheers* reference!), turned before his owner, with that open, canine joy at seeing a friend. Not so Ed. Despite the pleasure he took in schooling the next generation of law enforcement, he looked significantly less happy than he had behind the grill a few hours ago. "Some big night out for you two."

"Yeah, well," I replied with a shrug.

The incident could only add to Ed's serious and frequently stated concern about my involvement with Joe. While he had no question about Joe being a standup guy, he had plenty of doubts about whether a prosecutor could give Henry and me the appropriate level of time and care.

Normally, of course, I'd be thrilled to see Ed. He and Garrett are two of the most important people in my life, not to mention just being fun to have around. But I sure didn't need Ed to see Joe working a scene when the two of us were supposed to be enjoying a romantic dinner at Due Fiori.

Especially when Henry was spending the night at that big grandkids' sleepover at Garrett and Ed's house.

Somebody was going to have some explaining to do. And that somebody, at least for now, was me.

The social niceties might buy me some time.

"Well, first," I began, "Retired Trooper Sergeant Ed Kenney, I'd like you to meet Joe's college friend, Easton Jeffries. He's an architect who's working with Temple Beth Shalom."

"Ed. And this fella is Norm."

The big dog raised his head again at the mention of his name.

Easton Jeffries shook Ed's offered hand and beamed down at Norm. "What a great dog."

"We think so."

"Norm—as in *Cheers*?"

Ed grinned. Hallelujah for dog people. "You bet. He loves to meet new people. Just let him sniff your hand."

"My daughter's golden is the same. I swear she'd stop a burglar by loving him to death."

Small, not inappropriate chuckle. Even Colby smiled.

As the laugh faded, though, Ed's natural cop sense kicked in, and he looked closely at Easton. "So how does an architect end up in the middle of this mess?"

"I found the guy." Easton's easygoing calm wavered a bit. "I have no idea what happened to him…I was just taking a look around the building when I almost tripped over him."

"No fun," Ed said.

"Not even a little."

"What's up, folks?"

Add one more to the party. EMT Captain Tiffany Medina, my other really close girlfriend, walked up to us, tackle box in hand, game face matching her uniform. Her bright lipstick was the only sign she'd also been enjoying a date night before the call—I recognized the long-wear matte because I was wearing the same brand in a different shade. On her advice, of course.

"Hey," I said. "Your date night scuttled, too?"

"Jorge and I had just poured the wine when the phone rang." A sigh. "There'll be other nights."

"What I'm telling myself," I said.

Ed looked from Tiffany to me, and his scowl deepened as he patted Norm.

"So?" Tiffany asked.

I gave her a significant little glance. It was enough—she returned with a carefully small grin.

"Well," she continued, "Chief DiBiasi said there was a diabetic who might need a look."

"That's me," Easton said. "I'm okay. Dr. Shaw's getting me a snack, and I'll be fine."

"Sounds good. You need me to come in with you and check you?"

"I'm really okay." His voice came out a little too sharp.

"Let her do her job," Ed said in the command tone that ended the debate.

"You're right, Sergeant Kenney," Easton replied.

"I'm always right." Ed held my gaze. "Even when I'd rather not be."

I didn't take the bait. "Come in for some coffee, Ed?"

"Nah. Norm and I need to get back. The grandbabies are staying up late, whipping Garrett at Monopoly—he'll sign over the house if I don't stop him."

"Okay." I smiled. When Henry joined forces with Ed's other grandkids, it could get very wild, very fast.

"We'll see you on the original plan," Ed said, with a wry brow flick. "Make sure you get a decent breakfast, at least."

"Sounds good."

Ed leaned in for a half-hug, mindful of crime-scene demeanor, nodded to Tiffany, and walked off with Norm.

I turned to Easton. "You don't look great."

"Honestly, I don't feel that great."

"Bet your numbers are dropping," I said.

Tiffany patted his arm. "Let's get you inside."

Maybe ten minutes later, Easton was enjoying a mug of blue sports drink and an almond-butter granola bar, and Tiffany was sipping half a cup of coffee while she watched him. I poured myself a full cup and joined them.

By mutual unspoken agreement, we made small talk about kids and gardens rather than anything that was happening outside…or the indoor activities earlier in the evening.

When Easton crumpled the granola-bar wrapper, the Empress came bounding out of her window and into the room, clearly hoping for treats.

With Easton and Tiffany settled, I let the Empress lead me down the hall to my office, where I kept a packet of her favorite Savory Salmon Bites. She accepted a few, and a pet, and rewarded me with a trilly little purr.

Less than a minute later, she'd had enough and hopped down to wander off into the darkened regions of the building. Typical Empress.

I'd just rejoined Tiffany and Easton when we heard a perfunctory knock on the back door, and Joe walked into the workroom.

"Numbers back up?" he asked Easton.

"Yeah. They're taking good care of me, and we're talking kids."

"We've decided on a family picnic," I said, pouring Joe a cup from the carafe.

"Maybe next week," Tiffany added. "As long as nobody brings zucchini anything."

"No zucchini." Joe was a little more emphatic than you'd expect, thanks to his deep and mostly inexplicable hatred for the green squash.

"Coffee." I handed him the cup.

"Thanks." He took a sip. "That helps."

Tiffany, Easton, and I waited.

"I think we might want to hold off on the family picnic for a little while," Joe said. "This is going to be a mess."

"Oh?" I asked.

"Well," Joe turned to me. "The victim's the director of the play on the Green…and he was just outside his trailer."

"Hell." I took a sip of my own coffee. "Sir Jeremy. That's too bad."

"In more ways than one." Joe, who'd heard more than a few tales of the director's unreasonable demands, shook his head and then turned to Easton. "And you had to find him."

"It's not like I planned it," Joe's friend reminded him.

"I know." Joe made careful eye contact with Easton. "Don't get me wrong, nobody suspects you, Ease, but Major Crimes is going to be grilling you for every little detail that might help—and the local media will want anything they can get."

"Not just the *local* media," I said.

"That's right." Tiffany nodded. "My sister—you know the one who watches all the entertainment shows—asked me about him. Apparently, there was some gossip item about him leaving London after an epic and public breakup."

"Public breakup?" Joe asked.

"It's on one of the gossip sites—some kind of hissy drink-throwing extravaganza. Some other famous person was there and got caught in the tequila and glitter crossfire."

"Yuck," said Joe.

"Oh, I get the glitter," Tiffany said. "I'm not sure about the tequila."

We all suppressed inappropriate chuckles.

"The breakup was spectacular, but having worked with him, the relationship is what I really don't get," I said. "Who'd want that at home?"

Tiffany shrugged. "My mom likes to say there's a shoe for every foot."

"Mine says that, too." Easton chuckled.

"What kind of breakup?" Joe asked.

"I think a divorce," Tiffany said. "I'm sure I'll be getting an upset call from Jen in the morning, so I'll ask what she heard and where."

"Thanks." Joe's expression was still a bit awkward. "Um, do you know divorced from whom…I mean, a man or a woman?"

"Nope. Never cared enough to ask."

Joe looked to me.

"I could guess, but I'd probably be wrong." I shrugged. "I guess it's good that we've come far enough that nobody's sure and it doesn't matter, right?"

"Yeah, except it makes it pretty tough to know where to start with suspects."

"Spouse is always the first, right?" Easton said. "Somebody's got to know you really well to want to kill you."

"Pretty much." Joe sighed. "Looks like I have a lot of questions to answer."

"Well," Tiffany said, taking one more look at Easton as she put down her cup, "this lovely gentleman seems to be fine, and I have a bottle of wine and a firefighter who doesn't have to get up in the morning waiting for me."

"Good for you," Joe said.

"Nice meeting you, Captain," Easton said.

"Next time under better circumstances." Tiffany picked up her tackle box and gave me a look-over. "You. Walk tomorrow?"

"Sounds good. We'll text."

"Not early."

"No way."

She winked and walked out the back. I heard Colby wish her a good night in an adoring tone. Tiffany has that effect.

"Some night." Joe stretched a little, drank a bit more coffee.

"Got that." Easton took another sip of sports drink. "Stuff actually tastes a lot better than it looks."

"Has to," Joe said, sitting down on the cold radiator near the door. "Once you're feeling okay to drive, Ease, you can go home whenever you like."

"Are you clear from the scene?" I asked.

"Clear enough. M.E.'s crew is doing their job, Crime Scene has secured everything, so I can go get some sleep."

I looked down at my coffee.

"Oh, no," Easton said. "You guys weren't on date night?"

"Guilty as charged." I tried not to sigh like a Victorian heroine.

Easton turned to Joe. "Marry her. Just go find a J.P. right now and make it official."

Joe blushed. I kept my eyes on the cup.

"After what Amber put you through, dude?" Easton laughed and patted my arm with a reassuring glance. "Trust me, Doc, you're all set. Can't wait to dance at the wedding."

"Well, thanks," I said, with as much diplomacy as I could manage. "Let's work out that family picnic first."

"Fair enough." Easton shook his head at Joe and rummaged his car keys out of his pocket. "At least try to get a little alone time."

Joe and I nodded.

"Good meeting you, anyhow," I said. "Hope I'll see you around the temple while you do your work."

"Oh, you will."

"Then you'll have to join Rabbi Aaron and me for slushies some afternoon. Kule's always has at least one no-sugar-added flavor, and it's all tasty."

"Sounds good. Talk soon, Giuseppe."

Easton and Joe exchanged the kind of warm half-hug, half-handshake thing men do with their longtime friends, and Easton took off.

Joe and I sat there for a moment in the quiet workroom, the blue and red lights still reflecting through the window.

"C'mon, *Dottore*, let's go home."

"Together?"

"Hell, yes, together."

"That's all right, then."

Chapter Five

Pasta alla Homicide

"We never got dinner," Joe said as we walked into the foyer, now flooded with silvery moonlight. "I'm sorry."

"Nothing to apologize for." I took his hand.

"I'll owe you, Due Fiori." He pulled me close.

"I'll hold you to that." I leaned my head on his shoulder.

Good way to end a horrible night.

"How bout I cook us some pasta?" he asked. "Made a bunch of Mama's pesto last weekend because I had a lot of basil."

"Sure. Can I watch you cook?"

"Be disappointed if you don't."

Cannoli appeared as we headed back, clearly more interested in attention than treats. Joe picked him up, and the miniature dog happily snuggled into his shoulder. The humans weren't the only ones who needed reassurance.

The kitchen is the only truly comfortable and homey room in Joe's showplace of a house. Everywhere else was decorated in high-end bland beige by the ex, Amber, who'd left for greener pastures when Joe traded a white-shoe partner's share for a prosecutor's salary. Joe made a principled choice after the drunk driver who nearly killed his brother got off because of bad lawyering, but Amber hadn't signed on for principle. She landed in husband number two's waterside manse in Southport. Joe kept the house for their daughter's visits—and its proximity to his mother.

And, just in case you're keeping score, Joe and Amber are impressively civil for daughter Aly's sake. My job is to stay out of the whole thing as much as humanly possible, even if I think Amber's behavior was shallow and cruel. My real concern is fifteen-year-old Aly, who's delightful. We've been slowly building a warm and friendly, but not especially parental, relationship.

Despite its status-brand stainless-steel appliances, the kitchen is warm and welcoming, with a light wood farmhouse table and matching chairs with blue gingham seats. In the center of the table was a big jar candle, probably from the town farmers' market, in brown sugar cinnamon, just because he likes the scent.

Joe set Cannoli down on one of the chairs, and the dog curled up on the seat, happily observing the scene with his bright black eyes. After he'd settled in, first Joe, then I, gave him an ear scratch.

The only sound for a while was comfortable kitchen noise: running water, the click of the gas stove lighting, squeak of the corkscrew, and then the glug of chianti as Joe poured two generous glasses.

I lit the candle with a match from the box on the candle trivet.

Joe handed me a glass and sat corners so we were close. Reached over with his free hand and toyed with a curl that had fallen out of my clip, then ran his hand down my bare arm. "Hell of a night."

"It is." I took a sip of wine. Just right. As you'd expect for a New Haven Italian man, Joe knows good chianti. "But we're here now."

Rueful smile as his hand rested on my arm. "One of the things I love most about you. You just deal."

I took his hand and laced fingers. "Dealing is one of my best things."

"That it is." He squeezed my hand, then took a sip of his own wine. "So I'm going to presume on privilege."

"Privilege?"

"Significant others aren't necessarily privileged, but—"

"Privileged as far as I'm concerned," I said.

"That'll do for now." He smiled. "Plus, of course, the privilege of having a brilliant woman in my life who happens to have a professional connection to our victim."

"Ah." I sighed. "Him."

"Him. The fingerprints identify him as one Gerald O'Hara, originally of Dublin, and his UK passport is a very good fake."

"No Hightower? No title?"

"Nope." Joe chuckled. "A really masterful reinvention. Though, you'll notice he seems to work mostly in the U.S., where we don't know enough about titles to ask awkward questions."

"Oh, hell." I'd done a basic background check on Hightower, but since the Shoreline Shakespeare Festival had hired him, I'd figured he was okay. Also, importantly, my full retainer had shown up promptly in my PayPurse account. "He didn't raise any obvious red flags."

"Anything off at all?"

"Not really." I thought about it. "The accent was right—BBC standard diction, upper-class word choices, no obvious howlers. Definitely knew his stuff with theatre. Talked the right talk with the right terms."

"That's not a surprise. He really is—well, was—an experienced theatre director."

"Experienced, but definitely not easy to work with," I said.

"Well, no." Joe had heard enough stories from the front. "But while he wasn't who he said he was, he did seem to be *what* he said he was, at least for the last twenty-five years or so."

"Before that?"

"Still waiting to hear from the Irish authorities. UK records have him as a British resident from the 1990s, eventually a naturalized subject. Current legal residence in London…but seems to have been over here for most of the last year."

"The infamous breakup with tequila and glitter."

"Yeah. We'll have to nail that down."

"I'm sure it's good. Tiffany's sister is a celebrity gossip expert."

"I'm sure. At some point, I'll get to the tabloid sites. I've just got a lot to check out with this guy."

"If I have time tomorrow, I'll take a look—or reach out to someone who does."

"Thanks."

I drank some wine. "Do we know why he originally left Ireland?"

"Between time zones and the weekend, we haven't been able to connect with anyone in the Garda yet."

"Look at you, knowing the right name for the Irish cops," I teased.

"Not bad for an Italian guy, huh?" He grinned as he stood. *"Radiatore* okay?"

He held up a packet of the little radiator-shaped pasta.

"Perfect...but I want you to say it again."

"Radiatore." He pronounced it perfectly as he shook the pasta from the bag into the water. Joe doesn't make a big deal about it, but he's bilingual thanks to his Italian-speaking parents. He's even sexier in Italian, as he reminded me when he continued, *"Radiatore, radiatore."*

"Oh, yess..." I sighed. "I'll want these again when we're not in the midst of such a serious conversation."

Joe stirred the pasta with a wooden spoon, turned it down a little, and returned to sit with me, petting Cannoli as he spoke. "Takes longer than you think to get a perfect *al dente*, but it's worth it."

"Like so many things."

"Oh, so true." He took a sip of wine. "So what can you tell me about your buddy the director?"

"Not my buddy. All due respect to the dead, he was a jerk."

"What kind of jerk?"

"Arrogant. Demanding and abusive, too."

Joe's eyes narrowed. "What kind of abusive?"

"Power stuff."

He held my gaze, raised an eyebrow. Cannoli alerted, too. "Any, um..."

"Sex power stuff?"

"Yeah." Sheepish shrug as he took my hand. "Suddenly feels weird talking about this with you, y'know?"

"Kind of." I squeezed his fingers. Inevitably, events earlier in the evening had changed the balance of our relationship, but I hadn't expected this.

"And I might want to slug him if he creeped on you," Joe said. "Which doesn't help when I have to think of him as my victim."

"It's okay," I assured him. "He wasn't that kind of creep. Not at all. Different thing—self-important. So superior to everyone else. And extremely demanding. I went four rounds of email with the guy over Hero's sleeves, and we were still wrangling earlier today."

"Sleeves?" Joe's eyes widened, but he wasn't as shocked as he might have been. Costuming, including sleeve detail, often came up on the productions I consulted on, so he was used to hearing me talk about odd little clothing facts.

"Yes," I said. "This is an early-Victorian production. 1848, the year of all the European revolutions and the Chartists in Britain. Clothes were very fussy and feminine at the time. So there are a lot of sleeve treatments, puffs, and such. And Hightower got all snotty, because he thought the sleeves on Hero's gown looked too Renaissance."

"Too Renaissance?"

"He was afraid people would take this for, quoting here: 'an ordinary Shakespearean production rather than a new critique of attitudes on sexuality.'"

"Good Lord." Joe took a generous sip of his wine. "Do you have any idea what he was getting at?"

"I don't think *he* was a hundred percent sure what he was getting at, honestly, but I'll take a stab at it."

Joe winced, and so did I.

"Sorry."

He reached over and patted my hand. "Anyhow, go on."

I laced fingers with him. "Basically, the Victorian clothes were intended as a statement about restrictive sexual mores in the nineteenth century and the plot of the play, which, as you know, turns on questions about a woman's chastity."

"Right." Joe got up and stirred the pasta. "I don't really remember it in a lot of detail...but this is the one where the girl is falsely accused of cheating and dumped at the altar, right?"

"Yep. Then, of course, cleared and happily married off to her one true."

"Can't argue with the one true part," he said with a little smile, taking an aluminum mesh pasta strainer from the rack. "I guess I can see where he was going. Prudishness and sexism and such."

"Exactly. That much is valid. But he was really demanding and mean getting there."

"All due respect to Victorian statements and whatever, but that's a far more useful line of discussion. What kind of mean?" He settled the strainer in the sink.

"Dismissive and occasionally verbally abusive to just about everyone but me."

"Good thing," Joe growled.

"Yeah, well." I shrugged. "I think my doctorate backed him off a little. And of course, I always addressed him appropriately as Sir Jeremy, which set the right tone."

A buzz from the counter. Joe's phone. He read the text and sighed. "Well, we know who he broke up with."

"We do?"

"Major Crimes found the contact info. The husband or ex-husband—it's unclear where they were in the process—is flying over. They think he'll be here around noon."

"Lousy trip," I said.

"Got that." His gaze moved from the screen to me, and he put down the phone. "Could you—"

"I'm not the Ambassador from Widowhood."

My voice had a little more edge than I'd intended.

Joe blinked, startled.

"I didn't mean to suggest you were," he said, reaching for my hand.

I twined my fingers with his. "And I didn't mean to snap at you."

We both took a long breath.

"Sometimes it feels like we're building a house on a minefield," he said.

"We are." I squeezed his fingers. "But I'm sure glad we're building that house."

"So am I." He squeezed back, released my hand, turning back to the pasta.

"Now let's get some dinner."

"A good meal helps everything," I said.

"Exactly." He fished out a piece, blew on it. "Mama taught me well."

"That, she did." I watched him as he tested it.

"What?"

"You're pretty terrific, you know."

"So are you, *cara*."

Shared smile. Exactly the sort of moment we should have been having on this night.

"The *radiatore* are ready." He grabbed a couple of mitts and picked up the pot.

"Want me to get the pesto?" I asked, standing and walking over to the big shiny fridge.

"Sure. And grab the chunk of parm, too."

For the next couple of minutes, I happily watched Joe flip the pasta back into the pot, dress it with pesto, and finally grate a snow shower of parmigiano on top.

Cannoli accepted a piece of Fakin' Bacon (Big Taste Treat for Tiny Dogs) and toddled off, back to his TV shows.

"*Radiatore*," Joe said as he handed me one of the bowls, then grinned. "*Radiatore, radiatore…*"

"Nice." I moved back to the table with my bowl in one hand and the bottle of wine in the other. "Top off your glass?"

"Yes, please."

After, I set down the bottle and picked up my glass. He clinked his against it. I must have looked shocked.

"Because no matter how bad it is, it's better together, *cara*."

"True that." I clinked back. "*L'chaim.*"

"*Alla nostra.*"

"To us." I translated.

"Common Italian toast. But so much better tonight."

"Yes."

He took my hand. "I think it's been a couple of hours since I told you I love you."

"I love you, too."

"Forgive me for being a stereotypical male, but everything feels different now. *We* feel different."

"Women fall in love to have sex, men have sex to fall in love?"

"That's the one. My sister and daughter would say it's sexist and heteronormative, but here we are." He looked down at his bowl for a moment. "You know, I did already love you before. I mean, we knew it was big and serious."

"We did…and we do."

"This mess tonight isn't making you reconsider?"

"Not even a little."

"Good. How long should I wait to propose?"

He said it with a teasing smile, a joke, but not a joke.

I responded in kind. "Well, I'd hold it for now, since we don't want the *radiatore* to get cold."

Grin. *"Radiatore, cara."*

Chapter Six

Welcome to the Morning After

Joe and I—with Cannoli curled up on the bed corner by his feet—managed a few fitful hours of sleep before the phones started making noise again. Joe's first call was the Medical Examiner with an unsurprising preliminary ruling: cause of death: massive blood loss from a slash to the neck, contributing head trauma, manner: homicide.

But Dr. Alexandre also had some kind of concern about the murder weapon, and told Joe she'd be sending photos when she had time.

My day started with a text from Henry, a cheerful note that his numbers were fine—which I already knew from the app on my phone—and Uncle Ed was making his famous green eggs and ham for the kids. I sent an equally cheery reply, telling him to enjoy the morning and give hugs to Garrett and Ed. I did not give away Ed's secret: green eggs are actually eggs Florentine, a sneaky use of a Dr. Seuss reference to get the kids to eat their spinach.

The next message was much less pleasant.

Dina, who had only the small gravel road circling the Green between her temple and the murder, broke her usual Sabbath tech rules to send me a text asking if I knew anything about it. I called her right back.

"Oh, honey," she said as she picked up. "I didn't want to interrupt anything. I just wanted you to get back to me when you can."

"You didn't interrupt," I said. "The party's over."

"They called in Joe." She sighed. "Oh, honey, I'm sorry."

"Yeah. I got called too—because the police needed the Society driveway."

"So you're both in it up to your eyeballs."

"Afraid so."

"Is everything okay with you two?"

"More than."

"Yeah?"

"Yeah." No need to be graphic, but a little clarity wouldn't hurt. "We… uh…didn't get to our reservation."

"No?"

"No. Let's just say the main purpose of the night was accomplished before the phone rang."

"Excellent. I assume all went well in that area."

As a woman of the cloth, Dina wasn't interested in the dirty deets, but the relationship dynamics. I assured her, "Very well indeed."

She let out a tiny, girlish giggle. "Glad to hear it."

"No worries there, anyhow," I said.

"Speaking of worries—" she began.

"The victim is Sir Jeremy Hightower."

"The play director?"

"That's the one. And—there's nothing in the early info to suggest it has anything to do with the temple."

"Well, that's a relief."

"Definitely. Easton Jeffries, the architect, found him near the backstage area while he was walking around the temple."

"You mean after dinner with Ben and me?"

"Yes. Apparently, he was just getting a sense of the building when he tripped over the body."

"How awful for him. Lovely man, you know."

"I do. He's a college friend of Joe's," I said. "We met while the police were working the scene."

"Really? Well, we are definitely going to have to get everyone together for dinner. We invited his wife and daughter last night, but there was some kind of dance team thing."

"Dance team?"

"No idea. The twins were basketballers." A breath and change of tone. "Look, I have to start getting ready for the morning service. Want to swing over for some cold-brew this afternoon?"

"Sounds good," I said.

"And don't think I'm not going to ask for some details over the coffee!"

"Maybe we invite Tiffany for a walk first, and I'll bring you both up to date at once." My offer wasn't entirely serious, but Dina didn't take it that way.

"Works for me. I'll buzz her after services, since you're hopefully going to be busy."

"*Shabbat Shalom*, Rabbi," I said.

"And also to you, Christian. And that big gorgeous guy of yours."

"Thanks."

As I hit end, I looked up to see Joe rolling up the sleeves of his blue check oxford. "Sharp-dressed man."

"Not sure who I'm going to see today, so better look decent."

"I like you better when you're indecent."

"The feeling is mutual, *Dottore*." He bent down to kiss me and touched my messy curls. "I like you with bed hair."

"With any luck, you'll get to mess it up again soon."

The second light kiss might have become something else if both our phones hadn't chimed.

"Dr. Shaw, what on earth happened?"

The frantic voice of Shoreline Shakespeare Festival Director Julia Henshaw exploded from my phone.

I only barely recognized her. Julia is a lifelong arts manager and pretty much unflappable. All you need to know about her is that she treated herself to a little diamond pendant on her sixtieth birthday: two stencil zeroes, for Zero F**ks Given, Zero BS Taken.

Only the violent death of her director could shake Julia.

"Well, Sir Jeremy was found stabbed on the Green last night," I said. Julia, like everyone else who'd seen Joe dropping by the Society for a morning coffee, knew about us and was probably assuming I had inside knowledge.

"I *know* that." She took a deep, ragged breath. "Chief DiBiasi called me at midnight."

"Well, then you know what I know," I said.

"Oh. Do they know why?

"Too early to know anything." What part of *you know what I know* is a problem?

"But why…what…"

"I've got nothing," I said. "I honestly don't."

Casting about for ways to calm her down, I turned to see Joe looking at his phone.

"Christian." Joe's voice was gravelly.

No nickname. The listen-up tone.

Oh, holy hell.

"I'll call you as soon as I know anything," I promised.

Hit End. Looked to Joe.

"We need to get to the temple now," he said.

Chapter Seven

Evil Among Us

When we arrived, the Green was once again packed with police cruisers.

This time, it looked like they were all state police, except for two nondescript dark sedans that were probably Major Crimes or maybe even federal. After what Joe had shown me on his phone, the Feds were a definite possibility.

One sentence from Dr. Alexandre: "The knife has a swastika on it."

We hadn't spoken since he showed me the phone. I'd quickly scrambled into the clothes from my overnight bag, and we'd taken off, me wrestling my bed hair into a clip as he drove. I wasn't sure if I wanted to throw up, punch somebody, or curl into a ball and weep.

None of those options was available at the moment, though.

Joe drove with cool precision, periodically glancing over at me and patting my arm.

He got it.

Whatever had happened on that darkened Green, the marking on the weapon made it personal for me. Even more so for Dina and the congregation. Some things are just part of the soul, and the sheer chemical revulsion of any Jewish person—or anyone who loves one—to a swastika is one of those things.

As far as I was concerned, whoever had chosen to do murder with that weapon was coming for my boy. Of course, my friends, too—and probably me—as the mother of a Jewish boy, I didn't doubt they had a spot on their wall for me. But above all, my baby.

By the time we got to the Green, my blood was at full boil.

Before Joe even set the parking brake, I jumped out.

"*Dottore!*" he called as I ran for the columned portico.

Colby and Sergeant Ellis were at the base of the stairs, while a couple of state troopers were further up at the door to the sanctuary.

"Hey, Dr. Shaw," said the sergeant, a Black woman in her thirties with braids in a low knot and the graceful posture of a ballet dancer. "Sorry to bother you last night.

"Not a problem. Glad to pitch in."

Ellis nodded. "Everybody's okay here. This is just a precaution."

"Thanks. I figured, but—"

"Yeah, I don't blame you." Her mouth tightened in a scowl. "My church got a threat a few years ago. Ugly racial stuff."

"I'm sorry. Creeps everywhere, aren't there?"

"True that, Doc. Hey, Mr. Poli," she said as Joe reached us.

"Hi, Sergeant."

"Poli, what is going on here?"

I recognized the big voice from last night's phone call. State's Attorney Amelia Porter was walking away from one of the unmarked cars, with a big, nondescript guy who was probably a Fed a few steps behind her.

In a navy-blue linen suit with cream-colored trim and buttons, finished with brilliant red lipstick that made her coffee skin glow, Porter was summer flawless, taking charge of the scene through sheer command presence without saying a word.

"Hello, Ms. Porter," Joe said, holding out a hand for a formal shake. "Thank you for coming down."

"Of course. Dr. Alexandre actually interrupted your call. I appreciate both of you taking appropriate action. Any time there's potential hate crime involvement—"

"Exactly," Joe said.

Just then, the bell at the nearby Episcopal church began to chime. The big doors of the temple opened, and a few older people cautiously stepped out onto the portico.

"What's going on?" asked Gerry Diamond, a slight, older man with huge glasses, a member of the board and past president of the Temple Brotherhood.

"Police?"

The word came first in an elderly female voice and quickly bounced around a few times in a low, nervous murmur.

"Let's find out what happened." Dina's calm tone carried over the buzz as she walked to the front of the group.

While she's barely five feet tall, Dina is one of the most formidable people I know. In a prayer shawl embroidered by her grandmother over a simple navy summer dress, she was in full Rabbi Mode, an impressive and inspiring sight.

"So, *nu*, Ms. State's Attorney?" she asked, gazing up at Porter.

"Well, there's a possibility of hate-crime involvement, because of a swastika on the murder weapon."

As the people behind Dina gasped, and she bit her lip, I noticed the Episcopal tower had stopped chiming and realized how early it still was. This wasn't the main service crowd. It was the Torah study group, a small number of especially committed and observant folks who enjoyed coming together to discuss and analyze.

"What on earth?" Dina asked, her eyes moving to Joe, seeking reassurance from a friend.

"We're still sorting it out, Rabbi," he said. "But Ms. Porter and the relevant authorities are acting with an abundance of caution."

"Poli's right, Rabbi," Amelia Porter agreed, putting a soothing hand on Dina's arm. "This is not one we want to get wrong."

"I agree." Dina nodded. "We have about an hour until the main Shabbat service. We'll be happy to have an increased security presence."

"And we'll make sure you have it." Porter and Dina moved seamlessly into a handshake, and I realized they must know each other.

"Thank you."

"Of course." She turned to the big guy. "I'd like you to meet Agent Wisnewski."

As Dina made acquaintances, Joe touched my arm.

"You okay?"

"Yeah. It's just—"

"I know," he said, then shook his head in correction. "I mean, I don't *know*, but I get it."

I nodded, leaned in close so only he could hear. "Damn, I love you."

"Back at you."

We pulled apart so quickly nobody noticed—other than Gerry Diamond.

"Glad to see you two here," he said. "Better under different circumstances."

"Got that," Joe agreed, holding out a hand.

As they shook, Joe's phone buzzed.

"Sorry," he said.

He pulled it out of his pocket. "Dr. Alexandre just sent me an image of the weapon. She says it appears to be an antique pewter dagger."

"Antique?" State's Attorney Porter turned back to us as Agent Wisnewski continued his reassuring conversation with Dina.

"Antique, the M.E. says," confirmed Joe. "May I show it to my in-house expert?"

Porter turned to me with a carefully calibrated smile. "Dr. Shaw, I presume."

I held out my hand for a shake. "Yes, Ms. Porter."

"Would you mind offering some informal insight? I'm assuming Poli is not dragging you in under duress."

"Not at all," I said. "May I see it?"

"Here."

Joe turned the phone to me.

At first, it was just what I expected to see: a dull-gray metal knife with a symbol carved in the hilt. The symbol I expected.

The gut punch I should have expected.

But as I looked at it, I realized something else.

"This isn't what you think," I said.

"What do you mean?" Joe asked. "Of course it's a swastika."

"It is, but it isn't." I pointed. "It's not a Nazi swastika."

"There are other swastikas?" asked Agent Wisnewski, turning away from Dina and, with her, joining the conversation.

Dina and Gerry glanced at him.

Maybe a little concerning that a guy who was involved in investigating a hate crime case didn't know the swastika had existed long before it became a symbol of evil. Or maybe not, as long as he understood how to stop the hateful people who used it.

I motioned to Joe, who turned the phone so the others could see it. Dina winced visibly, as I had, but then focused on the screen, nodding.

"See how it's backwards?" I asked, pointing to the direction of the spidery arms.

Joe and the others followed my gesture.

"You're right." Porter squinted at it, then returned to me. "Does that mean something?"

"I think so. Before the Third Reich, the swastika was a good-luck symbol in some cultures. The Russian Empress Alexandra used it, and so too did some other people at the time."

"And then, of course," Dina added, "it became something else."

"Right," Agent Wisnewski said. "That part we know."

"I'd have to see it in person to be sure, but this looks at lot like a turn of the 20th century letter opener we have at the Society. So I'd put it at roughly the same time period."

Porter's eyes narrowed. "You have one like this?"

"Yes. It's in a drawer in the front parlor. I don't feel comfortable leaving it out, considering, but it goes with some of the other writing utensils in the room."

"Do they have swastikas?" Porter asked.

"No, just various geometric motifs. It's not a married set."

"Married?"

"It's a jewelry term, but we often use it in the context of household items.

It means something of the same design made at roughly the same time to be used together. These pieces are similar but not the same."

Porter nodded.

"So, it's not a real swastika, then," Dina said.

"It's a swastika but not a swastika." I nodded to her.

"Can you get the one from the Society?" Porter asked. "For comparison?"

"Sure. I'll go over right now."

"I'll go with you," Joe volunteered.

"I'll come too," Porter said. "I'd like to take a good look at the piece."

"You're welcome, of course." I motioned toward the building.

"Before you go, though, the big question remains." Dina glanced at me, and then Porter. "Does this change the hate crime factor?"

"I don't know," I said. "It could be a hateful misdirect. Or the killer could have deliberately chosen that weapon."

"Or it could be something else." Porter shook her head. "We have to assume the worst and hope for the best."

"That we do," Agent Wisnewski said. "This is not one we want to get wrong."

Dina looked across the small crowd of law enforcement. "Well, then, it looks like we're getting extra guests for Sabbath services."

"*Gutte Shabbes,* Rabbi," Porter said.

"We can only hope so," Dina replied.

Chapter Eight

Parlor Games

Joe and Porter made the short walk to the Society with me, while Wisnewski and the assorted officers followed Dina for a tour of the synagogue.

Empress Frederick met us at the door. Joe and I had left her some extra treats in apology for invading her space last night, but she was clearly not a happy girl. Though she enjoys being adored, at a distance, by any and all comers, she does not appreciate changes to her routine. Her Imperial Majesty was happy to share her displeasure, yowling at us as we walked into the front hall.

"What an adorable little kitty," Porter said, her severe and regal expression softening as she bent to admire the Empress, holding out a hand so the cat could take a sniff.

Our small royal could just as easily have hissed and flounced off. But she clearly sensed a kindred spirit in the regal State's Attorney, and she leaned into the offered hand, then accepted a pet.

"Well, I've seen everything now," said Joe, whose relationship with the cat consisted mainly of glances and sniffs even though she seemed to like him.

"I'm a cat person, Poli. We understand each other."

Wisely, Joe merely nodded.

The ruler of the building duly greeted; we moved into the parlor.

"It's like stepping back in time," Porter said. "Did you set up this room yourself?"

"With plenty of help from the volunteers and my assistant, Lewis Barnes," I replied. "We have a really nice collection here."

"And she arranges it beautifully." Joe didn't quite do the *Price is Right* model sweep, but it was close.

His boss sent me a little grin. "Nice to have a fan club."

"I think so." Of course, I was blushing and, of course, she clocked it. To dilute the embarrassment at least a little, I moved on with the mission, leading them to the small table in its spot near the window. With the sun picking up the shimmer of the intricate inlaid wood top, it was a lovely piece. "This is really more of a writing table than a desk."

"I see that," Porter said. "When you said 'desk,' I envisioned one of those rolltop deals."

"We do have one, but it's in the library across the hall. This is an elegant space where the lady of the house holds court. A writing table is for social letters and invitations...the big rolltop is where the husband would do business and keep household accounts."

Porter's eyes sharpened. "So, are you saying the letter opener could be a woman's weapon?"

"Well, now, it could be anybody's weapon. The M.E. would know better than I do, but I don't think you have to be all that strong to stab a smallish, older man in the neck." I opened the drawer. "Back when it was made, it probably would have been a weapon of opportunity."

"Now, it sure seems like a statement," Joe said.

"Just about has to be," Porter agreed.

I looked down in the drawer. A small silver tray with an elaborate antiqued border that looked like an unusually elaborate Greek key design. A rectangular pen box with the same design. And a cylindrical holder for a roll of stamps.

No letter opener.

Uh-oh.

"It's gone," I said. Honestly, it wasn't really a surprise—how many swastika letter openers can there be?

Still, I had plenty of other questions. Starting with who would have known it was there, who had a chance to take it, and why? Question for me, too: I often get a vibe from objects, and I'd never sensed anything from this. It's not really paranormal; it's just kind of a mental picture of who might have owned the piece and what they would have done with it.

Maybe I hadn't wanted to get a vibe from a piece with a swastika. Even a backwards one.

Much to consider, and not just for me.

Porter and Joe looked down in the drawer, then met my gaze.

"Could it be somewhere else?" she asked.

"I don't think so…but other staff and volunteers do come through here."

"It's not a really secure area," Joe said.

"Living history can't be," I added. "The most valuable items, like the 17th-century Bible, are in special, secured cases. And rooms are organized to protect the fragile pieces. Otherwise, we don't take a lot of precautions."

"Deliberately, as you said." Porter looked around the room. "Too much security would ruin the moment."

"Absolutely. I want people to feel like you just did—like they're stepping back in time—not like they're walking into a museum."

"It's good," she said. "But if it's your knife, it's going to mean a huge suspect pool."

"True."

"Is there a way to tell if it's your knife?"

"Well," I said, unable to stop a bit of edge from creeping into my voice. "First, it's not *my* knife. It belongs to the Society."

"Of course." Porter gave me a careful nod and sharp glance as Joe's eyes widened at the momentary tension between us. It wasn't anything serious, just two professionals making sure everyone knew the boundaries, but it might have looked like more to Joe, with his interest in both sides.

"Thanks," I said, giving the State's Attorney an encouraging smile, which she immediately returned.

Peace restored.

"Do you mark the Society's inventory in some way?" she asked.

"I do. Most pieces get a label with a number. Our catalogue is on the computer now, but we still have the old paper binders down in the basement."

"You document a lot on each piece, don't you?" Joe's proud tone warmed my heart.

"I do." I nodded. "We record who donated it, a short description of the provenance, any restoration work, and where it's displayed."

"I'm sure Dr. Shaw can give us copies of the documentation."

"I can get that right now," I offered. "Easy enough."

"Thanks, Dr. Shaw." Porter nodded to the drawer. "Do you log when something is moved?"

"Not as strictly as we could," I admitted. "We're pretty loose about that, honestly. It's part of the openness. I often show special pieces on tours or bring out items for local artists or students. But I don't usually write down what I brought out for each individual session."

"No?"

"If it's a special event, sure. But if I just bring out a christening cap for a grandma who's working on a project, no."

"Can people take things home with them?"

"No." I shook my head. "Students can take digital pics, and we have wonderful software that generates patterns, but the objects stay in the building."

Porter looked down in the drawer. "They're supposed to, anyhow."

"We run on a lot of trust," I admitted. "I don't think that's a bad thing, overall."

"Neither do I," the chief prosector assured me. "Especially not with things like this."

"Really?"

"Really." She gave a sheepish shrug. "Honestly, I like the idea that there are people like us, still out there, living on the honor system."

"Glad to help restore your faith in humanity."

I was being a bit snarky, but Porter gave me a rueful little smile. "Something has to."

Chapter Nine

No Shalom Here

An exchange of texts and photos with Dr. Alexandre quickly confirmed that the swastika knife was ours, with the Society's small cataloguing mark still intact. A few minutes later, Porter and Joe left with copies of the documentation forms for the piece, and I headed over to the temple.

Dina had gone back in the building, standing in the entrance surrounded by the morning minyan, the Fed, and a growing assortment of understandably upset congregants.

Normally, it would never have occurred to me to darken the door of the sanctuary in casual summer clothes. But I suspected my presence was more important to Dina than any deficit in dress. The Talmud probably has something to say about appropriate female attire for worship…but it also has plenty to say about consoling people in pain or sorrow, and that seemed to be the more important value.

As I was learning in my Wednesday evening chats with Dina, an informal conversion course on Henry's Hebrew School nights, the proverb "two Jews, three opinions" is nothing more than a statement of fact.

For Dina, so too is the idea that community and care for our fellow people almost always supersedes any given rule.

When she saw me, Dina patted the arm of the older woman she'd been reassuring and walked right over to me.

I'm not normally a hugger, and neither is she, but we both held out our arms.

After the embrace, she looked up at me with something almost like her usual grin. "Must look like one of those comics of the big twin and little twin."

"Well," I said, "I could be the one hundred and fifty percent version of you."

We shared a small rueful smile.

Our height difference and similarities in hair color and texture were a running gag between us. Corny little way to lighten the moment.

Better than nothing. Much better.

"How are you holding up?" I asked.

"Well, I suppose the law-enforcement presence should be soothing, but it isn't."

"Too much history, right?"

"Got it in one, pupil of mine." She shrugged. "Don't get me wrong, I'm very grateful to have the protection, but the whole thing is a pretty grim reminder."

She didn't have to say "reminder" of what. Nothing really good for me to say here, so I merely nodded.

"So what are they thinking?" she asked.

"Right now, they're just gathering information." The door opened as I spoke, and a couple of older ladies walked in, one a docent who shot me a nervous smile.

"The sooner we have some useful information, the better," Dina said. "The Senior Brotherhood is already organizing a watch."

"Oh?"

"Gerry Diamond is the young whippersnapper of the group at eighty-five. If we don't get some clarity on what's happening here, I'm going to have a bunch of nonagenarians sitting out front with World War Two sidearms."

"Yikes."

"Yikes indeed." She held my gaze squarely. "What's your radar say?"

"Really?" I asked my supremely rational rabbi friend.

"Really." Nervous shrug. "You call it radar, I call it gut feelings. Whatever it is, it's all the stuff our brains pick up that we can't necessarily process consciously. We can't necessarily quantify it, but it's often useful."

"O-kay."

"Especially in matters like these. Women tend to pick up real threats to their families and communities much better than men do."

"Sexist much?"

"Not even a little. It's thousands of years of biology and history of being the ones left behind at the village while the men went out to fight the barbarian hordes. We're just wired to catch subtle signs of danger and react."

"Well, then." I was more than a little stunned at Dina's logic. But I couldn't argue it. She's right. Reverse sexism or not, the women I know often do have a tendency to see trouble well before men do.

"And so, my dear Celt, your radar is extremely important right now. Picking up anything?"

I took a deep breath and thought for a moment. "I'm not picking up much. Except that I'm not as upset as I should be."

"Yeah?"

"Yeah. A guy was stabbed to death outside our door with a knife decorated with a swastika, and I'm not very rattled at all. I'm angry and sickened and sad for the loss of life, of course, but there's a level—"

"Weird. I'm feeling the same thing. I put it down to the fact that the knife may not really be a swastika."

"It's a real swastika. Just a nineteenth-century one."

"Which doesn't mean the same thing it did in the 1930s."

"Exactly." I shook my head. "There is a lot of noise here."

"Noise?"

"Noise. All kinds of extra happenings that may or may not have to do with what happened out there last night. It could be a hate crime. It could also be some fool grabbing a weapon of opportunity."

"You mean the killer might not even realize it was a swastika knife?" She pushed her hair back. "Seriously?"

"Never discount the power of stupid."

"Well, there's that." She glanced back at the congregants. "You're staying for the service, right?"

"I'm not dressed…"

"This is not the Presbyterian Church in Mars, P. A., honey. This is a Reform congregation in New Haven County. Your shirt's clean and your hair pulled back. You'll more than do."

"And it's not about how I look anyhow, right?"

"Oh, so right, my giant *shikse*." Grin. "I have to go calm some folks down. We'll be starting in a few. Text your fella and tell him where you'll be, and I'll see you inside."

"Good call," I said. Joe probably would be concerned if I just disappeared.

After a quick exchange of texts, I started for the sanctuary, once the home of a two-hundred-year-old Congregational church. As I turned, I felt a hand on my arm.

"Christian, dear."

Amy Taylor, nonagenarian war bride, Historical Society docent, and recent bat mitzvah girl, gave me a warm smile. "Gerry is busy at the barricades, so why don't you sit with Elaine and me?"

"I'd love to. Henry is at a sleepover."

Elaine Dietz, Henry's Hebrew School teacher, gave me a twinkly smile. "He's been talking about it for weeks. Loves spending time with his cousins."

"He does, that," I agreed. Henry had settled on that description for Ed's other four grandkids, because it was easier than explaining, and fit the relationship. "Ed's making green eggs and ham."

"Spinach?" Amy asked.

"I used to do that, too." Elaine, mother of two college-age sons, nodded. "Sneaky brilliant."

"Absolutely."

We continued in light, inconsequential conversation as we walked to our seats, in unspoken agreement to keep the tone pleasant and comfortable. In the sanctuary, we took seats on the lower level to spare Amy the stairs, even though Henry and I like to sit up in the balcony together, unless he's hiding out in a top corner with his Hebrew School pals. I felt underdressed in my summer clothes, but Dina was right, I didn't really stand out as scruffy.

She was also right that it didn't matter once the service began.

Growing up in fundamentalist Western Pennsylvania, I'd been to revival meetings, and even my mother's presumptively mainline Presbyterian church was very conservative. In college, I'd taken to going to Mass with a friend occasionally, just to feel God in the room.

But I'd never felt I *belonged* the way I did at the temple.

Not just God in the room, but community, too.

Don't get me wrong, I'm sure everyone gets the same feeling of rightness when they're in a good spiritual place. This is just mine.

On that particular day, the service was exactly what the congregation needed, every one of us. The well-worn forms, and Dina's short, but pointed, comments on the importance of being together on this day, in the face of these particular events, brought us both comfort and new energy.

Always good to get a little *shalom* with your Shabbat.

Chapter Ten

Never Saw Him Coming

Outside, the morning sun had given way to the heavy clouds and leaden sky that suggested the forecasters would be right about late-day storms.

As it turned out, while the literal storm didn't come until later, the metaphorical one didn't wait.

Though police tape was still up at the base of the stairs, the crime scene van was gone. Nearby, Officer Colby was standing at attention, even though there was a bench within easy reach. Ah, youthful energy.

A few yards away, the back of the open-air seating area, Joe and State's Attorney Porter were surveying the scene, with Joe pointing out the various features of the stage setup.

As the temple crowd filtered out, the two prosecutors turned.

"Ah, there's your fella!" Amy crowed, elbowing me. "Cute as a button."

"And there's yours." Elaine nudged her, nodding to Gerry Diamond, who was standing at the base of the portico stairs with several other oldsters, all with pugnacious stances and scowls that dared anyone to mess with them. They may have been a half-dozen little old men in polo shirts with Sansabelt slacks up to their armpits, but they clearly saw themselves as the return of the Maccabees.

More power to them.

Amy, Eileen, and I exchanged quick goodbyes, and I zipped around a couple of bubbes to give Dina an encouraging pat on the arm before running down to the authorities.

"Ah, Dr. Shaw," Porter said. "How is the congregation?"

"Reasonably okay. Pretty resilient folks."

"Because they've had to be." Porter nodded. "I'm sure the prayers helped."

"Prayer always helps," I said.

"We agree." Porter offered a small, dry smile. "Whatever else happens, I'll be at my church tomorrow morning."

"Anyhow," Joe cut in. His religious history is at least as complicated as mine, and he's not into talking about it. "I've been showing Ms. Porter around the stage area, and I think we have a pretty good sense of the geography. When do rehearsals start today?"

"They had scene work scheduled for noon," I said, thinking about the calendar pinned to my office board. "I'm not sure they'd go ahead under the circumstances."

"I'd guess they'd have it just to give people a chance to get together and grieve." Porter's expression suggested she'd seen plenty of events affected by violent death.

"That's what I would do. But they may prefer to stay away from the scene for a day. Maybe somebody sent word..." I pulled the phone out of my pocket and took it off airplane mode. Before the service, I'd sent Henry a quick message letting him know I was staying, so I wasn't worried about him. But with everything else going on, there had to be plenty of other folks looking for me.

The phone lit up like a Christmas tree, as emails and messages poured in from the server. I saw Julia Henshaw from the Shoreline Shakespeare Festival, Tiffany, and most of the Historical Society board. It was going to be a very, very long afternoon.

I was just tapping on Julia's text, which started with an all-caps "WHAT," when we heard a squeal of brakes.

Everyone turned toward the sound, in time to see a big shiny black SUV slam into Unity's tiny electric cruiser.

"NO!" Officer Colby let out a noise like a wounded animal and started running toward the crackup.

The empty cruiser, which I had to believe Colby had parked, was accordioned into a blue-and-white ball, hissing and sparking. The SUV looked barely scratched. Before Colby reached the scene, the driver's side door opened, and a man with floppy wheat-colored hair in khaki shorts, a loose French-blue striped oxford, and boat shoes without socks bounded to the ground.

"Good lord, what *else* will happen today?"

The accent and demeanor were unmistakable, at least if you lived within a fifty-mile radius of an Ivy League school. Admittedly, the boat shoes and floppy hair should have been a clue, but even here, real, old-school yacht boys have become pretty rare.

Joe, who'd climbed over a few of these guys to get to Law Review and that old job at the white-shoe firm, tensed immediately. Neither I, the hill-country girl, nor Porter, raised by a widowed mother with three jobs, were thrilled, either.

But we were better at hiding it.

"Who..." Joe asked.

"No one I know," I said.

Porter shrugged.

"You, young man!" said Yacht Boy, waving imperiously at Colby.

"It's Officer Colby, sir."

Good on Raggedy Andy for standing up for himself.

"And isn't that nice for you," our new arrival said. "Who is in charge here?"

Colby glanced about, seeing no other uniforms, clocking Porter and Joe, and then returning to the guy. He drew himself up a bit taller. "Well, I'm the officer on duty at the moment."

"You?"

"Yes, me." Colby held the guy's eyes with his best cop gaze for a moment. Ed would have been proud. He let the gaze sink in before speaking again, in the same sweet, friendly tone he always had. "But maybe you'd like to talk to the State's Attorney?"

Porter, with Joe and me a half-step behind, had already started moving toward them. Her normally regal bearing had taken on an additional sheen, making it clear to Yacht Boy who was in charge. Joe's jaw had slipped forward just a bit into a lightly pugnacious scowl. A twinge in my back told me I'd drawn myself into a far more upright posture than my usual.

Our old money scion was about to get a lesson in manners.

"May I help you?" Porter asked, punching the "may" just slightly and holding Yacht Boy's Atlantic-blue gaze with freezer-burn cool.

He took a breath and opened his mouth.

I'm sure we were all preparing for some imperiously asinine comment.

But that wasn't what we got.

Instead, he choked a question and burst into tears, crumpling into Porter's arms like an upset child.

Pretty much the last three words we expected from an arrogant, overbearing, old-money yacht boy:

"Where's my husband?"

Porter, who was a couple of inches shorter than the guy, shot Joe a 'help me' glance over his head and cautiously, if rather reluctantly, patted his back.

Joe looked at me with the horrified and helpless expression most men have when any adult person cries in front of them.

This was a job for the Ambassador from Widowhood.

"I'm so sorry," I said, gently taking the man's arm and peeling him off Porter. He didn't fully fold onto me, just draping himself over my shoulder, still breathless and nonverbal from sobbing. "Why don't we just go over here and have a seat on the bench?"

Thank heaven for the town fathers who'd managed to find the money for four iron-and-concrete benches at the sides of the Green most of a century ago. Also, thank heaven I am not a small or weak woman. I guided the guy to the bench, noticing up close that he was older than I'd thought—only a few years younger than Sir Jeremy—slim and wiry, and used a bit too much of a strong citrusy aftershave.

I recognized it as Number Six, George Washington's favorite, still sold by Caswell-Massey Apothecary. Old-school indeed.

"What can I do?" Joe asked.

"Should I call a medic?" Colby asked.

"Is he okay?" asked Porter.

With my hand on the guy's back, I could tell he was breathing okay, and he didn't seem in physical distress, just emotional.

"Let's hold on the medic," I said, "Maybe get him some water?"

"I've got some in the…" Colby started, then looked at his car. "Oh."

"The theatre people keep a cooler backstage," I said. "There's probably something left."

"I'll go." Joe stalked off toward the tent.

"Thank you." My new friend pulled back and slumped over on his side of the bench.

I patted his arm. It didn't seem appropriate to rub his back the way I would Henry's. "Of course. Loss sucks."

The blue eyes held mine. "You know…"

"I know enough." I nodded. "Just keep breathing. Take a moment so you can get yourself under control a little."

He blinked agreement. Took a deep, ragged breath.

Another, a little less ragged.

Finally, another.

"Here." Joe handed him a bottle.

He took a sip and spat it out, most of it on my shoes.

"What the hell is that?"

Joe shrugged, looked at the label. "Kombucha refresher. Only thing in the cooler."

"Ugh."

Neither Joe nor I could argue.

"Sir," Porter said, "would you mind telling us who you are?"

"Oh, jeez. I'm sorry. I'm Hitch Cotton. The Third, if it matters."

His obvious misery prevented us from snickering at the ridiculous old-money name.

"Forgive me if I don't shake hands," he continued, fluttering his fingers to indicate the tears and worse that had coated them during his outburst. "I'm sorry about the police car…I just ran out and started driving when I tried to call Jeremy, and the guy at the medical examiner's office picked up…"

He drooped again.

I patted his arm. "I'm sorry."

Joe and Porter made appropriate sympathetic noises, and we all waited quietly, his breathing loud in the thick air, the silence heavy.

"Get that man-stealing twink of a yacht queen out of here!"

Everyone turned in the direction of the shout.

Stepping out of a big midnight-blue car, door held by a driver who looked like he was working on his own case of PTSD, was a man in a bright satin caftan. It could have been a giant poppy print, or just a bunch of red-green-and-yellow blotches with some black swirls. Whatever it was, it was definitely a statement.

Especially on a guy who was built like a linebacker and carried himself like a gangster. Imagine a mob enforcer in a sweeping robe, and you'll be in the neighborhood.

Porter was the first to recover the power of speech. "And who might you be?"

"I *might* be the Second Coming," he said with a pronounced and unmistakable Jersey accent.

Well, that was a stopper.

"I might also be the Wicked Witch of the West," continued our new visitor. "Or, perhaps, more appropriate to this production, I might be Don Pedro, the Prince of Aragon."

The ruling prince in *Much Ado About Nothing*.

"You!" Hitch gasped, jumping to his feet, almost knocking me over in an effort to get to our latest arrival.

"Yes, me, the true widower of the lamented Sir Jeremy Hightower, that bigamous and duplicitous son of a—"

"Behave!"

Porter snapped the word as she stepped between the men.

They clammed up immediately, as people generally did in response to that tone. Someday, I'm going to get Joe to have her teach it to me.

He and I exchanged glances as Porter took charge, squirming a bit like a couple of high schoolers watching the principal lay down the law with the burnouts.

"All right," she said, with a nod to Hitch. "We know your name and how you got here. How about you, big fella? What's your story?"

"Well, obviously, I've just flown in. Your people called me last night."

"You were in England?" I hadn't intended to say out loud, but the shocks of the day had clearly loosened my boundaries a bit.

"Yes, Orphan Annie, they permit Jersey guys into the King's domain. The Queen was far better, but of course, beggars can't be-"

"Stop." Porter shot me a glare as she snapped at him.

Joe scowled at the guy. "So you're the emergency contact the police called last night."

"That's me. Vic Nero. Originally of Newark, lately of Mayfair, thanks for asking. Got the house in the split. I like London."

"No doubt." Porter nodded. "Was your divorce finalized?"

"Not quite."

"That's not true!" Hitch snapped. "We got married a month ago in Maine."

"I don't care what you did in Maine, pal. The divorce isn't final."

"He said you were still sorting out the property settlement, but he was free to marry."

"Well, surprise, sweetcheeks, he lied to you," snapped Vic. "He wasn't free to cross the street, never mind marry anyone."

"Oh, no." Hitch crumpled back onto the bench.

I did rub his back then, like I would Henry's when he had a nightmare. I wanted to smack the smile off Vic's face. He might as well have kicked a puppy.

Porter glared at Vic. "I think we need to get you fellas over to the police station for a little talk."

"What?" Vic bristled. "Do I need to call my barrister?"

Hitch just shook his head.

"No, no," Joe said quickly. "This is just to sort out who's in charge of what and talk through the next steps so you can make arrangements and such."

"Arrangements?" Vic let out an operatic cry, his voice cracking on the last syllable, and he moved toward Hitch and me. "Out of the way, Orphan Annie, I need a hug."

I ended up between Porter and Joe, as the two men, who'd been ready to slug it out seconds ago, collapsed together in a weepy embrace.

"Um, what the…"

Colby asked, but we were all thinking it.

"Loss doesn't always make sense," I said. The Ambassador from Widowhood was back.

"Any chance you have a few minutes to come along, Dr. Shaw?" Porter asked. "You seem to have a bit of a rapport."

Joe's gaze moved from Porter to the sobbing husbands, to me. A silent plea for help.

"Sure." I glanced from the men to the prosecutors. "I have a few minutes. But if the big one calls me Orphan Annie again, I'm slugging him."

Porter nodded. "Entirely fair."

Chapter Eleven

A Lovely Afternoon Walk

A surreal hour later, I was thrilled to use Dina's text, asking me if I wanted to walk with Tiffany, as an excuse to slip away from the police station. Hitch and Vic had decided to fill out the first batch of forms together and fight out the legalities later, in a surprisingly calm and adult fashion.

I figured it wouldn't last.

I also figured I didn't want to be there when it fell apart.

Over at the old rectory, Dina and her husband Ben were sitting in two of the worn-in Adirondacks in the garden, chatting quietly.

"How go the wars?" I asked as I opened the gate in the white picket fence and slipped inside.

"Nothing new," Ben said, managing a weary smile. "We're down to one statie from the hate crimes unit out front, and the feds on speed dial. I think we're supposed to feel protected."

"I'm trying to see it that way," Dina agreed. She'd changed into khaki capris and a chambray shirt, so she was comfortable for the walk—and the rest of the day. "But it's not easy."

"Not at all."

"What about you?" she asked. "I saw some of the drama on the Green."

"Not the play," Ben added.

"Shakespearean enough," I said. "Sir Jeremy, the victim, apparently had two husbands."

"Two husbands?" Tiffany asked as she walked into the garden. In civvies, she was cute and comfortable, wearing long denim shorts and a sun-protection tee emblazoned with giant flowers in shades of pink, her caramel hair loosened to free some strands around her face. "Really?"

"Really," I said. "It's not talking out of school since they had it out on the Green in front of everyone."

"True." Dina stood and picked up her big smoke-framed sunglasses.

"And we're all more than capable of keeping a confidence," added Tiffany.

Ben picked up his bottle of lemon soda. "Suddenly I'm feeling a lot better about everything."

"What do you mean?" Dina gave her husband a very dubious scowl.

"Well, the fact that the victim is a bigamist with few, if any, connections to the temple sure points away from us." He took a sip. "I'd say the same thing of a straight bigamist, by the way."

"The bigamy's the issue, not the orientation," I said.

"Exactly."

"He's right," Dina said. "A person who can lie about something as important as marriage to someone as close as a partner could be doing any number of bad things.

"True that," Tiffany agreed. "It speaks to the person."

"But," Dina added quickly, "it does not mean anyone had a right to harm him, particularly in that disgusting fashion."

"No way."

Ben, Tiffany, and I sounded like some kind of round in our unintentional near-unison.

"I'm afraid the police—and Joe—have their work cut out for them," Dina said.

Until that moment, I'd been a pro. Focused on the homicide at hand and how I could help those affected or left behind. Not a thought about last night or even a trace of a blush.

But somehow, whether it was Dina's mention of his name, or the way Tiffany's brow flicked, suddenly, the realization hit that it was the morning after the Big Date, and I was standing here with my girls. And inquiring minds wanted to know.

I didn't blush so much as I erupted. Mount Saint Freaking Helens.

Dina and Tiffany exchanged glances and smiles.

"Well," Ben said, in his best avuncular rabbi's husband tone, though there was no way he could *not* have noticed, "the Mets are the early game, so I'm going to go enjoy that nice big-screen TV my lovely wife bought me for my last birthday. Have a good walk, ladies."

If there was a twinkle in his eyes as he nodded to us, we were able to play it off with friendly goodbye waves.

"All right," Dina said, grabbing my sleeve and steering me toward the fence, "you have some talking to do, young lady."

"Darn right you do," Tiffany opened the gate. "Let's go."

The Green was finally quiet. Colby had returned to his spot near the temple, on foot patrol now that the cruiser had been towed off to the public works garage. There were a few other walkers, glancing and pointing toward the backstage area, where one small space was still police-taped. No one seemed to pay much attention to the temple, other than waving at the three of us when we appeared from the side path.

Good. Word hadn't gotten out yet.

It would, of course, but surely we deserved a little normal friend time before the onslaught.

Famous last words, I know.

I knew all too well, because DiBiasi had put out a one-sentence press release confirming an apparent homicide on the Green and the legal name of the victim. As soon as the newsrooms checked their email, we would be the center of the local media universe. We might even get some interest from New York or the national celebrity websites.

I gave it until the evening assignment editors came on duty.

Maybe midday, since the few remaining local news operations often didn't have reporters until later in the day on weekends. My late husband Frank had been one of the last print breaking news reporters here, and the media scene had not improved. These days, on Sunday mornings, the TV stations usually ran a headline package recorded the night before.

But everything changes with a big story, and I had to figure some enterprising young journalist was going to try to make her bones on this.

Soon.

But hopefully not too soon.

"All right," Tiffany said, as we walked onto the little gravel road that ran between the Green and the buildings, including the temple and the Society. "How was the evening?"

"Well…we never got to the restaurant."

"Ah, yes, that's right," Dina said. She waited.

"Well, we got distracted."

Tiffany and Dina exchanged smiles. Then they both turned to me.

"So?" they asked.

"Well, he brought out candles for me to light, and one thing led to another." I glared at Dina. "You're the one who told me it's one of the Shabbat pleasures."

"What?" Tiffany had a puzzled expression.

Dina drew herself up to her full height and gave us both the rabbi look, clearing her throat. "It is considered a blessing to enjoy any number of physical pleasures, of course, in an appropriate and ethical way, on Shabbat. It's part of celebrating the Lord's many gifts to us. The love of a partner, and the physical expression of that love, of course, is a great gift indeed."

"I can agree with that." Tiffany grinned. "I'm going to use it on Jorge next time we have a night off together."

"Happy to help." Dina winked at her, then turned to me. "Now, of course, it's also the man's duty to make sure his partner is satisfied. Jewish law is very clear on that—"

She broke off in a giggle. Tiffany snickered.

"Nothing to worry about there," I said, before collapsing into giggles too.

The shared laughter was warm and wonderful, just what we needed after the last horrible day.

"All right," Dina said. "Then we can safely assume you two have safely crossed that bridge."

"That's it?" Tiffany asked. "Crossed the bridge?"

"Well," Dina said, an uncomfortable expression creeping up her face, "don't we want to respect her privacy?"

"Yeah, sure." Tiffany brushed it off.

"I'm not going to draw you a diagram," I said, attempting a tone of great dignity, "but let's just say I was literally swept off my feet."

"Oh?" asked Tiffany.

"Yeah." I beamed at my buddies. "Scooped me up and carried me right up the stairs."

Tiffany clapped her hands, then smiled wistfully. "Wow. Jorge hasn't done that in ages. It's awfully nice."

"Yeah." So what I sounded like was Marcia Brady. I'd earned it.

"Really?" asked Dina. "That's so—old movie."

"And your problem is?" Tiffany asked.

Dina contemplated for a moment. "Feels kind of sexist, I guess."

"Not if everyone involved is into it," Tiffany said.

"Right," I agreed. "It's all about consent and what's fun for you."

"Hm." Dina reflected. "I wonder if Ben even could—"

"If he hasn't, don't try it now," Tiffany warned. "Do you want to know how many people I have to transport with slipped discs after they try some kind of caveman situation? It's not fun when we get there…and a lot less fun at the ER."

Dina and I winced.

"Fair enough," Dina said, "We do just fine anyhow."

"I'd say, twenty years' worth." I nodded to her anniversary band, a thin but noticeable circle of light above her wedding ring.

"Twenty-four." Her turn to blush a bit. "We're spending a week in Tahiti next year."

Tiffany and I ooh'ed appropriately.

"Anyhow, the point is made," Dina said. "I'm glad you two got the good part of the evening in before the trouble started."

"Yeah—after everything you've been through, you deserve it." Tiffany patted my arm.

"He is pretty great."

"Don't be surprised if he starts talking about marriage." Dina's voice had a warning note.

"Jump back." Tiffany shook her head. "Little early, don't you think?"

"Well, he has, in a jokey way…" I started.

Dina gave a wise nod, Tiffany stared.

"Testing the waters," Dina smiled. "Old-school guys are so predictable."

"Not a bad thing," I said.

"Yeah?" asked Tiffany.

"A lot to work out," I admitted. "But yeah. I think we all know where this is going. Just not in any rush."

"Excellent attitude, Dr. Shaw." Dina gave me a wicked grin. "I love a good interfaith wedding."

"Cool off, Yenta." Tiffany elbowed her. "Remember that not-rushing thing?"

"Yeah, I know." The rabbi nodded. "But love is good, and there's not nearly enough of it in the world."

"Well, maybe Sir Jeremy had a little too much," Tiffany said.

"Sure sounds like it."

We all glanced over at the Green, still empty, even though I would have thought the company should be coming out by now. Just then, a single mournful chime rang through the air.

"Is it one o'clock?" I asked. I should probably touch base with Julia Henshaw at some point, to find out what happened.

"Yep." Tiffany looked at her phone. "Gotta go. Is Henry going to that STEAM Storytime at the Library this afternoon?"

"Sure is." The town library did a great job with summer programming, including frequent late-afternoon events on Sundays, to help with the weekend wind-down. "I need to get over to Garrett and Ed's and pick him up now so we can have a little time."

"Ava's all excited…apparently, there are experiments. She's been checking the flyer all weekend."

"Henry was too busy with the sleepover, but I'm sure he'll be into it now."

"Have fun," Dina said.

Tiffany and I both caught something in her voice, and we gave her the same look she'd given me a few minutes ago.

"Oh, fine." Her turn to blush. "Let's just say the rabbi's husband isn't going hungry."

Chapter Twelve

Too Many Husbands

Tiffany gave me a ride to Garrett and Ed's because it was on her way home, saving me a few minutes.

Henry, Garrett, and Norm were in the front yard, doing batting practice, their thing of the moment. Henry's not really a sporty guy, but since we figured out that he bats left even though he's right-handed, he's come to love it. Garrett pitched on his college baseball team, decades ago, so he was happy to dust off his skills. It's become special to them.

As I climbed down from Tiffany's SUV, Henry connected with a big swing and sent the wiffleball flying toward the back.

"Nice!" crowed Garrett.

Norm sped off after the ball, barking happily, as Henry threw down the bat and clapped his hands.

"Great job!" I called, holding out my arms.

"Ma!"

Henry ran over and tackle-hugged me. Someday, he's going to be too big for that...or I'm going to spend a lot of time on the ground. Just good to enjoy it while it lasts.

"Hey, fella."

"Well, look who's here." Garrett smiled. "How go the wars?"

"Could be worse." I pulled back and ruffled Henry's hair as he took off for Norm.

"Could always be worse." Garrett took off his ballcap and wiped his forearm across his brow. "Norm gets the ball, and I don't have to worry about hitting this when I mow later."

"Good catch."

Eyebrow flick and smile at the small pun. "Gonna warm up the tractor in a little while. Ed's taking Jana's three back down to Fairfield. Dave's daughter had to leave early because she had a game."

"So, it's yard work for you."

"And then a quiet night for the old coots." He put his State Police Spouse hat back on and settled it carefully. Garrett, as a very proud late-life husband, can never resist merch.

"After hosting five kids under ten, you've earned it."

"Damn right we have."

"And you wouldn't have it any other way."

"Not even a little." He beamed as he nodded to Henry. "He had a good night. No issues with the numbers."

"Great."

"And his mom?"

"Not nearly as bad as you'd think with the murder."

Garrett beamed. "Excellent. You know, Ed's not too thrilled."

"Reminded him of everything he doesn't like about Joe."

"Got it in one. How do you folks feel about dinner in the garden tomorrow?"

"Sounds good."

"Tell Joe he has to eat."

Meaning it's a command performance. "Okay."

"Not the zucchini, but he has to eat."

We smiled. For some reason, Joe has an open, loud, and very strong distaste for zucchini. Garrett finds it hilarious...and he's been known to tweak him on it.

"He does. And we will. Henry and I are seeing Mom for brunch in West Haven tomorrow, so we'll bring back some of those great steak tips from Pilato's."

"Works for me." Garrett nodded. "Ed's just watching out for you."

"I know."

"So who killed that jerk?"

"No obvious suspects yet, but there are two husbands."

"Two…hmm. Probably at least one too many."

"Probably," I agreed. "Jury's still out on that. They both seem to be decent guys, even if they're a bit over the top."

"Over the top, how?"

"Different ways. One is an old-money yacht boy. The other one is—well—kind of weird."

"What's weirder than a yacht boy?"

"A Jersey mobster in a caftan."

"Huh?"

"Carries himself like he just stepped off *The Sopranos,* but he was swathed in multicolored satin."

"Oh, my. I'd love to see that." He chuckled. "They do grow them weird in Jersey."

"He's the one who was living in Sir Jeremy's house in London," I said. "Apparently, he kept the Mayfair house in the split."

"The infamous glitter and tequila breakup?"

"Don't tell me it got to your corner of the internet."

Garrett beamed. "Oh, yes. It's a classic. Made me rethink my opposition to margaritas."

"You've never had a problem with glitter under the right circumstances."

"Of course not." His smile faded quickly. "Anyhow, it sounds like Joe's got a fine mess on his hands."

"You know we're all going to be involved in this before it's over," I said.

Norm and Henry loped up to us.

"Yeah, probably." Garrett patted the dog. "But at least you won't have to hear about puffed sleeves again."

"I may wish for puffed sleeves."

Chapter Thirteen

Storytime Prompt

Henry and I enjoyed a couple of hours at home getting re-scented by Cookie and relaxing together before STEAM Storytime at the library. If he had any questions or thoughts about my night out with Joe, he didn't share them, being far more interested in catching up with his kitty. Our fuzzy attention sponge wasn't happy at being left alone for a night and clearly wanted to ignore us to express his displeasure. But that lasted exactly as long as it took Henry to shake the bag of tuna surprise treats. Bribery helps.

It didn't hurt, either, that we had one of those short, loud summer thunderstorms and Cookie needed a lap, which we were happy to provide.

Storm over and everyone back to relative normal, it was time to zip over to the library. When we walked up, Jorge was dropping off Ava. He shot me a wave as the kids joined hands and ran for the door.

With an hour and a half to kill, I decided to head over to the Green, just to see if maybe I'd missed something. And, okay, to see if maybe Joe was there.

He'd texted me a couple of times, just to let me know he was going to work through dinner, so I had no concerns. But we'd still just crossed the bridge, as Dina so neatly expressed it, and I wanted to see him.

Joe wasn't on the Green, and neither were any of the theatre folks.

I thought.

"Christian!"

The shout was the only warning I had before I was tackle hugged.

I had my hands up, ready to fend off what I assumed was an attack, when I realized it was Julia Henshaw, the Shoreline Shakespeare Festival COO. A regal sixtyish Massachusetts native who wore her silver hair spiked into a crown and blazing burgundy lipstick, she tolerated no nonsense—and was not normally given to excessive drama. Ironic, I know, but a less florid style is actually extremely helpful if you're managing drama types.

And she essentially wore a sign warning everyone she was not to be messed with—that wild 00 pendant: Zero F's given, Zero BS taken.

That, though, was before her show director's violent death, which had clearly been triggering. I honestly didn't blame her, though Henry was normally the only person permitted to tackle hug me.

"Um, Julia…" I said, as I regained my balance.

She didn't detach. Here we go again. Somehow, I've been promoted to chief comforter.

"It's just so awful, Christian." Julia gasped, pulling back a little. "I'm sorry."

"It's okay," I said. "No apology needed."

Julia patted my arms and then straightened her shoulders, a partial return to her usual magisterial style. "I'm okay."

"No, you're not."

"Not even a little." Rueful smile.

"But you will be." I rested my hand on her arm and made deliberate eye contact.

She nodded, took a breath, and touched her pendant, maybe using it as a talisman to remind herself who she really is. Then gave me a searching look: "You're too good at this."

"Earned it the hard way," I replied.

"I know that one."

Julia had been through a series of tough losses herself in the last year or two—I'd gone to calling hours for two of her relatives—and we shared a mutual understanding and respect.

"Bet you do," I said. No need for either of us to pursue that line of conversation. "Are you here for rehearsal?"

"No." An annoyed head shake. "Checking out the area ahead of the company meeting."

"Meeting?" I realized I should have watched my texts while I was relaxing with Henry.

"Tomorrow at noon. Give everybody a chance to drink and cry and whatever tonight, then get back to work." Her tone suggested she favored more rehearsing and less drinking and crying—and had been overruled.

"Makes sense," I said. I wasn't a fan of drinking and crying either, after all. "You're going forward, then?"

"We have to." Her voice wobbled again, but she kept going. "We're a small company, Christian. Cancelling could put us out of business."

"Oh, hell. I'm sorry." What a rotten situation.

"I think we can do this." She took a breath. "I've already heard from Sir Jeremy's husband. He's willing to take over."

"Husband?" I asked. I wondered *which* husband.

"Yes. Lovely man by the name of Hitch. Says he knew Sir Jeremy's vision, and he'll step in and carry it out."

If Vic gets involved, I thought, it won't be a vision being carried out. But I wasn't sure how much she knew, and I didn't want to prejudice anything. I tried for a neutral response. "That could work."

"Hopefully. We'll work it out at the meeting tomorrow. Will you come?"

"Sure. Glad to pitch in."

"And maybe give an update on the investigation—the process, at least?"

"I have no official standing," I reminded her.

"No, but you've been here for the whole thing, and you have a connection to law enforcement. In a way, it's better coming from you, because you'll help damp down any speculation.

"Okay. But I probably won't be able to do much beyond confirm the identity of the victim because it's public record—then describe the investigative process. I'll turn it over to you for discussion of what happens next with the show."

Since I'd seen DiBiasi send out the press release (and even proofread it for him), I knew I would be safe to acknowledge what everyone already knew.

And I could certainly give them some insight into how investigations unfold.

"That'll do." Julia started walking toward the back of the theatre space, and I followed, since I was free for the moment. "Thanks."

"Glad to help."

"I'm glad I ran into you."

"Oh?"

"I actually have to ask you another favor."

That didn't sound good. "What?"

"Come here." She motioned down to the base of the stage. "I need somebody I can trust to take over the prompt book."

"What?"

"Sir Jeremy did it himself. He was really crazy about it—and this." She walked to the stage and picked up the big volume I'd last seen in Sir Jeremy's hands. "I don't think it's a great idea to saddle the husband with that."

I didn't think it was a great idea to give either husband a potential weapon, but it wasn't the time to say so. "Probably true. But I'm an historian, not a lit person."

"Oh, come on. How many of our productions have you done?"

"As a consultant on costume and cultural things, not dealing with the language. I haven't read Shakespeare since grad school."

"Puts you ahead of most of the company—including the ones onstage."

"It would be funny if it weren't true," I admitted. Most of the company was young, and it's fair to say the canon isn't big with the Gen-Zs. Unless it's the kind they shoot in a video game.

"Please, Christian," Julia said. "We need someone who's familiar with the material, and it *is* a slow time at the Historical Society."

"Oh, all right."

It did not escape my notice that the prompter's seat was an ideal place to gather information.

"Here's the book." Julia handed me the doorstop.

The weight threw me off balance for a second. "It's a monster."

"Isn't it? I think it's an old one from a 19th-century production. Very old, anyhow."

"Wow."

"Wow indeed. Apparently, the Victorian edition of the play was important to his vision. He'd lock it in the box office desk at the end of each rehearsal. Drove me nuts, but I understood. There's no safe in his trailer, so…"

"Yeah. Gotta be careful."

"Exactly. I probably don't want to know how valuable this thing is."

"You're right." I tried to get a grip on the behemoth, wondering why on earth Sir Jeremy used it. Extra—just like him, I guessed. And from my limited general knowledge of old books, probably worth a pretty penny. "Doing his own prompting—and with an antique book. That's a lot."

"I'd guess a control issue." Julia shrugged. "Anyhow, look it over when you get a chance tonight, and we'll see you at the meeting tomorrow."

"Sounds good."

We exchanged a half-hug, and I assured her again that she'd get through this.

Then, the Ambassador from Widowhood had to get moving toward her next assignment.

The sheer size and elegance of the antique prompter book was unusual. Last summer, I'd helped with the set dressings for a between-the-world-wars *Henry V* and spent an afternoon sitting with the prompter. Her "book" had been a black ring binder with laser-printed pages, lots of highlighter, and scribbles in the margins. The outside of it had been decorated with a patchwork of vintage cigarette cards and Playbills.

This was an ornate, deep green leather-bound volume, heavily embellished with gold leaf. Folio-sized, it was heavy, unwieldy.

And way more than just a script and collection of notes.

I needed to take a good look. This volume had far more significance than a sheaf of photocopies. It was too heavy to study while I walked. I hefted it and started heading away from the stage area.

The walk back to the library took me past the spot where Sir Jeremy was found. I hadn't seen it in daylight. I didn't cross the police line, just looked over it.

The grass was still crushed in the shape of his recumbent body. It was wet, not just damp from the brief thundershower, but soaked like it had been hosed down. I doubted either Julia or town officials had the presence of mind to call in one of the cleaning companies, so I supposed someone in the show had done it. Maybe a gesture of respect.

As I walked past, the late-afternoon sunlight sparked off something at the base of the curb. Awkwardly shifting the weight of the book, I bent down to take a look. A cufflink.

Not the kind I expected, though. I'd seen plenty of Sir Jeremy's links when he shot his cuffs for emphasis in the middle of a tirade, and he wore a few high-end sets: silver and lapis lazuli, onyx and mother-of-pearl inlay, heavy gold with a coat of arms—but not the same one as his signet ring. I'd had no idea whether any of the heraldry was real, and honestly, hadn't much cared. Might be worth a look later.

Right now, the issue was the cufflink at the curb: two vintage buttons fastened together. The buttons were pearlescent bright green acetate, with crystals embedded in a swirly pattern. High-style, somewhere between the 1930s and 1950s.

Definitely from a woman's blouse.

Maybe or maybe not the killer's.

I wasn't falling into the sexist trap of assuming stabbing was a male purview. Until Dr. Alexandre weighed in with more specifics on the angle and force, we had no way to know. But the backstage area was very well traveled, and our stylish lady could very easily have wandered by anytime.

The link had been washed into the roadside, and I probably wouldn't ruin its evidentiary value by picking it up…but I really didn't want to do that.

"Dr. Shaw!"

I turned to see Colby, after-shift scruffy in navy basketball shorts and a Police Academy tee, walking toward me, looking, if possible, even younger out of uniform. I swear he could have been a middle-schooler.

"Hey. What's up?" I asked as I stood.

"Thought I'd take one more look at the scene before I went home." His rounded face was tight, with a little puffiness under the eyes.

"Too tired to sleep?" I'd had that problem occasionally in grad school…and later.

"That's it, exactly." Sheepish shrug. "It's my first homicide."

I nodded.

He blushed. "I mean…"

"I know what you mean." I patted his arm. "Look, would you mind doing me a favor?"

"Sure. What?"

"I just found this cufflink washed into the road, and while I'm sure there's no evidence still on it, we still have to record it properly, just in case."

"Cool." Colby's face lit up, and he swung his backpack to the ground. "I have a couple evidence bags in here—"

"You carry evidence bags?"

"Sure. You never know."

"Guess not." I pointed to the piece. "See? It's from a woman's cuff. It might mean something."

"You mean it might be the killer's?"

"No idea," I said. "The full autopsy report isn't in yet. So all we know is that somebody used that knife."

"That horrible knife."

"Yeah." I sighed.

He shook his head as he knelt down to neatly grab the cufflink by using the bag as a glove, then flipped it inside.

"Slick," I said.

"You don't want to know why I'm good at that."

"Either walking a dog or doing cat litter."

Grin. "Both. Mom has a dog, and Dad has a cat. They would say both belong to me."

"Or you to them."

"That's closer to the mark." Colby stood up and pressed the bag closed. "Let me get a pen, and we'll sign it, and then I'll take it to Chief DiBiasi."

"You don't mind?" I knew the answer, but I wanted to give him a chance to say it.

"Nope." He grinned. "I'm bringing evidence to the Chief. That's pretty great. Should I tell him to call you if he needs to verify?"

"Sure." The church steeple bell chimed. "Yikes. I have to get back to the library."

"Okay. Thanks, Dr. Shaw."

I was smiling as I walked over to collect Henry.

Chapter Fourteen

Late-Night Talking

At the library, Henry and Ava were all charged up with scientific inspiration, and he spent the walk home burbling about his plan to fly to Mars.

It wasn't the time to point out the Type-1 was probably a dealbreaker for NASA...but it did remind me I should introduce him to Easton soon. Be really good for him to see an adult with Type-1 and an interesting and active professional life.

Back at the house, I threw together simple salads, extra grilled chicken for Henry, extra cherry tomatoes for me, and a separate plate of chicken chunks for Cookie. The real ruler of the roost was very unhappy at being alone most of the day and not shy about expressing it.

After his first batch of chicken was gone, supplemented by a bite from Henry, and several from me, Cookie decided we'd suffered enough, and settled onto the couch between us, purring. By the time Henry was enjoying the dark chocolate square that was his usual evening treat, the cat was snoring contentedly, curled back into his boy's leg.

After I finished the cleanup, I popped a bottle of my favorite tangerine seltzer and returned to the couch, grabbing a book and settling in to hang for a while. Other than that hour before the library, Henry and I hadn't had any real mom and boy time since Thursday night, and it seemed like forever ago. A treat to just sit together in our living room, read and watch a planet documentary, with the sunset breeze filtering through the screens. Relaxed and happy and safe.

Together.

Since it was still only Saturday night, I let Henry stay up a little later, tucking him and Cookie in with the window locked open a couple inches so they could sleep to the chirps and twitters of the night birds.

Once he was down, I poured a glass of chianti and stretched out on the couch with my book. As I sat, I caught a glimpse of the prompt book on the small table by the door, where I'd left it with my keys and bag. Should I have put down the wine and done some snooping through the prompt book? Absolutely.

Was I a little too fried to deal with it? Absolutely, also.

My read wasn't completely without merit, anyhow. A study of how 19th-century clothing styles evolved, I'd ordered it on interlibrary loan after Sir Jeremy's first email, in which he held forth at great length about women's dress, how it reflected the sexual mores of the time, the themes of the play, and how he wanted to illustrate all of this with the costumes.

Despite more than a decade of reading and writing in academe, I'd found Sir Jeremy's screed tough going. Worse, he insisted I take the email to Alannah, the costumer, and read it with her. She'd been even less enthused than I was, but our chat over coffee gave us a chance to reconnect from earlier productions, so all good.

I wondered how Alannah and her husband, Sean, the actor playing Hero's father, Leonato, were doing. A lot of other people associated with the show had been pouring out their emotions in the company group chat.

Even Julia had put up a few words about tomorrow's meeting, the devastating loss, and a couple of crying emojis.

Not Alannah, though.

Based on her warm, blunt personality and her clear antipathy to Sir Jeremy, I wondered if maybe she'd just decided she couldn't fake an appropriate level of upset.

Not that I blamed her.

Despite that, I doubted she'd been involved. Way too obvious and easy.

Not to mention a rather petty motive for murder, even considering theatre folk. I mean, if she'd killed Sir Jeremy over his stupid costume demands, Major Crimes could lock her up by morning, and we could all go back to our lives.

But she probably would have done it years ago. She'd done several shows with Sir Jeremy, and she knew exactly what she was getting. Not that she liked it, but Alannah and Sean had to draw some benefit from working with him.

There were several others in the company who would have made equally obvious suspects, thanks to Sir Jeremy's demanding nature. But, unlike straightforward Alannah, they were all participating in the virtual keening. I supposed I should look at it later, to see if anyone was overdoing it to divert suspicion.

Right now, though, I was more than happy to go back to Victorian attire.

Thankfully, the book was far more interesting than Sir Jeremy's thoughts. Lively and well-written, with plenty of fashion plates and photos of actual garments, it was a marvelous read. So marvelous, I lost track of time as I squinted at the edges of my reading glasses to get a closer look at the details of a corset.

The soft knock at my door startled me.

But I knew who it had to be.

Ten pm wasn't really that late for grownups. Especially right after crossing a bridge.

Smiling, I checked the peephole and opened the door.

"Hey."

"Hey, *cara.*" Cannoli trundled in, followed by Joe, looking adorably scruffy in long basketball shorts and a Yale Law T-shirt. "Had to walk Cannoli, and I thought I'd see if your light was on."

"My light's always on for you," I said, glad I'd taken a couple minutes to shower before dinner and put on the nice house outfit—green-striped pajama bottoms, matching camisole, and a thin oatmeal-colored cardigan.

"Good to know." I walked over to the kitchen and pulled out the little glass prep bowl I keep for Cannoli's visits and filled it with water. "Here, fella."

The tiny dog looked around to be sure there was no sign of Cookie, and then happily started slurping up the water. I hoped Cookie was deeply asleep enough he wouldn't notice the smell of dog seeping into his space.

Joe, who'd been watching with a smile, pulled me in for what was probably intended as a simple greeting kiss. Of course, it didn't stay that way.

All of a sudden, we were right back where we were before Joe's phone rang.

The events of the last twenty-four hours vanished in a flash, and the only words we exchanged for the next little while were his asking if the master bedroom door locked, and my assurance that it did.

Good thing Henry and Cookie are deep sleepers.

"I really didn't intend that," Joe said, when conversation was possible again.

"No complaints here." I snuggled in, resting my head on his shoulder.

"Good. I can't stay...or at least I shouldn't, but I really wanted to see you."

"Same here." I looked up at him. "Shouldn't?"

"Well, I figured you wouldn't want Henry to see me staying over..."

He knows me too well.

"I want you here." I took a breath, thought about how to choose the next words. "I want to be with you."

"But you're not sure how to explain to Henry."

"Yeah. I don't know what the thinking is, but..."

"I'm sure there are plenty of kids in his class whose parents have social lives."

"You're not my social life."

"No, I'm not." Joe kissed the top of my head. "You want to wait until we have something definitive to say?"

"I don't know." I leaned into his embrace. I knew what he meant by definitive. And I also knew it might be too soon. "We've only been together since May."

"But we know."

"Yeah, we do."

"So now we have to work everything out," he said.

"Exactly. But we did stay at your house when I had the concussion. And that was no big deal for him." I remembered the night after I'd been hurt helping break up a plot against Amy Taylor. Joe had brought us to his house so he could watch over me. The next morning. Henry had happily gone along with the sleepover as if it were routine. "Maybe we're overthinking it."

"Yeah?"

"Kids are adaptable. We know you're going to be here. So maybe you're just…here."

"I am here, for both you and Henry. As long as you'll have me."

"Right. So be here." I kissed him. "And maybe we worry about the explanations later."

"Ma!" An upset cry from Henry's room.

Maybe now.

I grabbed the first piece of clothing I could find, Joe's T-shirt, and ran. Henry was sitting up, looking very upset.

"What's wrong, sweetie?"

"Cookie clawed me." His voice came out small and much younger. "I moved, and he clawed me."

"Aw, honey." I sat down on the bed and pulled him in for a hug. This wasn't the first time Cookie had gotten feisty with Henry, and it always blew over. "C'mon, let me put a little disinfectant on it, and tuck you back in."

"Okay." We crossed the hall to his bathroom, and I was spraying the barely visible scratch with antibacterial when we heard a yowl and a yip from the kitchen.

Another run, this time for Henry *and* me.

Cookie was standing in the center of the small galley in fighting stance, hissing. Cannoli was cowering in the corner between the cabinets.

Since Cookie is about twice the size of Cannoli, the dog had every right to be scared, even if I knew Cookie couldn't kill a sock, never mind an actual living creature.

"Cookie!" I snapped. "Be nice to the poor little thing."

Cookie hissed and moved toward Cannoli. I scooped up the cat. The dog ran between Henry and me and scooted down the hall.

"What's Cannoli doing here, Ma?" Henry asked.

While I patted Cookie and tried to come up with an answer, another voice replied:

"Being scared out of his little mind, apparently."

Joe walked into the kitchen, and the tiny dog snuggled into his bare shoulder. Thankfully, he'd taken the time to put his shorts on, but there was still no doubt he was casual and comfortable here.

Talk about cat out of the bag.

Cookie, damn him, started purring.

"Hey, AlysDad." Henry greeted Joe with the same cheery smile as he would at a much more decent hour, in more decent attire.

"Hey, buddy. I was walking Cannoli and just came over to see your mom for a while."

"Cool. Next time, come early enough to see me, too." Henry yawned. "Tuck me back in while Ma talks to Cookie?"

"Sure."

Joe shot me a grin over Henry's head and followed him back to his bedroom. While they had their man-to-man, I put out a little wet food for Cookie and took the pitcher of homemade lemonade from the fridge.

Lemon- or limeade was my yard work day treat. Henry hated the stuff, so I could make it with regular sugar, and even a little twirl of honey from the farmers' market. It had been such a crazy week that I'd forgotten I had it. It was exactly the right thing to offer right now, when it was really too late for wine, with Joe back to the case later in the morning.

By the time Joe returned, Cannoli still snuggled in his shoulder, I was at the table with two freshly poured glasses.

Cookie looked up from his treat and hissed.

Cannoli yelped.

"Cookie!" I snapped.

The cat flicked his tail, the feline equivalent of a shrug, and stalked off toward the living room.

Joe sat at the table, still patting Cannoli.

He met my gaze with a grin. "I guess the cat is out of the bag."

"In more ways than one."

"Seems like Henry's okay with it," he said, reaching for the lemonade with his dog-free hand.

"It does, at least for now."

"So we've crossed that bridge."

"More bridges than one the last day or so," I said.

"*If ever two were one, then surely we.*" He put down his glass and rested his hand on mine.

"The Reverend Donne has returned."

Shy smile. "Yeah."

We bent our heads together, a nice, warm couple moment, even with Cannoli's little snuffle in the background.

"I love you, Giuseppe," I said.

Joe's eyes widened, and he pulled back. "How…"

"Easton called you that. I figured it was just a nickname." I shrugged. "A nice one."

"It's my actual name. Mama insisted…but Dad made her put 'Joe' on all the school forms."

"Very cool."

"Yeah?"

"Definitely. Always good to honor your heritage. My name is a very old Scottish one, you know."

"I didn't. I just thought it was an unpronounceable version of Christine."

We shared a smile, happily gazing at each other across the table.

Cannoli squirmed up into Joe's jawline, breaking the moment.

We pulled apart, both laughing.

"Hell of a weekend," he said.

"And it's only half over."

"Tomorrow's going to be a mess. Going to have to talk to the husbands again. And hopefully we'll get the full report from Dr. Alexandre."

"Pay attention to the angle and depth of the wound."

"Why?"

"I found a woman's cufflink near the scene today."

"How do you know it was a woman's?"

"You know any man who'd wear an acid-green vintage button with crystal swirls?"

"Just met one today."

"Oh, hell." I sighed. Of course, he was right. I'd missed it. "Okay, so we have to keep the door open for a very fabulous gay man."

"The only one in the picture was in London when the murder happened. That at least seems to be verified."

"I think that would be hard to fake." I drank a bit more lemonade. "And there's no guarantee that the cufflink is even related. People do come through the Green a lot, especially with the play production."

"Where'd it end up?"

"Colby happened by when I was leaving the company meeting, and he whipped an evidence bag out of his backpack and scooped it up. He took it to the police station."

"Good. So if it's important, it's admissible. Nice catch, *Dottore*."

"My pleasure."

"Ah…don't give me ideas."

"Why not?" I batted it back with a little spin but no intent.

That part of the evening was over, and we both knew it.

"Well, I'm going to have an interesting Sunday, too," I said.

"Yeah?"

"There's a full company meeting at noon, and I've been asked to pitch in as prompter."

"Well, that will be interesting. Is Henry coming along?"

"Yeah. He'll be fine with a book, and maybe my phone." I smiled. "It'll feel like a treat."

"True."

We sipped our lemonade in pleasant silence for a moment.

We really are a good fit.

Once the lemonade was gone, he set the glass down with a rueful smile.

"So, I have to get out of here and get a little sleep." He held my gaze. "As much as I'd like to sleep here, I need to look decent to talk to witnesses."

"You know," I began, "maybe you want to keep a few things here."

"You could keep a few things at my house, too."

For a moment, we stared at each other.

"Little moves in the right direction?" he asked.

"I like it."

"I love you, *cara*."

"Back at you, Giuseppe."

Chapter Fifteen

The Show Must…Well, You Know

One weekend morning always belongs to my mother, who lives in a senior community near the water in East Haven, about twenty minutes away. We usually go out for a leisurely brunch with the Mad Knitters, her two best buddies.

Mom had been suspiciously willing to shift the time when I'd called last night, and I found out why when we arrived at Pokey's Diner at the ungodly hour of 9 a.m. to scoop up a surprisingly good table. At least I had a nice breeze off the Sound for the proceedings, which made the Spanish Inquisition seem like amateurs.

I probably should have been annoyed at Mom for tipping off her pals, but I'd been the fool who let slip that Joe and I were finally having a big date night, so it was really my own damn fault.

Suzanne Luciano, who took a special interest in Henry because she has only granddaughters, brought him a new Lego minifigure set, which distracted him from the "girl talk." Peggy, the naughty redhead of the trio, jumped right in with her best Torquemada, and Mom and Suzanne quickly joined the party.

I never thought I'd be grateful for the murder, but it gave me a convenient excuse to shut down the interrogation. While they were still giggling about us skipping dinner—all the detail I intended to give—I quickly pivoted to the phone calls that scuttled the end of the evening

It worked even better than expected.

Until the very end, as I packed up Henry, when the ladies announced they were trying to get tickets for the show. Their hopeful tone suggested they hoped I might have some inside pull to get them seats, though the production had sold out months ago.

Even if I had, I wouldn't.

"Would be such a nice night out," Mom said wistfully.

"And maybe we'll get a chance to meet Joe, too." Peggy gave me a fetching grin.

"Nice Italian boy," Suzanne added approvingly.

"I just want to see how he looks at you, sweetie," Mom assured me.

No sane person would put their new partner through that—even before the addition of a homicide investigation.

Since it was past 10:30 and I still had to stop at Pilato's Market to pick up their famous beef tips for tonight's garden dinner, I mumbled something agreeable and just kept going.

By the time we were back in Unity, beef tips duly procured and dropped off with Garrett, who was busy swearing at the Sunday news shows while Ed took Norm to the really good dog park over in Alcott, I'd decided the theatre company, no matter how dramatic, was a significant upgrade from the Mad Knitters.

Famous last words.

I gave Henry my phone and pointed him to a spot in the far upper corner.

I pulled the prompter book out of my bag, remembering that I really needed to give it a good look-over. Even a cursory examination suggested it was more than the usual piece of show equipment.

Books can be hard to date, because they were so precious and expensive until at least the early 19th century. People prized them, repairing and re-covering them, often very long into their useful lives. The binding on the prompt book, dark-green Morocco leather with embossing and remnants of gold leaf, probably dating from the turn of the 20th century. The pages inside looked much older, but that might not mean much. Victorian publishers sometimes reprinted classics, like Shakespeare or translations of Greek philosophers, in the style of the original. Nailing down the age might well require careful study, like a magnifying glass or even a microscopic study of the typeface and printing process, or even lab tests of the pages and the binding.

Many more questions than answers on first look. One thing I could say with certainty: this was a very valuable piece. I didn't know what it meant, but anyone with even a passing knowledge of the investigative process has to wonder when a murder victim was in possession of a valuable antique. And I wasn't really sure I wanted to be the next person holding it.

Carrying the precious book only a little nervously, I slipped down to the front, toward a side seat. The spot let me see everyone as they entered and still kept Henry in the corner of my vision. As I tried to sit, Julia Henshaw zipped across to me.

Before I could raise the idea of handing off the book, she started talking with wide, concerned eyes:

"Christian, did you hear about the second husband?"

"There was some talk…" I offered noncommittally.

"Well, there's going to be more."

I waited.

"They're both coming today."

"Both?"

"Both. The second one called me a few minutes after you, and I talked. I'm not at all sure what's going to happen when they get here."

Based on the way those two had behaved yesterday, I wasn't optimistic. "If you're not sure, maybe you should ask the cops to drop by."

"You think? Do they even have someone to send with everything else going on?"

"I don't know, but maybe the chief could roust Colby the rookie."

"Good idea." Julia rummaged her phone out of her red-strapped canvas tote. "I'll call and ask."

As she stepped away, I saw the curtains move on the dressing room tent, and a small, slim woman with green, blue, and aqua ombre hair emerged. Like many costumers, Alannah usually prefers very simple black clothing, today a capri-length jumpsuit topped with an open cardigan, but she likes to play where she can. I don't think I've seen her with the same hair color twice.

I waved.

She walked right over, and as she got closer, I saw her eyes were smudged and her face tired, a jarring contrast to the fun mermaid hair. "Hello, Christian."

"Hey. How are you holding up?"

"Oh, just a little wretched." Alannah's accent was a bit like Niamh Stanley's, lilting and musical even in her sadness. "Terrible thing."

"Absolutely terrible," I agreed.

"I'd like to say I can't imagine who'd wish him dead, but I'm afraid the list of people who didn't is shorter."

"I'm afraid you're right."

Alannah shook her head, and the mermaid waves flowed. "He was a horrid and exacting man, but he didn't deserve to have his throat cut."

"Just so." The group chat had chosen the neck wound as the cause of death, so there was no guilty knowledge in her comment. I took a deep breath and patted her arm. "The police will figure it out."

"Do you think we're safe? Sean and I drove past around noon yesterday and saw the police car at the temple."

"They're doing everything they can," I said.

"I heard on the news they were looking into the possibility of a hate crime. Have you heard anything about that?"

Since I knew police often held back a key detail, I didn't want to give out the swastika knife. But I also didn't know what Alannah's religious and/or ethnic background was, and I had to give her the chance to protect herself. I chose my words carefully: "The authorities think it's a possibility. So they're being extra cautious."

"Makes sense to me. Glad to see they take that sort of thing seriously."

"They do. For a small local police force, they're awfully good."

"Thanks, Christian. You've been a help," she said, holding my gaze for a moment, then turning as her husband emerged from the curtain. "Sean, love, let's take our seats."

Sean, a tall, spare man with salt-and-pepper hair, movie star cheekbones, and pale blue eyes, shot me a shy smile as he allowed Alannah to herd him toward a spot. Onstage, he lit up, one of those rare actors with a truly compelling presence. Offstage, though, he was low-key to the point of self-sabotage. I suspected he had some kind of social anxiety issue, because he rarely said more than a few words to anyone.

The rest of the cast and crew were wandering in now, mostly college or grad students working the summer festival for tiny wages and academic credit. There were also a few pros like Alannah and Sean, mid-career folks in key production positions, willing to accept what the Festival could offer because of the prestige and two expenses-paid months on the Connecticut shoreline.

That was the main draw for many: the Festival had a deal with a very nice waterfront resort complex, which put the company up in return for good seats for the paying customers. The Festival is a rep company, usually doing three productions a season in three different locations across the shoreline. Unity gets them every four years or so.

Somewhere back there, most of the town had been thrilled to have the mid-August production. Summer theatre productions usually do well anyhow, and by that point in the summer, dog day boredom had set in for folks who weren't taking long vacation trips, which was everyone I knew, for different reasons.

There were probably a lot of people who would be grateful the show would go on. And Julia was right, even though they're pretty stable as arts groups go, the Festival could not afford to lose a full week's receipts.

From the looks of the company, going on would be good therapy for them, too. Most of the young actors were red-eyed and dazed, and I guessed there had been some pretty serious therapeutic drinking last night. Maybe still this morning, I thought, as the two female leads passed one of those giant insulated mugs back and forth. One of the male leads swooped between them and grabbed it, taking a sip before handing it back to the girls with a bow, and they all managed a smile before he climbed over a seat and sat down beside them with the other cast members and stagehands.

The college kids seemed to be mingling without any regard to divisions of actors versus crew, but the grownups clearly wanted to hold their own space. The set designer, Alannah, and Sean, and the "swings," a few older community theatre folks who played a slew of small roles, were in the opposite section.

I probably should have taken a spot with them, as the prompter and an adult, but I preferred to observe.

Julia had just stepped into the center area under the stage when we heard a commotion at the front of the theatre.

"All right, people!"

The Jersey-flavored shout could only be one person.

And indeed, it was.

Vic Nero, now in the marginally less insane attire of a multicolored awning striped linen pajama set, marched down the center aisle, with Hitch Cotton in his wake. Hitch looked almost exactly as he had the previous day, though his shorts were washed red instead of khaki. Still Yacht Boy vibe, though.

Julia stared.

Clearly, she'd been told about the husbands without actually getting a look at them. This could be fun.

"Gentlemen?" asked Julia in a slightly tremulous tone.

"Hello, Ms. Henshaw," Hitch said. "Thank you for inviting us to take over."

"What else were you gonna do?" Vic asked.

Julia flinched.

"Seriously, though," Vic continued, diluting the menace with a friendly pat on her arm, "we're grateful for the chance."

"Very grateful." Hitch turned to the company, which, vets to rookies, pros to community theatre folk, was transfixed.

"All right! Eyes here." Vic called, completely unnecessarily.

Julia backed off and almost fell into a seat close to mine.

"Wow."

I wasn't sure if her comment was for me, or a general observation.

"So we all know a terrible thing has just happened. And we're all grieving,"

Vic said. "We're gonna take that as read."

"We're all grieving," Hitch cut in. "Especially us, the closest to him."

"About that," Vic said with a scowl at Hitch. "We're his husbands, and we have a better idea than anyone what his vision was for this show."

"Husbands?"

The squeaked question came from either Hero or Beatrice—I couldn't tell the young women's voices apart.

"Yeah, Cinderella," Vic replied. "We're sorting that out. All you need to know is we've agreed to work together to carry out Sir Jeremy's vision."

"And get his fee," whispered Julia

That explained some of it, I was sure, but I still had plenty of doubts.

The actress nodded.

Everybody else, properly chastened, just kept staring.

Those whose jaws weren't gaping already were struck dumb as Vic continued: "Awright, then. Sir Jeremy conceptualized this production as a commentary on Victorian sexual mores amid the uncertainty of the 1848 revolutions. As you know, we're using the story of Hero as a way to interrogate the role of women and the societal emphasis on heteronormative chastity…"

The expletive Julia breathed under her breath was far closer to what we'd expected of Vic. Though maybe I should have seen it coming, given that Zero-Zero pendant of hers. Sir Jeremy's senior husband went on in this vein for a good two minutes before he turned to Hitch.

"Now, while I'm taking charge of the overarching themes and the general style of the production, Mr. Cotton here will be working with you on delivery. The iambic pentameter of Shakespeare can easily sound like nursery rhymes if you're not properly schooled."

"And schooled," Hitch said, stepping into the front, his droop suddenly replaced with cool assurance, "you shall be. I'm sure you've all done Shakespeare before, but you've never done it for us."

He took a breath, and his face softened for an instant, then continued.

"My master's thesis is on Renaissance English. Sir Jeremy planned to bring me in for the final stretch of rehearsals, and we'll just start work now."

Nods across the theatre.

"Also, company," Vic said, "we're lucky enough to have an expert on Victorian life, and we'll be using her expertise as well."

Whaa...

"Dr. Shaw here has served as a consultant on a number of film and television productions. Ms. Henshaw has enlisted her to be our prompter, but she'll also be keeping an eye on you."

I will? I shot Vic a stunned glance.

He ignored it. "She'll be watching to make sure you're period-consistent in movement and demeanor. It's a very important part of the show. Remember, something as simple as striding across the stage floor the way you do offstage can ruin the illusion."

Vic was right, of course, but this was a whole new level of aggravation.

"We'll pay you more," Julia whispered.

I gave her a dubious look. She was going to find more money for me in a production they needed for survival?

And what kind of a jerk would I be to take it?

"You are Victorian ladies and gentlemen," Hitch said, backing up Vic. "Keep it in mind and act accordingly onstage."

"And she's nice." Vic shot a thumb my way. "If we have to tell you, you're really not gonna like it."

I had a sudden, terrifying vision of Vic trying to teach the girls to walk like ladies.

"Anything to add, Dr. Shaw?" asked Vic.

I coughed. Cleared my throat. Finally found my voice, and a word. "Delicacy, ladies."

"Good one, Doc." Vic made a fist and nodded in agreement. "That's the one. Be del-i-cate. And boys, ya gotta think elegant."

He swanned across the floor, moving with surprising grace, like Jackie Gleason in the old *Honeymooners* videos.

"Elegant," Hitch cut in, sending Vic a discouraging look. "But not swish, guys. Think manly. Sword on your hip, strong stance. This is a man's world, and while you are a gentleman, you're still very much a man. I want to see that Y chromosome action."

I fastened my eyes on the grass below the stage.

If I made eye contact with anyone, I would absolutely explode in inappropriate giggles.

Y chromosome action?

Heaven help us all.

Mercifully, that was pretty much the end of directing for the moment.

"All right," Vic said. "We've all got a lot to do right now, but we'll come back here and work scenes in an hour. Get yourself some coffee or breakfast or whatever you need and get back here, ready to work." He pointed to Hero and Beatrice. "Except for you two sweethearts. We need you."

He took a long look at the company, and his mob capo drill sergeant demeanor slipped just a tiny bit. "You're probably not feeling great right now. None of us are. This is a terrible loss. But there's a reason we say 'the show must go on.'"

The tough guy tone softened.

"We go on because it's the only thing we can do. We go on because it's the only way to keep moving forward. And we go on because it's the best thing we can do to pay tribute to the one we lost."

He took a deep, haggard breath.

And, shockingly, couldn't go on.

"Loss is the price of love." Hitch put an arm around Vic, his voice clear despite tears spilling from his eyes. "We're all paying that price today. And one way we can make it hurt less is to keep going."

Vic coughed, a huge, ugly, consumptive noise.

"Awright, you mutts, let's get ready and get back to work."

Chapter Sixteen

Delicate Ladies

Not being mutts, Henry and I started to make our escape, only to be stopped by our new overlords.

"Doc, I know it's Sunday," Hitch said.

"And I'm sure this fella has something fun to do," Vic continued, with a surprisingly approachable smile at Henry. "Do you play Dragon Race?"

Henry shot me an uncertain glance.

I nodded.

"Yeah. Was just playing it on Ma's phone."

"Here, then." Vic reached into his canvas tote and pulled out a large, top-of-the-line tablet. "It's on this—my nephew plays."

Henry's eyes widened. "Can I, Ma?"

"I assume this means you two need me?" I asked.

"I saw the way Hero and Beatrice walked in," Vic said. "We gotta get those girls into some skirts pronto. That's why I asked them to stay."

"They don't move at all appropriately," Hitch agreed. "I'm hoping, if they do their scene work in skirts, it'll help."

The offenders were still sipping on that shared drink. I thought it might be better to settle for sobriety first and work on delicacy later.

But they sure weren't going to find a good performance at the bottom of a giant go-cup.

"I'm sure it'll be easy enough to get them into the petticoats and slippers anyhow." I waved to Alannah. And perhaps they'll be buzzed enough to be docile, I thought. If not especially coordinated.

"So," Vic said, "Do you think you'll be able to give them an hour or so on general demeanor?"

For a moment, I looked at Henry, silently calculating how much he'd eaten at breakfast and how his meter was set. "Sure."

I handed Henry one of the granola bars I always kept in my purse, patted him on the head, and told him to have a good time playing. The only warning I offered was to be careful of Vic's tablet.

No need to make a big deal of Henry's condition if I could avoid it. It shouldn't always have to be the first thing people know about him—or us.

"What's up?" Alannah asked as she crossed to me.

"We'd like to get the girls into skirts for a little movement session," Vic said. "Can we dress 'em up?"

"Absolutely. We'll put them in the petticoats and slippers." Alannah motioned to her assistant, a normally sleepy-looking girl who was also playing a couple of bit parts. Today, like most of the company, the assistant was shellshocked and barely hanging on.

"Excellent. Thank you so much." Hitch patted Alannah's arm, then made encouraging eye contact with her minion, which a director didn't have to do. Sir Jeremy certainly would not have bothered.

While walking over to the costume tent, I remembered I needed to send Joe a text about the garden dinner:

Grill in Garrett and Ed's garden. Ed notes that you have to eat.

Guess I do. Time?

6ish.

I'll be there with ice cream. Love you.

Love YOU.

Within ten minutes, Hero, a self-possessed blonde Yale Drama student from the Berkshires, and Beatrice, a feisty redheaded NYU senior from Brooklyn, were appropriately kitted out and joining me for a promenade on the Green. We took it out there because the set crew was working on the main stage.

As requested by Vic, Alannah had scared up a full skirt for me, too, so I could demonstrate. My summer ballet flats were close enough to period to work—and Alannah didn't have anything in my size anyway. Tall girl blues or salvation, I wasn't sure.

The skirt, a blue tartan plaid intended for someone shorter and wider, felt heavy and awkward. This was before the crinoline, so the fullness came from many petticoats, and thanks to Sir Jeremy's obsession with authenticity, each costume came with a half-dozen or more layers of starched cotton lawn. For dress rehearsal and performance, the women would wear authentic underwear as well: chemises, corsets, pantalets, and stockings.

Amazingly, my leading ladies seemed entirely sober. I debated being impressed by their alcohol tolerance or worried about their livers and decided it was better to get down to business.

"All right," I said, as we lined up. "How do you feel?"

"Clumsy AF," Beatrice said, smoothing her green sprig-print skirt.

"Like I'm going to trip." Hero fussed with her white-on-white striped mull.

"You've both worked in costume before, right?" I asked.

Annoyed mumbles from both actors. Only then did I get it.

"First leads for both, right?"

They nodded. As I looked at the two of them standing awkwardly in their skirts, I understood. In the run-throughs I'd seen, I'd noticed only that they were very talented and had a good grasp of Shakespearean delivery. But now, I noticed something else: their size. Out here in the real world, they'd probably be considered normal, or maybe—just maybe—a tiny bit zaftig. But it was likely different in the cutthroat world of professional acting. They were probably steered to character and supporting roles, and I'd be willing to bet the farm they'd been fat-shamed in ways subtle and flagrant that I couldn't begin to imagine.

Sir Jeremy, whatever his faults, had clearly been making another statement by choosing women who actually met the softly curved 1840s standard of beauty rather than the scrawny waifs who tend to get leading roles now. As the proud owner of a generous Scotch-Irish peasant backside, I heartily applauded the choice.

I might have to start liking Sir Jeremy, now that he was no longer here to annoy me.

Anyhow, my two leading ladies clearly needed a crash course in demeanor, and it was my job to deliver it.

"All right, ladies," I said. "Delicacy is our word for the day."

"Delicacy."

Near-unison as two pairs of nervous but determined eyes focused on mine.

"Let's walk. Keep your stride shorter, and don't swing your hips. We're not in the crinoline era yet. Glide daintily."

"Dainty I ain't!" Beatrice, real name Lita Kazmarek, laughed.

"Not even a little." Hero, born Caro Saxon, chuckled too.

"Well, guess what, ladies, you're going to be. If you're delicate and dainty in your mind, the audience will believe it. You have to sell it. And you wouldn't have made it this far as actors if you couldn't."

Alannah shot me a glance and rolled her eyes as she pulled a pack of cigarettes from her pocket. From her skinny frame and the beginnings of lip wrinkles, I suspected she kept her weight down with nicotine. Not an unusual vice—or motivation—in her world.

I was thinking about my own favorite vices as I continued: "Tiny steps. Straight backs. Hands folded at your waist unless you're making a deliberate gesture."

I demonstrated. At my height, I probably looked like a giant teapot sailing down the path. But I did at least know how to explain it and make it work.

"Let's go," I said.

The first walk was rough. As each tried to glide, I helped them rein in their stride and their movements and encouraged them to hold their posture.

By the third walk, they were floating—or darn close to it.

I stepped out of line and stood beside Alannah for the fourth run. She offered me a drag, and I shook my head.

"Never got the habit."

"Never? Not even pot?"

"Lord, no. I'm a country girl."

"What do you do?"

"Drink."

Shared smile.

"Well, we're already doing better than we were with that damn Englishman."

"Sir Jeremy was a bit much, rest him," I said, making mental note of the "damn Englishman" and the unexpectedly sharp tone in which she said it.

"That's a way to put it. These girlies have no idea how lucky they are."

"Oh?"

"He was a holy terror on the women the last time I worked with him."

"Really."

"Really." She took another deep inhale. I tried not to watch. Ten years from now, she was going to be one of those women who couldn't wear bright lipstick because it would ooze halfway to her nose. "Nitpicked every move they made, every word, everything."

"Why not this time?"

"Too early. They're both pretty good on the language, and they've memorized the lines, so the real trouble was going to come this week."

"When they got dressed and moving?"

"Exactly." Another drag on the cig. "Last time, it was a 1920s production, and the flapper girls weren't bold or sparkly enough. Kept yelling: 'I want to see you shine!'"

I rummaged some gum out of my jacket pocket. I needed something, even just sugar-free fake mint. "You figure he was going to go after these two?"

"I know he was. This was my fourth show with this bounder. He was going to climb up one side and down the other of those two poor girls. Probably the male leads, too."

"Not cool."

"The ones who stand up to it deliver a great performance. The ones who don't—"

"How bad?"

"I know of a half-dozen who've quit after working with him. One may have ODed."

"No wonder you're not weeping."

"Weeping? Hell, I'd like to set off fireworks, Christian."

"I think I've got it!" Caro, the blonde girl playing Hero, made a positively swan-like twirl and proceeded toward me.

She did indeed have it.

"Yes!" I cheered. "Dainty!"

"Now me!" Lita, our Brooklyn Beatrice, took a turn. A bit more spirited, as appropriate for her character, but still to period.

"Good job."

I applauded. So did Alannah.

"Would they have seen it coming?" I asked her.

"Maybe. He did go a little rough when they were doing fittings Friday afternoon."

"The sleeves?"

"The sleeves." She nodded. "Came up and ripped the ribbons off Hero's arm and fussed with them. Caro looked like she was going to cry."

"Ah."

"And then he turned to Lita and said something about too much red hair."

"Well, those are fighting words," I said.

"No kidding." She flicked one of her mermaid curls. "I'm usually a redhead."

If she wanted to consider fuchsia, hot pink, and a sunset ombre that made me think of tropical drinks, redheaded, it was her business.

"Well, our ladies are on point, anyhow," I assured her.

"Hero! Beatrice!" Hitch called, yelling from the stage area.

The young women turned to each other, then me.

"You're ready." I curtsied to them, then turned to Hitch with a flourish. "I give you two delicate ladies!"

"Thanks, Doc!" Vic appeared. "Now, can I get my tablet back from your kid?"

Chapter Seventeen

Motive and Mowing

We'd barely walked in the house and started the long process of appeasing Cookie when my phone rang.

"Hey, Doc." DiBiasi.

An operatic howl in the background, followed by a growled, "Hush."

Vic and Hitch?

"Hi, Chief."

"Question for you…Poli figured you'd know."

"Okay."

"Was Sir Jeremy wearing a signet ring the last time you saw him?"

"Last time and every time," I assured him. "Big old thing. I never got close enough to tell if it was the real deal or a reproduction."

"But a big gold thing, either way?"

"Yes."

"Thanks. Looks like we may have a motive."

"Robbery?"

"Could be. It's not in his personal effects. Thanks, Dr. Shaw."

"Glad to help."

"You really want to help, why don't you tell the husbands it's missing."

Another growl off-speaker: "Missing?"

"Did you incompetents lose his ring?"

DiBiasi had clearly turned the phone out to the two.

"It's priceless! It's his family crest!"

Definitely Hitch.

"It's a medieval signet," Vic cut in, "and worth a chunk o'cash."

"Um, Chief?" I asked.

"Sorry, Dr. Shaw. Would you mind calling Ed? He does a little victim service stuff sometimes."

Ed did, in fact, occasionally pitch in with victim services, especially with LGBTQ+ families…but, I suspected this was far more about giving DiBiasi some backup. "Be glad to. Good luck."

"Yeah, well. Thanks."

Like most suburban males on a Sunday afternoon, Ed was looking for a reason to avoid yard work, and helping the bereaved was just a good karma bonus. He was out the door before he ended the call—with a reminder to bring Joe to dinner in the garden, especially now.

Now indeed.

Ladies and gentlemen, we may have a motive.

I'd never taken a good look at the ring, and honestly, Vic and Hitch's claim wasn't worth much. If our victim was capable of faking his identity, he was perfectly capable of faking a priceless ring as part of the package.

With the thing missing, it was going to be really hard to track, unless Sir Jeremy had insured it. Then, we could count on photos, documents, and all kinds of verification. Maybe I could at least find a photo. Trace the coat of arms, perhaps.

While Cookie crunched away on his treats, under Henry's adoring supervision, I fired up the desktop to see if I could gain a little insight.

It will not surprise you to know I didn't have a phone full of pictures of Sir Jeremy. An email file stuffed with his many thoughts on 19th-century clothing and sexual mores, for sure, but no pics of the dude.

His publicity photos were the best I could do. There was a big one on the Festival website, along with a splashy graphic screaming: "ACCLAIMED DIRECTOR GRACES SHORELINE SHAKESPEARE FEST."

Enough for me that he was gracing the page. His Very Important Auteur pose was a closeup with his chin resting on his hand, his eyes off in the middle distance as he entertained creative thoughts. Fortunately, it was the right hand, with a good view of the ring and the crest. I took a screenshot and magnified it.

The ring was chunky, the design a bit imperfect in a way that suggested the handiwork of an artisan, rather than poor quality. Likely a very old piece, or a copy of one, I thought.

The design itself was simpler than I would have expected from Sir Jeremy: a shield with a diagonal slash across it, plus three balls above, and two diamonds below. Sir Jeremy seemed like the lion and banners type.

What it definitely was not, was the Hightower family crest.

There is, in fact, a Hightower crest, which makes perfect sense, considering the name came from an old Anglo-Saxon clan of petty kings. Petty King was a terrific description of Sir Jeremy, guilty as I felt about the thought.

But their crest was—surprise!—a tower. Whatever our petty king had been sporting, it was not the Hightower family crest. Not really a revelation, since we knew he wasn't really a Hightower. Still, a Hightower ring would have added to the illusion, so the signet had to have some other significance.

First, I'd have to figure out the design. Years ago, I'd studied a bit of heraldry when I consulted on a project that included a Victorian-style medieval costume ball, a hugely popular event in the period. Not that I remembered much.

The design was straightforward enough, but it was only half of the picture. Just about everything in heraldry depends on color. The diagonal slash in the middle, known as a bend, could come in any color from argent, silver, to rouge, or red, and almost every basic shade in between, all named in French because of the Norman influence, and each signifying something different.

Every aristocratic family had a unique crest, and sometimes each member of the family had different crests. Women's arms were usually on a lozenge— a diamond—rather than a shield. Often, the children of a particularly dynastic marriage would quarter the arms of their parents, combining designs. Go far enough with that, and you get something that looks like the Cadillac logo, I'm sure no mistake for General Motors.

It wasn't all about dynastic marriages, either. Royal or aristocratic bastards (the legal term at the time) would carry a version of their father's crest, with the "bar sinister," mark designating an illegitimate union.

Even the simple crest on Sir Jeremy's ring could mean literally anything.

I didn't even know where to start.

"Ma, can I have the desktop?

Henry's call broke my heraldic reverie.

"Um, no, sweetheart. We have to do yard work now, remember?"

I sent the screenshot to my phone for later consideration.

"Cool," Henry said.

He was still young enough to enjoy ripping weeds out of our few beds and sweeping the walk, taking pride in accomplishing his responsibilities. In the middle of this crazy weekend, it was especially good for him to settle back into routine.

Good for me, too.

Mowing the lawn with my small, low-powered electric machine is intense physical labor, which usually helps me relax and let my mind float. It's one of the few things I do that has extremely low stakes and almost no possibility of criticism. As long as you keep the mower on close to the right track, you can't really screw it up. And the lawn isn't going to complain to the board that your mowing is too "woke," whine that the rows aren't precise enough, or demand you explain your strategic plan for future cuts.

Yep, it's been an...*interesting* year with a few board members.

All that to say, mowing is my zen. And on that afternoon, I wished for a much larger lawn.

Chapter Eighteen

You Have to Eat

And on to family dinner.

Normally, we would spend Sunday evening relaxing after yard work, but Garrett and Ed's garden dinner was a nice treat—not to mention a requirement for Joe, who'd clearly understood the subtext in my message. At about 5:30, as I was trying to convince Henry to smooth down his damp hair instead of pushing it up into messy waves, Joe texted:

No-sugar chocolate sorbet and fresh peach ice cream.

Love you.

P.S. No short skirts since I have to behave around Dads.

I laughed out loud and pulled a pair of stone-colored capris and a semi-sheer coral-to-peach dip-dye sweater out of the closet. The sweater was soft, thin, and special; a very high-end brand I'd found at an insanely cheap price during a discount-store run for Henry's school clothes. A bit extra compared to my usual low-key style, and perfect for a night when Joe would see me. I was carefully dabbing on the long-wear coral lipstick I'd worn the other night when I heard Henry's cry from the living room:

"Ma! Cookie just threw up!"

So much for glamour.

By the time the hairball—giant and disgusting, a household hazard of having a big fuzzy cat—was cleaned up, and the container of freshly thawed shortbread cookies bagged up, we were running a bit late.

Turned out to be a good thing.

When we arrived, Garrett was composing a salad on the deck counter while Ed was grilling and chatting with Joe, while Cannoli sat on a nearby lawn chair happily sniffing the scent of cooking steak tips.

Dina and Tiffany and their respective husbands were nearby but not involved in the conversation, apparently enjoying their own round-robin on the possibility of rain later in the week, and its impact on their lawns and shrubs.

In suburbia, vegetation maintenance is always an issue by this point in the summer, for homeowners of all genders, faiths, and orientations. I would have happily joined in with my observations from the afternoon mow if Garrett hadn't caught my eye as Norm welcomed Henry with a generous licking.

Cannoli was too busy enjoying the steak show to notice anything else.

Henry happily dashed off with the big dog, following him to the patch of tall allium where Ava was playing with the dried-out blooms. I moved over to greet my beloved mentor with a hug.

"How go the wars?" I asked.

"Good here." Garrett returned to arranging his bowl of mixed greens, nodding toward Ed and Joe. "Better there."

"Yeah?"

"Yeah. I think those two might end up being friends…eventually."

"Eventually?"

"They've been talking about the theatre murder for the last ten minutes. Joe's bouncing ideas off Ed, and Ed's giving his thoughts. Pretty nice."

"Nice indeed." I looked over to the grill. Ed appeared to be explaining wound angles with his tongs.

"Now, we just make it last." Garrett smiled. "Our job is to not remind Ed how busy Joe is."

"Got it."

As he placed multicolored tomato slices on the greens, Garrett gave me a conspiratory smile. "We're gonna win him over."

"I take it you've made up your mind."

"If you'll recall, I was a holdout on Francis, so it's only fair for me to come over early now."

We shared a rueful smile. My late husband, Frank Glaser, had been a newspaper reporter when it was still a viable way to make a living. A damn good reporter, I'd add, a top-notch breaking news guy, who was almost always first on the scene, and always found a way to make every story fresh and immediate. The work was in his blood, as much a part of his DNA as his warm hazel eyes.

That was the only consolation when it killed him. One February night, he was driving to a triple-fatal fire, hit a patch of black ice, and spun into a power pole. Dead at the scene means no hope, but it also means no hard decisions or drawn-out waits. It also means no time to say goodbye. And no time to prepare.

I went to bed a wife and woke up a widow.

Frank's profession had been the reason Garrett wasn't too sure I should marry him. At the time, pre-Ed, Garrett was resigned to a single life punctuated by snacks, and he didn't put too much faith in the concept of true love. More, he was concerned I was moving too fast because I wanted to be a wife and mother, not necessarily Frank's wife.

He'd been wrong, and the first person to admit it after a long sit-down with Frank and, more importantly, a boozy brunch with me. And he happily served as my Best Person.

Now, more than two years after that terrible winter morning I got the call about Frank, both Ed and Garrett agreed I should be considering a new partner. Ed even agreed that Joe was the right kind of standup guy.

Everything else would just take time.

"Good call," I said, patting Garrett's hand. Thinking of Frank, even with the distance of time, always choked me up a little. But it wasn't raw pain now, as much as gratitude for what we'd had mixed with the sadness that it was gone.

Loss, as I had told Sir Jeremy's two husbands, is weird. And it sucks.

"Do you know how hard it is to make a salad in August without zucchini?" Garrett asked, a gleam in his eye as he enjoyed the misdirection.

"Still less painful this way, unless you want to hear Joe's lecture on why he hates it," I reminded him.

"Well, there's that." Garrett reached for a second bowl, filled with pale green shards. "I made a second salad—that shredded zucc thing Henry likes. Joe can ignore it if he wants to."

"That'll work." I took the zucchini salad and headed for the big picnic table, as Garrett picked up his big platter of squash-free veggies and followed.

Joe looked up from his conversation with Ed at that exact moment and grinned. The one I felt right down to my toes, that made the whole world fade into a blur around us, like some silly scene in a movie.

"Hey, Christian!" Ed called. "You can catch us up on the theatre folks."

"So that *was* you in the goofy outfit." Dina's husband Ben piped up. I'd heard a lawnmower while we were practicing, but I hadn't been able to place the sound. Ben, like me, is a Sunday yard worker and takes care of the lawn of the rabbi's residence.

As a top-notch eye surgeon and Yale instructor, he needs the break even more than I do.

"Yes," I said, with a flourish and a curtsy. "I was teaching Victorian demeanor to the leading ladies."

"Well, that must have been fun." Tiffany's dubious tone left no doubt of her views on Victorian demeanor.

"Do girls that age even understand what it means?" asked Dina, the mother of college-age twins, and frequent host to her kids' friends.

"These two do. High-end drama school students. This is their first lead, but not their first rodeo."

"Interesting." Tiffany's husband, Jorge, took another sip of the locally made lemon soda Dina and Ben always brought for these occasions. "Yalies?"

"One is."

"Good luck." The fire captain shook his head. "Let's just say they keep us busy at the station."

The glance he sent Tiffany suggested they'd had more than a few run-ins with *lux* and *veritas* during their time working together. When Ava was tiny, Tiffany had taken the EMT captain post in Unity so she could be closer to home. Jorge was still a New Haven firefighter, now running his own house—and so busy we rarely saw him.

"So, Victorian demeanor?" asked my guy, stepping over from the grill. He leaned down and took two bottles of soda from the case, handing one to me with a little flourish.

"Thank you, kind sir," I said, starting to turn the cap.

"Here, let me get that." Joe deftly popped it open and blushed as he realized everyone was watching him.

"Thanks," I said.

"Ah, the early days," Dina said with a laugh.

"Hey!" Ben turned to her with a wounded expression. "I still hold doors for you and tuck your afghan around you when you're studying."

"And I cook dinner at least twice a week." Jorge raised his soda in a half-toast, half-pointing gesture.

"We're proud of you back home, fellas." Garrett gave them a sarcastic little smile as he sat.

"Dinner's just about ready, folks." Ed reached for a big platter and started dishing the Pilato's Market steak tips, onions, mushrooms, and rainbow bell peppers onto it. Technically, it's a different dish from Italian sausage and peppers, so Ed can claim to be able to cook two things. But considering Ed's cooking technique: throw everything on the grill and watch like a hawk until it's done, it's really the same meal.

No matter. With some sourdough rolls from the bakery on the Green or a bowl of salad, depending on dietary needs, it was a perfect dinner.

Ed, as you'd expect of a good host, made sure everyone—canines included—had generous portions of beef and accoutrements before we all settled in to eat and converse. With the kids in the mix, the chat stayed light and fun, bouncing between baseball trash talk, classic sitcom plot points, and, of course, the usual New England complaints about the weather.

Only after the kids took their share of the ice cream in little paper cups and bounded off for a bit more quality time with Norm and Cannoli did we turn the tables to more serious concerns.

"Learn anything good at the rehearsal?" asked Ed.

"Plenty about the dynamics of the company, for sure," I replied. "Sir Jeremy's two husbands are running the show and actually getting along."

"I can't imagine that," Joe said.

"Whoa, back that truck up," Ben said. "The husbands are working together?"

"I know he was British, but isn't that still one too many?" Tiffany's husband asked and got a wifely elbow to the ribs.

"Apparently," I said, "Sir Jeremy convinced poor Hitch his divorce was final."

"Poor Hitch?" Ed asked. "He's the yacht-club guy, right?"

"Yeah. Hitchcock Huntingdon Cotton the Third," Joe couldn't get it out without a snicker. "He seems to be on the level and genuinely blindsided."

"What about husband number one?" Tiffany asked.

"That's the caftan guy, right?" asked Garrett.

The other men, gay and straight, winced in unison.

"Caftan?" Jorge finally asked.

"Caftan," I confirmed. "He showed up at the murder scene in a satin caftan in some kind of blindingly bright poppy print."

"What is he, swish?" asked Ed.

"Oh, not even a little," said Joe. "Think Jersey mobster swathed in charmeuse."

Ed's eyes widened. Garret snickered first, and then everyone else did, too.

"And these two mopes are running the show together?" Ed asked after favoring us all with a glare that looked a lot like Cookie's 'I meant to do that.'

"They are. And seem to be doing okay."

"Wow," Tiffany said first, and the others echoed.

"Yeah," I said. "I don't understand it, but I'm glad for it. Especially since I've somehow gotten sucked into being the prompter."

"Is that the thing where you sit just offstage and give people lines when they forget them?" Joe asked.

"Yep," I agreed. "In real theatres there's often a little pit for the prompter, but here, I'll probably just be in the wings."

He nodded, immediately absorbing the investigative advantages.

"Oh, that's going to be a lot of work," Dina said. "Sam and Syd were theatre kids. It will eat your week."

"How are you going to manage?" Tiffany asked. "Henry can hang with Ava tomorrow afternoon, but we're taking that midweek getaway special at Cosmic Castle up at Lake Willoughby with my brother and his kids."

"Jana took the kids there last summer," Ed said. "If you get a deal, it's terrific."

"That's what I've heard," agreed Ben. "Several of the families at the temple went last month. Almost made me wish the twins were little again."

"No, you don't." Dina sent her spouse a sharp glance. "They're much more fun now that they're real adult people."

"Maybe." Ben's face was a bit wistful as he took the last sip from his lemon soda.

"Anyhow," I cut in, "It's a slow week at the Society, and Henry's got one more week of camp. But the evenings could be interesting."

This was the part of the conversation where Garrett and Ed usually stepped in to offer their kid-watching services, to the delight of all involved. But somebody else beat them to the mark.

"I'd love to watch him."

As everyone turned to stare, Joe gave a sheepish shrug. "We get along just fine."

"You are in the middle of a homicide investigation," Ed reminded him with more than a slight edge in his voice.

"It's actually a lighter load than trying a case." Joe returned Ed's glare with low-key cool. "Right now, I'm mostly doing research and checking financials. Occasionally drafting a subpoena. Nothing that conflicts with spending time with Henry."

"Can you handle..." I started.

"Yep. Remember, I lived with Easton for a couple of years in school. I know about numbers and carbs and everything."

Garrett shot Ed a glance. Everyone else at the table understood it meant: butt out.

"Of course," Joe continued, turning to the men, "if he wants to come over to see you fellas and play with Norm or whatever, I'll bring him."

Garrett beamed. Ed gave a grudging nod.

"And he has Hebrew school Wednesday at six," Dina added. "So you can write some subpoenas then."

"Thanks, folks," I said. "I think I have to do this, in the interest of information gathering."

"As long as you're extremely careful," Ed reminded me. "You'll have your phone in your pocket at all times…and I want that new pepper spray in your purse."

Tiffany, Dina, and I all swallowed affectionate smiles. Ed had just recently presented us with our new mini canisters. He considered it his responsibility to keep the women in his life appropriately armed with defensive weaponry, and each year, on daughter Jana's birthday, she, and the rest of us, got our fresh supply.

"Absolutely," I assured him. "It's in my purse right now."

"As it should be." Jorge said it, but it was clear that all the other men at the table agreed.

"Did you get anything out of walking around in those skirts?" Ben asked.

"I learned a lot about the leading ladies," I said. "They're both from high-end programs and in their first really prominent roles."

"Really?" Dina asked. "My sense is that most people who go to college for drama have been playing leads all along. Especially if they're in a big program."

"You'd think so," I said, "But it seems like they've been tracked to supporting and character roles."

"I've seen them." Tiffany scowled. "It's about as looks-ist as it gets."

"Not cool," said Joe, a proud girl-dad who spent an awful lot of time and thought on making sure his daughter, very tall for her age, never felt anything other than beautiful.

"Nope," I agreed. "But an unfortunate reality. Whatever their instructors are doing, the business still tends to choose lollipops for the big roles."

"Lollipops?" asked Ed.

"Tiny body, big head," Tiffany explained. "It's not nearly as bad as it used to be. My sister Jen, the entertainment maven, stopped reading the sites for a while when she had some food issues a few years back. But it's still out there."

"It is, and it's not right," pronounced Dina. "And it's good to see these two healthy young women getting some play."

"It may be the only decent thing Sir Jeremy did." Even as I said it, though, I remembered Alannah's warning about what might have been coming. "But it may not have stayed that way. He was known to be abusive of his leads."

"Just women?" asked Joe.

"Apparently not. I'll look for more detail on that."

"Goes to motive," Ed said. "And not just the girls. I know what I'd do if some jumped-up British egotist started pushing my daughter around."

Garrett was not the only person at the table to hide a smile. In so many ways, Ed was the fullest expression of the dad stereotype.

Bet that one comes as a surprise. Not.

"Well," Ben said, picking up four of the empty soda bottles left on the table with his long fingers, "I have an early cataract removal, and I'd better get some sleep."

Everyone else nodded assent. While Ben's schedule often brought an early end to our nights, most of us also appreciated the reminder to get home at a decent hour. Whatever we might have planned to do once we got there.

Within a few minutes, the evening had wrapped up with hugs, handshakes, and ear scratches, depending on the participant and relationship, and we were all heading for our respective corners. Joe, who'd come from the office with a quick stop to get Cannoli, had his car and offered Henry and me a ride. We happily accepted, especially Henry, who loved to share the backseat with Cannoli, since the little dog would sit on his lap and might even lick his nose. Even though Cookie would make him pay, later.

After Joe put the car in gear and the windows up, he glanced at Henry in the rear-view mirror, made sure he was busy, and spoke:

"I'm buying Ed breakfast tomorrow."

"Huh?"

"I need a man-to-man talk with him."

"Are you sure? He's starting to come around and pushing him is exactly the wrong-"

"Not that, *cara*."

"What, then?"

"I need some insight into gay life. This thing with the husbands working together seems really weird to me." Joe's face tightened. "My sister tells me gay men have a somewhat different understanding of fidelity and such than many straight couples."

"Ah." I figured his sister, married to a woman and active in some LGBTQ+ advocacy groups, might know.

"Not better or worse, I know, just different." A squirm. "Stuff I'm sure Ed would never discuss around you. And, honestly, that I don't want to, either."

"That's fair."

"Really?"

"Yup. I'm a realist," I assured him, patting his arm. "Ed will talk much more freely if you're alone. And not at the diner."

"No?"

"No. That's where he hangs with his boys. Meet him at the Bagel Box over on Route Ten. He loves everything bagels, and Garrett won't have them in the house."

"Why?"

"Messy and too much going on. One of those weird married couple things." I shrugged. "Anyhow, it's a little out of the way, so he'll be comfortable talking about the kind of things you're going to ask there. And he'll appreciate that you didn't want to talk about that stuff in his usual spot where one of his pals might walk in."

"Well, they're cool, aren't they?"

"They're cool with him being married to a man because he's Ed. They might not be so cool about sitting around discussing the finer points of gay life."

"Got it."

We rode in amiable silence for the next turn or two.

"You really okay with me watching the fella?"

"Absolutely."

"Good. I think it'll be good for us."

"So do I." I patted his leg. "Better not screw it up, though."

Chapter Nineteen

Man to Man Talks

Next morning, Henry and I woke up almost cheerful, thanks to a decent night's sleep. After I waved off the camp bus, I walked back to the Society to start clearing the paperwork I left for these slow summer weeks.

First, though, an important check-in.

My assistant, John Lewis Barnes, a Yale PhD student, was working on a new exhibit in the front room as part of his dissertation. It would be our marquee event in the fall, and a sizeable chunk of his final coursework.

"Hey, Doc," he said as I carefully closed the big, heavy door behind me.

"Hey, Lewis."

The Empress yowled a greeting too, from the stairs.

"I fed Her Majesty when I came in," Lewis assured me. "I think she's a little upset from all the upheaval. I apologized to her, but…"

I walked over to scratch the kitty behind the ears, which she grudgingly accepted. "It started long before you got here."

"Oh." His amiable face turned serious. "The murder."

"Yeah."

"When, exactly, did it happen?" he asked.

"Friday night. She was in the window watching the scene for a lot of it." I kept scratching, and the cat started purring. The Empress has a funky trill-purr, which we don't hear all that often, so it was a treat. "And people were in and out all weekend."

"I know it was pretty wild when I dropped by Saturday afternoon to get my lists." He shrugged. "Honestly, I was busy thinking about the research I needed to nail down at the library. They could have been doing the New Year's Eve fireworks, and I probably wouldn't have noticed."

"It wasn't that dramatic," I said, "but there were all kinds of police and forensic crews coming through all weekend. And then of course, the theatre company came back to work yesterday."

"Couldn't prove it by me," Lewis said. "Except for the Saturday stop, I was at the library nailing down the sources for my catalogue commentary."

"Still mastering the source list program?"

"Probably still be mastering it when I retire."

I just smiled. Better not to point out to him that back in the day, we didn't have a word-processing program to organize sources for us.

Lewis looked around the room, which was currently in its neutral, between-exhibits configuration. "Do you have some time this morning?"

"Absolutely. I'm doing paperwork, so peel me away anytime."

He looked down at his legal pad, on which he'd drawn the shapes of pieces of furniture, looked at the room, and back to me. "Sounds good."

"Still working on the catalogue?"

We both turned at the sound of the voice.

"New Hampshire!" Lewis called a cheery greeting to Faith Stowe, one of our best volunteers, a fiber arts expert, Lewis's work buddy, and a Granite State native, hence the nickname.

"Hi, Faith!" I returned her smile, noticing she looked a bit tired. "You look like you need coffee, too."

"Weekend with the grandbaby. Definitely need a boost."

"Don't we all." I didn't elaborate because I didn't want to waste any brewing time. "I'll get a pot going."

I walked back to my office, and into a surprise.

Sitting in my desk chair, neatly framed, was a 19th-century melodrama poster, featuring a lovely maiden swooning in the arms of her hero:
ROMANCE! DANGER!

EAST LYNNE
NOW PLAYING AT POLI'S WONDERLAND!

The "Poli's Wonderland" was in big red letters, jumping right out at the viewer, even if the viewer didn't happen to have a partner of the same name. Poli's Wonderland was an old New Haven theatre—no connection to Joe, whose family had come over after World War II—and we had a lot of ephemera from them, because people saved programs and posters from special experiences.

"New Hampshire and I thought you could use a little art for your office." Lewis nodded to Faith. The two have an unexpected and wonderful friendship, cemented over a shared love of restoring apparently hopeless pieces and hatred for Patriots legend Tom Brady. And, one can assume, the joy of tweaking their hapless boss.

They shared a grin, waiting for my reaction with only a little trepidation.

I laughed. How could I not?

"Nice." I blushed, which only added to the fun for them. "I suppose I yapped an awful lot about my big night out with Joe last week."

Faith, who had told me about the tragic loss of her first husband when I was dithering about getting involved with Joe, patted my arm. "Not too much. I hope you two got the date before the murder."

"Only part of it," I said before I thought.

Two pairs of eyes widened, and my light blush turned into a full volcanic eruption. I threw my hands up and joined the laugh.

"So, all good?" Faith asked.

"All very good." I picked up the poster and nodded to a blank spot on the wall. "I'll hang this later."

"We did talk about displaying more of our ephemera at the last board meeting," Faith reminded me.

"We did. And we all have work to do, don't we?"

She shifted right into brisk restoration mode. "I'm just putting lemon juice on the new tatted tablecloth and sitting it in the sun for a good bleach. Maybe Lewis will join me tomorrow to assess it for repairs?"

"Yes, please. Save me."

They were chuckling together as they left the office. I set the poster on one of the already book-filled guest chairs. I'd have to dig out a wall mount, but it was absolutely worth it.

For the next hour or so, I plowed through donation records, requests for the meeting room, and a weekend's worth of emails. Mostly useless, but a few interesting things: a request for a blurb from a pal on the women's history faculty at Shoreline State, a field trip query from a Jewish elementary school in the next town over, and a couple of preliminary feelers from potential clients for fall productions.

I put those aside for a fun break from the recordkeeping and buckled down to work.

Even though I could feel my brain cells dying every time I checked boxes and filled out spreadsheets, I must have been generating good karma, because as I finished the last new-donation form, I heard the door open.

"Hey, Mr. Poli!" Lewis's greeting was the tipoff, but I'd suspected I might get a later-than-usual morning visit.

From the sound of his voice, I wasn't the only one glad for any distraction. Might need to climb out of the paperwork and see how Lewis was doing. Not immediately, though.

I quickly got up and turned the Poli's Wonderland poster to the wall. With everything else going on, this wasn't the time to explain a good-natured goof, even though Joe would definitely appreciate it.

Joe, looking tired but awfully good in his usual summer work gear of light-gray suit pants and blue-check oxford, sleeves rolled up and collar open, walked into my office and put a small bag on my desk. "French Toast bagel with cinnamon brown sugar cream cheese."

"How did you—"

"Good guess."

I narrowed my eyes.

"Okay, Ed told me."

"And what else did he tell you?"

"Actually, a lot."

The Empress, who'd bounded down the stairs when she heard his footsteps, jumped up on the back of the guest chair and accepted an ear scratch before yowling and flouncing away. Her Imperial Majesty will never admit it, but she has a teensy crush.

"Got time to sit and tell me about it?"

"Not really.   Enough to say Ed and I had a very open and honest conversation, and I know a whole heckuva lot more about gay men than I did."

"Well, that's good."

He held my gaze. "That wasn't all."

"Oh?"

"Well, with all the boundaries coming down around the bagels, we got into the whole question of why he has such a problem with you and me."

"Really." I tensed.

"It's okay, *cara*. I'd be doing exactly the same thing if Aly were dating someone in law enforcement. He's right to worry. And to make sure I understand, you and Henry come first. Which I do." He reached for my hand. "I've already told Porter I'm going to be a bit less available."

"You are?"

"I've given the Trial Bureau far more than they deserve for the last few years. Earned some rope. Taking next week off, too."

"Really?" I asked. "Henry's out of camp, and I'm taking time."

"I heard that somewhere." He grinned. "How do you feel about a little getaway? Day trip or more?"

"I like it. But what about the office?"

"Well, all of this assumes we wrap up the theatre mess by the end of the week."

"Your lips to God's ears."

"Something like that."

Our eyes held.

No time for this now.

"All right," I said. "As long as you're not harming your career for us."

"I'm not." He twined fingers with mine. Smiled. "And Ed's given me his official blessing."

"Wow."

"Yep." He leaned in and kissed my cheek. "We'll talk—and not talk—more later. I need to get to the office."

"Yes, you do. And you don't have to worry about us."

"I know. Best thing about you."

Chapter Twenty

Slushie Break

Walking Joe to the door gave me a good excuse to wander into the front room.

"How go the wars?" I asked Lewis.

He looked up from the legal pad, which was chicken-scratched with arrows and shapes.

"Could be worse, I suppose."

"Tell me."

Lewis spent the next five minutes walking me through his concerns with the setup, while I listened and helped him talk it through. Nice to be able to help him.

Once the discussion was done, though, I had no excuse but to return to my office and the next thing on the list: some tax forms for donors.

"I'm sorry I didn't ask before," Lewis said as I turned to go. "What happened to Sir Jeremy?"

"Stabbed to death with what sure looked like our swastika letter opener."

"You mean the one with the backwards—"

"Yeah."

"Weird," Lewis said. "I saw that sitting out on the table Friday afternoon and wondered what was going on."

"You did?"

"Yeah. I know we keep it in the drawer unless it's being studied or part of a presentation, so it stood out."

"Which table?"

"That's what stood out. It was on the coffee table, like someone had picked it up, looked at it, and left it there."

"Really?"

"Yeah. I saw it when I came up from the basement a few minutes before the Regency tour arrived. My hands were full, so I didn't move it."

"And then the kids got here," I said.

"And we all know how that went."

We shared a dry smile. A small crowd of tenth graders looking for real things to match their Regency romance fantasies had actually turned out to be more of a handful than the whole squirrely fourth-grade class tour.

"So the knife was just sitting there in the early afternoon."

"And somebody took it to kill him," Lewis said, his tone quiet and sad.

"Do you remember if the swastika was visible?"

"I don't. I just always think of it as the swastika knife."

"So do I." And it always creeped me out, hence the fact that we kept it in a drawer.

But if it was sitting out there for anyone to grab with who knows what malicious intentions?

Well, we knew the evil action intended. We didn't know the extent of the evil behind it.

"Doesn't that suggest it wasn't any of our people?"

"How so?"

"If it was on the table, anyone could have grabbed it."

"Anyone who came through the Society. Not a happy thought."

"Except that most of the world came through Friday," he reminded me. "The theatre company's coffee machine was down."

"Oh, that's right." I only barely remembered; the mess had just added an extra layer to the chaos of the day, but now, it massively expanded our suspect list. "You probably need to talk to Mr. Poli at some point."

"Why don't I call him now?"

"You'd do anything to get away from planning, wouldn't you?"

Wry smile. "Don't get me wrong. I'm really looking forward to putting this whole thing together, but this spatial relations groundwork stuff is tedious."

"No more tedious than tax forms," I said as my phone buzzed.

Dina.

I stepped out of the front room and left Lewis to his work.

"What's up?"

"Actually, Easton Jeffries is." A bit of impish warmth in her tone suggested she was in a more optimistic mood this morning. "On the steeple."

"On the steeple?"

"Well, yeah. It's part of the inspection. Has to make sure the whole thing is structurally sound and that there's no moss, mold, termites, or whatnot."

"Whatnot?" I asked.

"I'm sure there are other things besides moss, mold, and termites, but I have no idea what they are. So, whatnot."

"Makes sense to me."

"Anyhow, I know he's all harnessed up, and I know he has an assistant with him, and I know we have police and medics and probably a Fed within shouting distance, but I'd feel a lot better if someone else could watch with me."

"Hmm…tax forms or standing outside in the summer breeze watching something cool…" I paused, strictly for effect. "Tough call."

"I'll throw in a slushie. I promised to take them to Kule's when they come down. Bring Lewis, too, if he has time."

"Sold. We'll be out in a minute."

I hit End, walked back to the office, tossed Joe's bagel in my mini-fridge so it would be edible when I had time for a snack, and grabbed my sunglasses, then waved to Lewis. "Rabbi Aaron is watching the architect inspect the steeple. Want to take a break and join us? There will be slushies later."

"You don't have to bribe me." Lewis grinned and set down his legal pad. "But it doesn't hurt."

Outside, Dina and Officer Colby were standing on the far side of the circular road around the Green, shading their eyes and gazing up at the steeple.

They were so absorbed in watching the show they didn't notice us until we stepped in line beside them and started looking up, too.

And no wonder.

At least fifty feet in the air, a man was rappelling around the steeple. Probably thirty feet below him, another man was holding ropes and watching him. Both were wearing harnesses and helmets. If I hadn't known the guy on the steeple was Easton Jeffries, I would never have recognized him.

Not just because of the distance, but because of the cool precision of his movements, absolutely focused and absorbed, the polar opposite of the easygoing fellow we'd met the other night. On-duty Easton was clearly far more intense.

One more way he was like the rest of us.

"Wow." I whistled under my breath.

Dina turned but didn't look away. "Amazing, isn't it?"

"Sure is." I leaned down and whispered to her, keeping my eyes on the steeple. "Lewis tells me he saw the knife sitting out on a table Friday. It may have been just a weapon of opportunity."

"You'll tell Joe."

"Yep. I'm sure they'll keep the security for now."

"Good."

She kept watching Easton, while I looked away for a moment to send Joe a quick text with Lewis's info on the knife. No immediate reply.

He was probably up to his eyeballs in a different corner of this mess.

Might as well enjoy the architect on the roof show. It really was cool, the way Easton nimbly rappelled around the steeple.

"I want to do that," Colby said, his cute Raggedy Andy face full of honest admiration—and a little envy. "I think they do those kinds of things on the Special Rescue Team."

"Probably," Lewis said. "I'm an academic, and I want to get up there and play."

"Right?" Colby nudged him.

Dina did look at me, then. We shared a smile. They may have been young professionals, but they sounded just like little boys. Suddenly, I was very glad Henry was at camp.

"Thank goodness Sam and Syd are still finishing their summer classes," she said. "Sam would be trying to climb up there."

"So would Henry."

We shook our heads together. Moms gonna mom.

"Nothing bad so far, Rabbi!" yelled Easton, with a thumbs-up.

"Thanks!" Dina called back.

For the next ten minutes or so, we watched with interest and only a little concern as Easton and his assistant nimbly worked their way around the steeple and roof, then finally rappelled down the ropes, floating gracefully to the ground.

"Wow." Lewis was the first one to say it, but we all followed.

"One of the coolest parts of my job," Easton said with a little Jimmy Stewart shrug. As Dina did a quick and friendly round of introductions, I reminded myself I really needed to get him and Henry together. Even at the risk of Henry wanting to start climbing steeples.

The short walk to Kule's Ice Cream, in an old Victorian mansion just past the outer edge of the Green, took only a few minutes, but it was enough for me to scoot between Easton and Lewis, who clearly had a bad case of the gee-whiz.

"Hey," I said.

"Hey, doc," said Easton. "Hope the rest of the weekend was decent."

"Had its moments."

Shared smiles. Lewis shot me a wink and moved on ahead.

"Y'know," Easton said, "Giuseppe has it pretty bad."

"Good to know."

"Something you should know."

I waited. A muscle in his jaw flicked—much the way Joe's did when he discussed difficult things.

"He and Amber are okay now, but she really hurt him with the whole packing up and leaving for a guy who was making the buck."

"I gathered that. Honestly, I think he's pretty great for being civil."

"Right? I sure wouldn't be able to."

"You would," I assured him. "If it's for your kid."

"Good point."

"And speaking of kids, I'd really like to get you and Henry together. I don't want to throw around words like role model, but—"

"Yeah, that's a bit much." Easton grinned. "But I'm coming back Saturday afternoon to double-check the measurements. It's the only time I have for a climb up that wouldn't disrupt the services. Maybe Henry would like to watch."

"Great idea."

"And when this whole theatre thing is over, I'm absolutely sure my wife would love to have you three over for dinner in the garden."

"We'll bring the ice cream and Italian ice," I said.

"As long as it's from here." Easton smiled as we walked up to the porch, "I've heard about it."

"It is, in fact, that good," Dina said. "And the slushies are ethereal."

"The rabbi's right," Lewis agreed.

As we headed in, Alannah and Sean were coming out, waffle cones in hand. I was glad to see them looking a bit more relaxed. More, with my romantic radar sharpened by recent events, I caught the way their gaze locked as he held the door for her.

Nice to see that kind of bond in a long-married couple.

"Ice cream helps with everything, doesn't it?" I asked.

"So true." Alannah held up her cone with a vivid green scoop. "Daiquiri ice. Tasty, and it's my favorite color."

"Too much for me," Sean said. "I'll stick with plain chocolate."

We laughed.

"I don't think you know each other. Easton Jeffries, meet Alannah and Sean Yard, costumer and actor. Easton's architectural firm is inspecting the temple."

"Wow," Sean said.

"How fascinating," Alannah agreed.

Easton tilted his head a bit as their eyes met. "Did you find what you were looking for the other night?"

Alannah startled. Almost dropped her cone.

A short but noticeable pause before she took a breath and nodded.

"Oh, that's right," she said. "You were going to dinner at the rabbi's when I had to run out to the craft store for some trims."

"You went to the craft store?" I asked, my curiosity piqued by her reaction—and the errand, somewhat odd for a period piece. "Thank heaven Sir Jeremy never found out."

"They carry some very credible glass beads, you know." She shrugged. "And I'm sorry, but the show budget did not extend to silk thread."

She and I shared a dry laugh about Sir Jeremy, and while the guys looked a little confused. I didn't blame her for trying to find good modern beads rather than sourcing vintage ones—we'd done the same in a few large restoration projects.

"Well, enjoy," I said, as the moment quickly passed. "We're going to get ours."

"And well you should," Sean said. "Too good to miss."

Inside, we caught up with Dina. She was working on filling out her frequent-cone loyalty card, and didn't mind picking up the fairly sizeable tab, but she was also happy to let me take care of putting a nice tip in the jar.

Once supplied with slushies, which are indeed ethereal, we wandered back toward our respective workplaces, chatting amiably.

Lewis and Easton's assistant, a fellow grad student, commiserated about their respective busy lives, while Dina, Easton, and I fell in step together.

Dina nodded toward the crime scene area, now without tape but still very well marked in all our minds. "Must have been awful for you, finding him."

"Yeah." Easton took a deep breath. "I'd never seen a body outside a funeral home. Gonna be burned in my mind forever, all bloody and twisted in the light of my phone."

The rabbi patted his arm. She hadn't been making casual conversation. She was trying to make sure he was all right. "Tough stuff. You know there's help for PTSD if you need it."

"Might ask you for some names. Or maybe just drop in for a coffee if it's cool."

"It's absolutely cool."

"She knows her stuff," I assured him. "And it's no surprise if it sticks with you. Most people never see this sort of thing."

"Yeah. I don't have a photographic memory, but I envision things in three dimensions, good for the job, you know."

"Better than you think." I nodded. "Henry *does* have a photographic memory."

"That must be interesting."

"It's usually good, but he sees the world a little differently than most."

"So do I," Easton said. "And I keep seeing the way the stabbing must have happened."

"Really?"

Dina and I spoke in unison, with probably different interests.

She was focused only on helping Easton deal with his trauma. I was concerned about that, too, of course, but also aware his impressions could be important evidence.

"Yeah," Easton took a sip of his slushie (no-sugar-added lemon) followed by a deep breath. "For some reason, I think he was attacked from below. He was already down when I got there, you know, but I have this mental picture of somebody reaching up and slashing at him. Maybe it's from the way he was bleeding or something."

"Ugh," said Dina. "Sometimes visualizing really helps when you're working out the trauma."

Certainly helped me. Dr. Alexandre was probably still diagramming the wound depths and angles, but it made me think one thing: a woman.

Sir Jeremy was a couple inches shorter than me, still taller than almost all the females and at least some of the males in the picture. Hitch and Vic were both taller, but they were out of the area anyhow.

It definitely did add weight to the idea that a woman who'd been on the wrong end of our imperious leader's wrath could have done it. Though I still had a hard time with the idea of a woman killing in such a bloody way. Sexist, I know.

Dina, good rabbi that she is, was far more focused on tending to Easton, asking him: "Do you have some time to talk?"

"I don't have to head for home for another half-hour or so."

"Well, I suspect Christian has a lot of work to do between the Society and the show," Dina said, sending a significant glance my way, "so maybe you and I could chat for a while."

"Sounds good, Rabbi."

Following Dina's lead, I took my leave—and my blue slushie—and headed back to the Society.

Despite my fantasies, the paperwork had not done itself.

But there were texts from Julia Henshaw and Hitch asking if I could get over to the Green to run scenes in an hour or so.

Thank goodness for another busy day at the ranch.

Chapter Twenty-One

Alert the Local Media

"Christian! Glad I didn't miss you!"

Niamh's cheery, Irish-flavored tones rang through the foyer as I walked in, carrying my half-empty blue slushie.

"Hey!" I closed the door and looked for a place to ditch the embarrassing treat, giving up as she laughed.

"Kule's?" she asked with a chuckle.

"Yep." I shrugged. "They're wonderful."

"I prefer the pineapple, myself. Just a bit exotic." Her eyes gleamed. "But I'd never judge anyone for their drink preference."

"Thanks. I have a thing for blue treats. Not sure why. They're just fun, I think."

"And a slushie should definitely be fun." She nodded toward my office. "The camera software is loaded on the desktop now, so you're all set to start taking and posting pics from the collection."

"That's great. Thank you so much."

"Of course. It's a pleasure to help." She looked past me to the Green. "Have they learned anything more about the murder?"

"You know it was Sir Jeremy."

"Yes, and don't I feel horrid about what I was thinking about him Friday afternoon." She shook her head. "Not that he hadn't earned it."

"He surely had," I agreed, thinking Niamh might be good for some basic insight, since we knew Sir Jeremy was originally from Ireland. "Even more than you know."

"How so?"

"He was Irish and lied about his background."

"Did he, now?" Niamh shook her head. "What part of Ireland…I assume you mean the Republic, not the U.K."

"Yes, indeed. He was originally Gerald O'Hara from Dublin. I don't know when he became a British citizen, but-"

"Christian, *acushla*, Brits aren't citizens, they're subjects."

"Oh, my." I shook my head, embarrassed. "Of course. Stupid error on my part, especially considering you folks fought for centuries to be citizens."

"Well, exactly. Even when I was a little girl, there was still a lot of bad feeling, usually just grumbling and such…but sometimes something more." She shook her head. "It's hard to imagine someone renouncing his Irish citizenship. At least in my family it is."

"You're a dual citizen?" I asked, quickly adding: "If you don't mind talking about it."

"Not at all. I'm proud to have dual citizenship. I was pleased as punch to raise my hand and take the oath—my husband and boys cheered me on at the ceremony—but I'd never give up Mother Ireland."

"Understandable. My uncle and his oldest son didn't speak for years after my cousin married an Australian and became a citizen there. He did it for the kids, of course, but my uncle took it as a betrayal."

"And you lovely lot are well over 200 years into your independence. So you can see how it would not be a popular decision."

"I sure can."

"Honestly, Christian, I'm hesitant to say this because I didn't like the man and I don't want to spit on his grave." Her amiable face tightened, showing genuine discomfort.

"Oh, I suspect spit will be the least of it," I assured her.

"You're not full Irish, so you don't understand, but running down the dead is far more than rude. It's bad luck. Me gran would probably say it might even make the unquiet spirit come after us."

"My grandma would probably have stopped at bad luck, but she was Scottish."

"Different kettle of fish. Pretty cold fish, honestly, from the ones I've known—no disrespect to your gran." Niamh shrugged. "Sorry to ramble."

"No worries," I assured her. "You have to talk yourself here."

"I do. But if I were your prosecutor friend, I'd be looking into whether the man had done something bad in Ireland. And whether anyone here knew or was affected by it."

"It's a very good point."

"Better than you know. No one is better at holding grudges than the Irish."

"Oh, the Scots are pretty good."

"Maybe. I can't say. What I do know is that you'd do well to chat with the Garda about plain old Gerald O'Hara of Dublin."

"I'll make sure Joe knows...he hadn't connected with the Garda at last call."

"That's also a point." Niamh's eyes narrowed. "Sure, they're swamped and all—every police force is—but the fact that they haven't gotten back to him yet suggests something."

"That they're not interested in Sir Jeremy?"

"Or they're glad somebody has cleared an old case for them...or possibly taken care of a fugitive they're happy to see gone." Niamh shrugged. "I don't know anyone in the Garda, but the foot-dragging seems unusual."

"Good to know," I said. "Thank you for the insight."

"Of course." She shook her head, as if to clear it, and when she spoke, her voice was a bit tentative. "You know I'm from Dublin, too. O'Hara's not an uncommon name. Do you know when he left?"

"I don't have exact dates. But his first London production was in the aughts."

"Ah. I was still in school. I don't remember much from that time besides cute boys and a lot of black eyeliner...not of it all on me." Good cheer restored with a girlish grin. "But a lot went on over my head, as it does with every kid."

"Isn't that the truth."

"You know, I'll call me Auntie Brig and ask her if she remembers anything involving a man named O'Hara back then. If the name Gerald O'Hara came up anywhere bad, she'll know of it."

"Well, there's one place it comes up," I said, unable to stop a snicker as the realization hit.

"What?"

"Scarlett O'Hara's dad in *Gone with the Wind*. I only realized when you said it."

"Heavens, you're right." Niamh's eyes widened as she processed it: "He changed a name that sounds fake to an even more fake one?"

"Maybe. Or maybe that was a fake name, too."

"Well, I can tell you for sure that recordkeeping wasn't what it is now, so it's at least a possibility."

"What's a possibility?" Julia Henshaw walked into the foyer, her tone cool, her demeanor calm, and her usual collected presence back with a vengeance.

"Well," I started slowly, "it looks like Sir Jeremy wasn't what he claimed he was."

"Oh, I know the title was fake." Julia shrugged. "I figured he got some sort of minor honor and overplayed it. Far from the first director to do that."

Niamh and I stared at her, stunned.

"Don't be so shocked. The guy was a name and a draw, and it was worth tolerating a certain amount of exaggeration to sell out the run."

"It's looking like more than that," I said. "Jeremy Hightower may have been a name, but it wasn't his."

"Oh, don't tell me we got taken by an impostor." Julia looked like she'd been slapped. "Is the real Sir Jeremy running around alive somewhere?"

Well, that was a possibility I hadn't considered. Add one more thing to Joe's list.

"You know, now that you mention it, I'm not sure. I was going on the assumption that this Gerald O'Hara person simply remade himself as Sir Jeremy."

"Gerald O'Hara?" Julia asked. "Like Scarlett's dad?"

Niamh smiled. "You got it right away."

"Oh, come on. Everybody read that damn thing at some point. Grandma raved about the romance, and I had to know, even if I ended up skipping over everything else because it made me sick." Julia's shudder wasn't white-chick guilt but genuine revulsion. I'd had the same reaction.

"It really is a horrifically racist book," I agreed. "But I read the Scarlett and Rhett stuff too."

"Much sexier in the movie," Niamh cut in. "Even though seeing the racial stuff is so much worse than reading it."

"Got that," I said, turning to her. "But you told me Gerald O'Hara isn't an uncommon Irish name."

"That's true. It could have been his real name."

"Or that overpriced freak could have been anybody," Julia said. "God, this nightmare keeps getting worse. What next?"

As an arts manager, never mind a lady of years and discretion, Julia should have known not to give the universe a chance to answer that question.

"What's that?" Niamh asked, looking out the door.

Julia looked. "Oh, holy frick."

She didn't say frick.

With her 00 necklace, you didn't really think she would, did you?

I muttered something equally unprintable under my breath, because a chunky white SUV with a great big blue NewsChannel 14 logo was pulling up in front of the theatre box office shed. At least one assignment editor had awakened.

"Well, this is going to be interesting," Niamh said. "Hope you ladies don't mind my abandoning you."

"I'd abandon us if I could," Julia replied.

As Niamh walked briskly to her car, fortunately in the back parking lot, a young woman climbed out of the van and started clomping over to us in impressively high heels. She was clearly hoping to work her way up to that big conservative network, because she was doing her best to copy the look: very blonde hair, cute little red dress with a skirt that was a couple inches shorter than practical for field work, and absolutely perfect makeup, complete with red lip to match the dress, despite the steamy day.

I was suddenly very aware of my wrinkled blazer and puffball hair.

I wanted to hide.

Julia, though, was ready for a fight. Considering what I knew of her political and social views, she'd probably been triggered by the Gadfly Network wannabee look. She had suddenly drawn herself up to her full height, eyes flashing fire, her burgundy mouth (I *have* to find out where she gets that long-wear lipstick!) curling into a small, wicked smile.

"Hello!" the reporter yelled. "Are you with the show?"

"We are." Julia walked down the steps with a cool air of command that would not have been out of place on either Queen Elizabeth. She shot me a quick glance, clearly an order to follow.

Like I would have missed this.

Not that I had any intention of serving as anything other than a silent lady-in-waiting.

"We would be happy to speak with you," Julia said. Royal we, I assure you.

"Oh, good." The reporter's careful expression cracked into a happy grin. She wasn't much older than Officer Colby. Probably just out of college.

I remembered Frank complaining about young and clueless reporters at scenes, replacing the seasoned pros he knew, thanks to media industry consolidation. How the mighty Connecticut media market has fallen, he'd say. This used to be a mid-career place, sometimes the last job before Boston or New York.

This pup had no idea what was about to hit her.

Julia held out her hand with a friendly smile. "I'm Julia Henshaw, CEO of the Shoreline Shakespeare Festival."

"Oh, wow. Just the person I wanted to talk to." The reporter pushed her hair back, and her fingers stuck in the strands for an instant. I knew it meant the fancy French manicure was press-on nails, because I'd worn a set for a family wedding last year. No great sin, just an interesting fact.

"I'm Lyman Damer from Channel 14 News," she said, quickly detaching the hair and taking Julia's outstretched hand.

Well, she had the memorably weird name part anyhow.

"Nice to meet you." Julia turned to me. "And this is our historical consultant, Dr. Christian Shaw. She had been working with Sir Jeremy on the production."

"Glad to meet you," I said, shaking her hand, though I was afraid of breaking her tiny bird bones. She had to be a foot shorter than me, with an extremely small frame

"Can I ask you a few questions for my story?"

"Sure," Julia said, nodding to the reporter's camera bag. "Whenever you're ready."

"One man band?" I asked her.

"We call it M.M.J.," the reporter said. "Multi-Media Journalist."

"Ah." I nodded. She was so young she didn't know the common industry slang from just a few years ago.

She pulled out the camera. The setup was faster than I'd expected.

Once she was ready to go, our visitor's hazel eyes sharpened, and I realized she was far cannier than I'd thought. "Do you plan to go on with the show despite the hate crime murder?"

"Really?" Julia asked, her tone cool and sharp. "Sir Jeremy's death is not being treated as a hate crime."

"So why did they increase security at the synagogue after the killing?"

The question told me two important things: she had done her homework, and the knife was not public knowledge. Which meant Joe and DiBiasi were doing a good job of keeping the information close.

One of the few advantages of our current desolate news landscape. Frank—and any other decent reporter who covered cops and courts regularly—would have known about the knife, because they had police, prosecutors, and medical examiner's office sources. Now, nobody had time to cultivate connections, and the authorities could keep things quiet.

Good for this case. Not for the world at large.

"They probably had a threat," Julia said. "Disgusting as it is, it does happen."

Lyman Damer wasn't sold, but she couldn't argue the point. "So the show must go on?"

"Of course, it must," Julia said. Her face changed, taking on a serious and resolute cast. "How better to pay tribute to Sir Jeremy's body of work than to complete this production that he set? And who better to do it than his husbands?"

"Husbands, plural?"

"It's a long story. There's some legal confusion about when the divorce was final. In any case, Mr. Cotton and Mr. Nero have agreed to work together to realize Sir Jeremy's last vision."

Lyman Damer lit up, as Julia fully expected her to do. "They are?"

"They are. I'm sure they'll be willing to talk to you at some point, as long as they can expect a respectful and careful interview."

"Oh, I can sure do that."

Julia's expression did not suggest confidence. "In any case, to answer your original question, the Festival and the *Much Ado About Nothing* company are absolutely devastated by the shocking loss of our director. We are amazed and inspired by the courage of his loved ones in working to keep the production going, and all we can do to support them is continue with the show as he would have wanted it."

The reporter's eyes widened.

"And," Julia continued, "I would remind you that while this is just a story to you, for all of us, it's the violent and shocking death of a colleague, and I hope you'll keep that in mind."

"Um, sure." She turned to me. "Anything to add?"

"No," I said. "Ms. Henshaw covered it magnificently."

"Well, fine." Lyman Damer turned off her camera. "Can you give me contact information for Sir Jeremy's husbands?"

"I'll have to ask them if it's all right. Come with me," she said, motioning to the box office shed. "I'll see if they're answering their phones..."

Julia shot me a grin over the reporter's head.

At least she'd won this round.

Chapter Twenty-Two

Home for Dinner

Mondays are often slow for rep companies, as actors do some scene work and refine their performances ahead of more focused rehearsals in the last few days before Thursday opening night.

That was good news for me, giving me a chance to get to Joe's by about six, meaning I'd only left him to cover for an hour and a half after Tiffany handled camp pickup. With the family trip, she really wanted to get Ava home and pack, so she handed off to Joe, who—she'd assured me in a text—was happy to take over.

I texted Joe to let him know I was done for the day and headed for his house, not that I'd been out of contact. After I texted him about the knife, he'd called for a quick confirmation, and he'd sent me a pic of Henry and Cannoli after Tiffany left.

But now, we were off duty.

Or trying, anyhow.

At the big vanilla brick house on Trelawney, I found Joe and a cheerfully grubby Henry on the front lawn, kicking a soccer ball back and forth, with Cannoli watching and cheering them on with yips.

"Hey, fellas!" I called as I climbed out of the car. "Who's winning?"

"Not me, for sure." Joe, who'd traded his work clothes for long shorts and a worn gray Yale tee, lightly kicked the ball back to Henry, who scooped it up.

"Hey, Ma!" He ran over and gave me a tackle hug while Joe smiled. "Good day at camp. We're starting a Gaga tournament tomorrow."

"Nice." I made a mental note to calibrate the meter for slightly more activity to absorb the local favorite pit-volleyball game and drop a few extra snacks in his bag. Never hurts to be prepared.

"What are you doing about dinner?" Joe asked, bending down to nudge the dog toward the door.

I shrugged. "Probably making chicken caesar salads."

"C'mon," he said. "Let me throw something together for us, and maybe we'll compare notes. I had an interesting chat with Dr. Alexandre today."

"I heard some interesting things today, too. Easton says hi."

"You saw him?"

"He climbed the temple today to check the steeple. It was pretty cool."

Henry's eyes widened. "Somebody climbed the steeple?"

"Joe's friend Easton, who's an architect," I explained. "It's his job."

"Wow."

"And, he's offered to let Henry watch him climb the steeple when he comes back Saturday."

"Really, Ma?" Henry asked.

"Yes, but only if we can work it out. Do you know what's really cool about Mr. Jeffries?"

"What?"

"In addition to climbing buildings, he also has Type-1."

"Seriously?" My boy's jaw dropped. I'm sure he was aware that there are plenty of adults with it, but he'd never met one outside a medical setting. "That is so cool."

"Easton is pretty cool," Joe said. "Is he okay?"

"Finding the body was a little rough on him," I said.

A concerned frown. "Probably would be."

"Yeah. He talked to Dina today, but it wouldn't hurt to have a word from a friend."

"Besides, I have to set up for Saturday." Joe opened his front door. "You're probably going to be busy with the show, so I'll work out the details."

"You just want to watch Easton climb the steeple."

"Oh, yeah."

"Saw that coming a mile away."

We shared a grin as Henry shot Joe a wink.

Cannoli trundled up to us, and Joe waved the dog through.

As Joe closed the door behind us, he held my gaze. "Should we exchange keys, maybe?"

Another corner for us, I thought. "You definitely need keys to my place, since you're going to be bringing Henry home."

"And you need keys for this place, too. I'll give you a set before you two go home tonight." He nodded to the kitchen. "Let's see about dinner. I made a batch of dough the other day, and I have some meatballs in the freezer…how do you feel about a pizza?"

"Sounds good to me."

"Now, you need some veggies, don't you?" He looked down at Henry.

"Got any zucchini?"

Henry's eyes twinkled as Joe glared.

"No, and you know why." Joe led the way into the kitchen. "Got some lettuce from the farmer's market, so it's salad for you."

"That nice butter lettuce?" I asked. "Garrett and Ed grow it, too."

"Good stuff, and it doesn't last, so we'd better eat it all."

A yip from Cannoli reminded us of our real mission. Joe fed him, and Henry bent down to pet him. We were going to have hell to pay when we got home. Even though Cookie was left with full bowls and plenty of water, he would act as if he'd been starved and abused.

Probably needed to give Joe the rundown on kitty care, too. I added that to my mental list…and smiled to myself about the exchange of keys.

While the stone in the oven heated, and Joe stretched the thin pizza crust on a peel, I pitched in on the salad, rinsing the leaves in the sink and taking the spinner out of the dish rack.

"Can I?" Henry asked after I loaded the leaves into the bowl.

"Absolutely, fella. Pitch right in." Joe looked up from smoothing out the sauce.

"Whee!" Henry attacked the spinner with glee.

Joe and I laughed together.

He picked up a knife and put one of the microwave-thawed meatballs on the cutting board, halving it in one neat stroke.

I must have winced a little at the sound of the knife hitting the wood.

"Knife?" he asked with a searching glance.

"Easton keeps visualizing the stabbing."

"Not unusual for people who aren't used to trauma," Joe said, pausing the slicing. "I had a hard time with my first homicide case."

I waited.

"Saw it when I closed my eyes, had some disturbing dreams, the usual. Amber…" He broke off, decided against finishing the sentence, and returned to meatball prep, not speaking again until he was laying out the first few slices. "Anyhow, he was right to talk to Rabbi Aaron."

"There's more." I flicked my eyes to Henry, who was stopping the spinner with the lock switch. "Sweetheart, how about you distribute the leaves into the salad bowls?"

"Good idea," Joe said. "They're right there."

"Sure."

Henry got down to work. I knew, from his serious expression and our home cookery, that he would organize the leaves with the precision of a medieval mosaic-maker.

While he was busy, I nodded to Joe. "There's something interesting in the way Easton is visualizing the stabbing."

"Really?" Joe picked up a ball of mozzarella and started slicing.

"He thinks Sir Jeremy was stabbed from below."

"Well, that would fit with what Dr. Alexandre is thinking." He placed the first slice of cheese and began moving in a neat circle. "She believes the killer was shorter. So Easton may be on to something. She should have the final wound angles and all soon."

"Points to the strength of the attacker, right?"

"Exactly." He turned to the oven and gave Henry and me a grin. "Showtime, folks."

Moving with practiced precision, he picked up the pizza peel and slipped the pie onto the stone.

Henry and I clapped.

"Hold the applause 'til you taste it," Joe said with a modest smile.

Just as he closed the oven, his phone buzzed.

"Uh-oh." He tapped on the screen, watching.

"What?"

"Channel 14 did a piece on the killing at six. Porter sent it to me."

"Oh, hell. The reporter came after Julia Henshaw while I was there."

"You're on the news, Ma?" Henry asked.

"No," I said, "I pretty much stood there while Julia talked."

"Boo."

"No, pal." Joe patted Henry's arm. "For most people, it's better to stay off the news if you can."

"Got that one right," I said.

He watched, keeping the volume to a low hum. "You're in the shot. Julia's ferocious."

"She is," I agreed.

At the end of the package, Joe tapped out a quick return text to his boss and put down the phone.

"If you need to talk to Porter..." I started.

"Nah," he said. "I actually think we're good for a while. The reporter is clearly all wound up over the tabloid angle of the two husbands, and she's not going to circle back to the hate crime deal for some time."

"By which time you'll hopefully have an arrest."

"Your lips to God's ears." He squinted at the oven window. "Pizza time, folks...hold your applause."

Applause, though, was entirely appropriate. The crust was thin enough that Henry didn't have to worry much about the carbs, perfect New Haven style, exactly the right base for the homemade sauce and meatballs. I suspected the meatballs and sauce were from Joe's mom, Lidia, a legendary cook, but I'd never call him on it.

Two slices of pizza and some salad later, Henry was fed and at the limit of his table manners. "Mind if I play with Cannoli?" he asked.

Neither Joe nor I let on we were glad for the chance to return to adult conversation. And we exchanged smiles at the sound of little-boy giggles as Henry got a good licking from the tiny dog.

We were going to be in such trouble when we got home to Cookie.

I divided the last of the bottle of San Pellegrino water, appropriate early-evening beverage for people who were driving and working, between our glasses. "You know about the knife, but I also turned up a bunch of new questions about Sir Jeremy."

"You're not supposed to be investigating."

"I'm not. When would I have time?" I held his gaze. "But I've been talking to people and, more importantly, people have been talking to me."

"Oh?"

"I've picked up some interesting insight on Sir Jeremy, well, Gerald O'Hara."

"That name is familiar for some reason. I've been racking my brain all day."

"Ever watch *Gone with the Wind*?"

"Yeah, Amber's mom loved it—had it up every damn Christmas. First time I said something, but after that…Scarlett's dad, right?"

"Right."

"Are we in the presence of a clue?"

"Maybe. Niamh—the Society's computer consultant, who came over from Dublin maybe twenty years ago—tells me it's not an uncommon name."

"I figured that. But…" He turned his hands up.

"Yeah, it raises some questions. Has the Garda ever gotten back to you?"

"Phone tag. Got the impression they weren't in a hurry."

"Niamh says that's unusual, too."

Joe took a sip of his water. Contemplated. "So maybe he isn't just not Sir Jeremy, but not Gerald O'Hara, either?"

"Or he's just some poor schmo who happened to be born with a sort-of famous name."

"Well, maybe I do a little online digging."

"Good idea. Niamh is also trying a different angle."

"What?"

"Irish aunties."

"Are they anything like Italian nonnas?" He grinned.

"I suspect older ladies who know everything appear across all ethnicities."

"So do I. And if I put Mama on a case, she'd have any information there was to know within a couple hours."

"Inside dirt from Dublin coming soon," I promised.

"Thanks."

"I won't say it's my pleasure…"

"That, *cara*, would be something else." He took my hand and laced our fingers. "And not tonight, when I have so much work."

"And so do I."

"Maybe I should stay over with Mr. Henry during dress rehearsal Wednesday?"

"And meet up with his mom after?"

"It would be more efficient."

"I like it." I leaned in and kissed him. "Something to look forward to."

"Lord knows we need it."

"Ma!" Henry called. "Can we go? I have to get ready for the gaga tournament tomorrow!"

"Hold that thought," I said to Joe, squeezing his fingers and stealing one more kiss.

"Gotta hold something."

Chapter Twenty-Three

Back to Poli's Wonderland

Next morning, Joe's mother and I arrived first at drop-off for the camp bus. Tiffany, Ava, and Jorge were off on their getaway, and Lewis's little cousins were on a family vacation, too, so his Aunt Ruby was enjoying a well-deserved break.

Since Lidia and I had been pals before I ever met Joe, hanging with her wasn't nearly as nerve-wracking as it might have been.

"You look tired," she said as I trailed Henry to the corner. Lidia has never entirely lost her Italian accent, and sounds like every stereotype of the adorable nonna, though she's anything but.

"Long couple of days," I admitted.

"Joe's looking tired, too. But happy."

"Good."

Shared grin. I didn't know how much Joe was telling her, but she'd clearly added up enough.

"You're good for him, Christian." She patted my arm. "I don't meddle, you know, but I'm glad you found each other."

"So am I. You raised a good one."

"Run! Run!"

We turned to see Sally Birdwell, the fullest expression of self-important suburban perfection, herding her children to the corner, kitted out in another of her matchy-matchy athleisure getups. This time, it was a charcoal gray unitard under a thin, oversized pink-and-gray striped button-down shirt, finished with pink-and-gray tech sandals, her black hair back in a matching scrunchie. Even so, the hair was recent-blowout silky, and her no-makeup-makeup was just perfect enough to be noticeable.

If the purpose was to make every nearby woman in her age cohort feel inadequate, the mission was more than accomplished, as I mentally compared her sleekness with my baggy khakis, rumpled vintage-linen blazer, and humidity-fueled copper puffball hair.

Lidia, cheerfully oblivious, not to mention low-key amazing, in a loose floral-print shirt over capris, elbowed me and rolled her eyes.

I returned the eye roll, with just enough time to pull my face into neutral politeness when the bus rounded the corner, kicking off the usual flurry of last-minute checks, hugs, kisses, and waves.

"So, has that D-A of yours caught the killer?" Sally asked me by way of greeting.

Lidia scowled.

"Police are working on it, Sally. Something like this takes longer to solve."

"Like what?"

"Crazy person from out of town," Lidia cut in. "Never know what's involved."

"She's right," I said.

"Well, I'll tell you one thing that's involved. That British guy was up to no good."

"Really?"

"Malcolm and I did a getaway at the Sand Dollar Spa in Old Saybrook last week, and we were having dinner at the Ebb Tide when we saw him."

It was a truly magnificent display of one-upping, dropping in the fanciest places in the highest-end resort town in the state. Unfortunately, there might actually be something to this, because the Sand Dollar was right next to the Old Brook Cottages, the place where the theatre company was staying. And Sir Jeremy, I had no doubt, would make sure he went to the best restaurant on the shoreline.

"Really?" I asked, doing my best to fake interest because she clearly expected it.

"Yeah. He was with his boyfriend, and they were having a fight."

"Boyfriend?" I'd better ask for a description. Sally wasn't exactly a paragon of enlightenment, no matter how much she enjoyed chatting with Garrett about gardening while he cooed about petunias in a way she never realized was ironic.

"Yeah. Some blond-haired yacht guy in shorts and a brass-buttoned blazer, if you can believe."

I could believe. Hitch. "That was his husband."

"Whatever. They were really getting into it. He said something like 'you're not who I thought you were,' and later called him a thief."

"A thief?"

"Yeah. Yelled it at him and stormed out. Really kind of ruined our apps. And we were having the raw tower with the caviar supplement, too."

Of course they were. If there were a way to have a gold-plated dinner, they'd find it.

"Wow."

Lidia sniffed, clearly unimpressed. "See you later, Christian. I have things to do."

It was entirely possible the things included watching one of the British murder mystery shows she loved or brushing her cat. Her tone, and the way she didn't bother to look at Sally, suggested just about anything was more important than talking to her.

Hard to argue.

"Anyhow, they should take a good look at the guy. It's usually the spouse, isn't it?"

If I had to be married to her, it sure would be. "Often. Sometimes I think you have to be very close to someone to want to kill them."

Sally stared for a second and then forced a little laugh. "Oh, that's funny. Anyhow, will you tell Joe about the fight?"

"Sure."

She beamed, thrilled at passing on the duty of a good citizen to someone else. "Thanks, Christian! I have to get my walk in. I'm showing a house on

Trelawney today, and you know how good a commission that will be."

I just nodded. I knew Joe's neighborhood was significantly pricier than my own, but unlike Sally, I was capable of forming a sentence that did not include reference to property values.

"Later!" she called cheerfully and started power-walking back the way she came.

At the Society, I was the first one in, not really a surprise because Lewis had been sitting in the front room with the beleaguered expression that portended a long night of consideration when I'd stopped by to pick up my purse after I finished running lines.

The Empress demanded her due, and I busied myself with small morning tasks for a few minutes while the coffee brewed, enjoying the quiet of the empty building and the pleasure of wandering slowly through the rooms of beautiful old things, straightening pieces, checking exhibits, and the information shelf in the foyer.

I'd treated myself to a pot of the extremely high-quality dark roast Italian coffee Joe brought me on occasion in lieu of flowers, and by the time I got back to the office, it was ready, perfuming the whole downstairs with the energizing scent of really good beans.

Filling my "We Are, in Fact, Amused" mug, which featured the only photo in existence of Queen Victoria smiling, I noticed the Poli's Wonderland poster. I really did want to put it up. Not only was it beautiful, but it was absolutely an announcement, in an "If You Know, You Know" way.

Better than going Instagram official, as the very online would do.

We had some of those no-damage wall adhesives in the workroom, and it took only a few minutes to hang the piece. One of those tasks that's more than a little fiddly and time-consuming for average people, but easy for me because I've done it so often.

I was just settling the poster in place when I heard a voice behind me.

"That's the theatre you told me about."

I hadn't heard Joe come in, but it was never bad to see him.

"Yep. Lewis and Faith brought it out…they're having a little fun with me." He grinned. "It's cute. And you're putting it up."

"A little If You Know You Know announcement, maybe."

He reached for my hand and pulled me in. "I like it."

"Good. Got time for coffee and a little intel?"

"Not really. Literally only a kiss—I have a motion hearing in another case this morning."

"Okay, then ask me later about a Sir Jeremy sighting in Old Saybrook. With Hitch, about a week ago. A dinner out that ended in a fight. No glitter or tequila, but plenty of drama."

"Good information?"

"I'd say. From Sally Birdwell, who never heard gossip she didn't like."

"Annoying human, but a decent source for this." He nodded, took a breath. "Where did you hide the paper cups now?"

"They ended up here after the board meeting last week." I pulled one from the small stack beside the coffee machine. "I'll even pour it for you."

"Thanks. Really appreciate it." He looked at the poster while I poured. "So do you have a bunch of posters like this?"

"We do. A ton of ephemera, from a relative of the Poli family who was a performer. Posters and programs…"

I trailed off and almost overfilled the cup.

"What?"

"The programs," I said. "A lot of theatre folks keep programs from every show, and sometimes people sign each other's at the end of the run. If you can find Sir Jeremy's, you'll learn a lot about who he is, and maybe any tensions or beefs, too."

"And maybe who wanted him dead."

"If you're lucky," I agreed. "While you're getting a more detailed alibi from Hitch, you might want to ask if he knows where Sir Jeremy's mementoes are."

"They could be in England in the home he shared with Vic."

"Could be. But he was living in New York with Hitch, so I'd guess he brought at least some things with him."

"What am I looking for?"

"The big one is, who's worked with him before," I said. "I know Alannah's done at least three shows with him, and so has her husband. The scene designer, maybe too."

"I looked at the credit list on his website, but I just haven't had time to cross-reference." He took a sip of the coffee. "You think the programs will help?"

"They could at least give you a direction." I looked down at my desk, where the prompt book was sitting on top of some stray paperwork. "I may have some time to do a little online research, too."

"I'll owe you." He glanced at my clock.

"I'll collect." I got on tiptoe and kissed his cheek. "Get outta here."

"I'm picking up Henry at—"

"Four-fifteen at the corner."

"Got it. Love you."

"Love you."

The exchange warmed me more than the coffee.

Chapter Twenty-Four

Paging the Ambassador from Widowhood

After a scintillating morning of paperwork (mine) and spatial relations (Lewis's), I was more than ready to spend the rest of the day with the theatre company.

When I headed over at around one p-m, the stage area was quiet. I could hear the boppy retro pop Alannah favored filtering from the costume shop, as well as some louder classic rock from the stage floor, where the hands were doing the final setup ahead of tomorrow night's full dress.

A long, long night of costumes, tech, notes, and prompting.

Yikes.

How on earth was I going to survive this week, even with help from Joe, Garrett, and Ed?

I must have been out of my mind to agree to this, I thought, not for the first time, as I walked past the back of the seating area.

"Dr. Shaw!"

Hitch was coming from the director's trailer—I couldn't really call it Sir Jeremy's anymore. Looking at him, I realized he was a lot like me in one respect: we both had a work uniform. Mine was a vintage blazer and khakis, and in cooler weather, one of my century-old men's dress shirts. His was a loose oxford, and long baggy shorts, in washed-out red or khaki, finished with deck shoes on his bare feet. The oxford, by the way, was Brooks Brothers, one of the very few brands that maintained the same high standards in fabric and construction into the twenty-first century, and it wasn't new. Not as old as mine, gathered from estate and yard sales, lovingly restored and maintained, but definitely something he'd had for a while.

The general state of his clothes suggested somebody who bought good things and kept them, which was consistent with the old-money background he claimed. So was everything else about him, but with all the questions swirling in the air, I should at least take a cursory look online.

I realized he was staring at me while I studied his clothes.

"Hi, Hitch," I said. "Just admiring your shirt. I collect vintage ones and wear them a lot in cooler weather."

He ran his fingers over the shirttail. "Nothing like good cotton well cared-for."

"No indeed."

"At any rate, you have no idea how glad I am to see you."

"Really?"

He threw up his hands. "Would you terribly mind dragging those girls through another deportment session?"

"Didn't stick the first time?"

"Not well enough, I'm afraid."

I sighed. "Well, let's ask Alannah to dress them, and we'll run their scenes and swan around a bit."

"Excellent." He studied me for a moment. "Would you like some coffee?"

"Yes, please." It came out in a desperate sigh, and I decided to go with honesty: "I didn't get enough this morning, and I'm dyin' here."

"I can fix that." Sheepish grin. "I decided we needed a decent coffee setup, and I ordered it in."

He motioned me toward the backstage area, where a couple of massive individual coffee machines stood majestically upon a large table, surrounded by every imaginable kind of milk and sweetener.

"Wow."

Hitch chuckled. "Every once in a while, being a trust-fund baby has its advantages."

"Guess so."

"Here," he said, walking me over to one of the huge machines, which had a large LED screen and more options than most café's. "Do you know how to work one of these?"

"Yeah…they had one like this at the history conference I went to in New York last year." I picked up a cup and started tapping through the display to make a latte with an extra espresso shot. "You're my hero."

As I waited for the machine to do its magic, Hitch started his own drink on the other one. "I've gone straight to the espresso."

"No wonder. It's been a rough week."

"Worst week ever."

My machine made a frizzling noise and finished my latte with a surprisingly credible layer of foam. I took it and buried my face in the steam. "Thanks."

"My pleasure." He watched happily as his cup filled with far more espresso than I would consider safe. Must have a high caffeine tolerance. "This whole thing gives me something to do instead of crying at home. Or worse, spending every minute of the day on the funeral arrangements."

"That is pretty ugly stuff," I agreed, feeling the muscles around my spine start to tense at the memory of Frank's shiva and the day leading up to it.

"We've decided to have a memorial in New York next week," he said. "A compromise. Vic wanted London."

"And you worked it out?"

"Surprisingly." Hitch picked up his cup and took a deep sniff. "We're actually doing well."

"You are," I agreed. "I can't say I thought you would."

"Neither did I. But the fact is, we've both been taken by Sir Jeremy."

"Both wronged parties," I said.

"I don't feel that way, honestly. I feel like the rent boy."

"Oh, no. Why?"

"Well, I'm the one who ran off with the married man."

"No, you're the one who believed him when he said he was free," I assured him. "You're the poor innocent led down the primrose path."

"Dr. Shaw, I'm a lot of things, but innocent isn't one of them."

"But even savvy people can get drawn in because they want to believe in love."

"There's that." He tried for a sip of espresso and backed off. "And I wanted to believe Jeremy was a good man."

At the comment, I tried to become very busy putting sugar in my latte.

"I know what that means," Hitch said. "The turbinado sugar is very nice, but it's not that interesting. You're trying not to tell me he was a jerk."

"I'm sorry." I tossed my empty sugar bags in the recycling bin. "A jerk is someone who leers at a cutie at dinner. A man who tells you he's free and marries you while he's still legally tied to another is something else entirely."

"I suppose." He tried again, took a nip of espresso, decided he couldn't quite stand the heat, and pulled away. "I should have known better."

"Did he tell you he was free?"

"Well, yeah."

"He lied to your face, and you're blaming yourself."

"Yes."

"So?"

Hitch's face relaxed into a sheepish, boyish grin. "Yeah. And he was ethically—slippery—in plenty of other areas."

"I don't like speaking ill of the dead," I said, "but he clearly didn't treat you right."

"Well, when it was good, it was *good*." Wistful smile as I prayed he wouldn't give me details. "It's true, though. I probably had a lot of the rose-colored glasses with him. Doesn't everyone dream about being scooped up by a naughty English lord?"

He clearly intended it as a laugh line, trying to sell it with a twisty smile and wide eyes.

"Well," I said, "he was certainly naughty. The English lord part, though…"

Hitch's funny mug evaporated. "What do you mean?"

"You didn't know he was using an, um, professional name?"

"No. He used to talk about growing up in shabby decadence at the family seat. Of course, I understood completely, as a scion myself."

"Oh, honey." My tone was the same as when Henry had a skinned knee.

"They're pretty sure he wasn't a scion."

"That was a lie, too?" Hitch buried his face in his cup.

"They're putting it all together, but he came from Ireland and-"

"Irish? He was Irish?" Hitch looked up.

"Yes."

"He said the Irish were pigs. It was his only prejudice." Hitch squirmed. "I don't want to tell you the words he used."

"I know most of them. I'm Scotch-Irish."

"Scotch…Irish?"

"It's a Western Pennsylvania Appalachian thing. Essentially, Protestant Irish people who stopped off in Scotland on their way here. Most other folks say Scots or Irish and leave it at that. There was plenty of anti-Irish bias here, too. Especially on my grandma's side—she was really Scots. So I've heard most of the slurs."

"I'm sorry, Dr. Shaw." Hitch blushed.

"Not your fault."

"I try to do better than my forbears on this sort of thing, I really do. And Jerry's talk about the Irish really bothered me." He took a breath and tried for a drink of the espresso. This time it was really cool enough.

While Hitch fueled up, I took a sip of my drink, too. The coffee itself wasn't nearly as magnificent as the Italian roast I keep for Joe, or even the 'Dark & Dangerous' my cousin sends from Seattle. But all the extras made up for it. Maybe I'd just needed a treat.

"Anyhow, Dr. Shaw, you really need to get those ladies back on the straight and narrow," Hitch said after his second generous slurp.

"I do." With some sugar and caffeine headed for my veins, I pulled myself back into proper posture and gave Hitch a confident smile.

"Thank you." Hitch held my gaze.

"You saved my life with the coffee," I assured him. "It's the least I can do."

"No. Julia told me about your late husband. I know you're paying it forward a little after everything you've been through—and I'm grateful."

"I am." Surprised that he got me. "And I'm glad it helps."

Now, back to corsets.

Chapter Twenty-Five

Put a (Signet) Ring on It

With us all facing a long day and night with final dress the next day, Vic and Hitch showed mercy and sent everyone home at seven.

I supposed I could have caught a ride back to the house, but honestly, it was still light and I was grateful for the chance to walk off the day. Henry and Joe were deep into a video game grudge match at the desktop, and barely looked up when I walked in.

Probably should have annoyed me, but the sheer normalcy of it warmed my heart.

"Dinner's in the fridge," Joe called. "Made chicken parm sandwiches with some cherry tomatoes. Open face for Henry, of course."

While I zapped my sandwich and nibbled on the mini tomatoes, the guys finished their battle—Joe, of course, lost—and drifted into the living room to wait for me.

The tomatoes were gone by the time the sandwich was heated, and I picked up the plate and a can of seltzer and joined them. We spent an hour in friendly family conversation before Henry headed off to bed.

Joe diplomatically became very busy catching up on news reports and email while I got Henry and Cookie settled for the night. Since he was tiny, my son has been chatty at the end of the day, whether just wanting some concentrated parental face time or needing to talk out something important.

He has unerring radar, always seeming to want a significant conversation when I'm at my most exhausted and desperate for quiet.

No real surprise, then, that he didn't open his book immediately that night, only holding my gaze when I sat down on the bed.

"What's the deal with AlysDad?" he asked.

I don't lie to Henry. Even when I had to give him the worst news, I told him the simple truth, answering his questions as honestly as I could. I'm not above shading or holding back details that might hurt or scare him, but I will not lie to my boy. Ever.

"Well, fella, we're seeing each other."

Henry waited.

"And it's serious."

"Do you love him?"

"I do. Not the same as I loved your dad because every person and every love is different, but yes, I love him."

His clear, wise eyes, so like his father's, held mine as he absorbed what I'd said. "I know he loves you."

"Yeah?"

"Well, I asked him."

"Of course you did." I managed to hold back a sigh or nervous giggle.

"Maybe you should marry him, Ma."

"Marry him?" My voice came out in a squeak.

"Yeah." He toyed with the cover of his planet book. "He's a lot better than that weirdo Emily Curtin's mom married. And he lives here, so we wouldn't have to move away."

"You've thought this through." The weirdo in question was a standard clueless bro his classmate's mother had grabbed in a rebound several months ago. And one of his running buddies had left last school year because his mom married someone she met online.

"Both points in his favor," I agreed. "And I love him, like I said. But what do you think?"

"He's pretty cool. Cooks better than you do. Makes me read like Uncle Garrett does. And he doesn't let me beat him at Dragon Race...but I usually do anyway." Henry moved a little, his foot bumping Cookie, and the cat squawked.

"All good qualities." I petted the cat, and he curled back into a ball. I returned my gaze to Henry. Even though he was talking about positive things, I knew something was bothering him. I took a guess. "You know, he will never take your dad's place. You're Frank Glaser's son forever."

"I won't have to call him Dad."

"Nope. Never. You already had a dad. And we miss him every day."

"Yeah, Ma. Yeah, we do."

I put a hand on his arm, and we sat for a moment.

Henry broke the silence. "Okay, then."

"Yeah?"

"Yeah. Let's keep him."

I did laugh then at Henry deciding our future the same way we'd decided to keep the stray Cookie when he turned up at our doorstep three years ago.

"I'll do my best," I assured him.

"Good." Henry picked up the book.

Dismissed.

I planted a kiss on top of his head, and went out to the living room, where Joe was watching the last bit of a package our beloved Lyman Damer had sold to one of the gossip TV shows. Good to know this was working out well for somebody, at least.

I reminded myself that if she was busy with the tabloid angle, she wasn't harassing Dina or mucking around in Joe's investigation. It could be a lot worse.

Coming up behind Joe, I kissed him on the cheek.

"All tucked in?"

"Yep. All good." I didn't want to get into what Henry and I had discussed right now—it would probably be better for everyone to let it settle.

"I should go home," Joe said, taking my hand and pulling me close. "But I need to ask you for some background on the signet ring before I talk to the British authorities."

"Okay. And I picked up some more insight on Sir Jeremy's impersonation, too."

"Then let me pour us a little wine, and we'll talk it out."

Joe got up and poured two half-glasses from the bottle he'd brought, and we sat on the couch together, taking a moment to just enjoy the wine and quiet.

"So I spent a while talking to Hitch today," I said.

"Grieving widower Number Two?"

"Bigamy victim Number One, we could also say." I looked at my wine in the low light. "He seems to be a decent enough guy, and he's got a good bit of guilt over this."

"Is that all?"

"You mean, am I picking up any vibe that he killed his husband?"

"That IS what I mean, yes. We know he was in the US when it happened, and so far we have only his word that he wasn't at the theatre Friday night. He claims he was walking on the beach and trying to relax ahead of the performance week."

"But?"

"So far, there's no evidence. Security cams show him leaving on the beach side of the building and coming back four hours later."

"That's a long time to walk the beach."

"But there are bars and such on that stretch of sand. He could have just gone for dinner or a drink. So, we have to find out if there's anyone who remembers seeing him."

"And it's also plenty of time to drive up to Unity, slash Sir Jeremy's throat, and get back."

"And take the signet to confuse the issue?"

"Or to sell because he knows how valuable it is."

"How valuable is it?" Joe asked.

"I'm still nailing down the details on that, but it could be anything from several hundred—the value of the gold—to much, much more."

"Can you try to get a little clarity on that? It could make a big difference in the theory of the case."

"I'll see if Garrett might have some insight," I offered. "He might have time to do more searching than I do."

"Good idea."

"What about Vic?" I asked. "Have you confirmed his alibi?"

"He really was in England when the notification call came. But someone with his background could have connections."

"You really think he's mobbed up? I think he's just posing."

Joe shook his head. "I honestly don't know. And I don't want to risk the next person's life on being wrong."

"Good point." I drank a bit more wine and rested my hand on his. "I'll call in Garrett in the morning."

"And watch out for yourself, huh?" he asked, lacing fingers with mine.

"Always do."

The comfortable silence fell again. When I was married, I used to love quiet late-night conversations. So honest and real, free of any expectation other than to enjoy, or acknowledge, or comfort each other.

Joe put down his wine glass and looked at my hand, one finger idly, but not really idly, toying with my wedding ring. Then a breath, as if he were making a decision. "What if, say, somebody gave you a ring? What would you do with this one?"

"Probably move it to my right hand."

"It'll always be part of you."

"Exactly."

"Do you think you'd want another ring sometime?"

"If the right guy came with it." I put my glass down and snuggled into his embrace, making no effort for eye contact. He was trying to ask without asking, and I didn't want to make it harder for him.

"Ah." He kissed my hair, rested his chin on the top of my head. "If, say, this right guy wanted to make it official with a big Italian wedding, could you handle that?"

"Might be fun."

"And if, say, this guy found a nice ring and wanted to propose in some really goofy old-fashioned way, like taking a knee after asking permission from your mom and your dads—"

"I think he might get exactly the answer he wants. If he's the right guy." I turned my face up to his and kissed him lightly. "He'd have to throw in a little John Donne."

Joe grinned. "I think that could be arranged."

Chapter Twenty-Six

What Would Tony Soprano Say?

The only difference between the final dress rehearsal and opening night was the timing: in a small show of mercy to the exhausted cast and crew, final dress was an hour earlier, so we might get home in time to sleep.

It took a long day of work at the Society to get there, though. Garrett happened to be walking Norm when I dropped off Henry, and I was able to ask him to nose around about the signet ring, sending him the screenshot and what little I knew.

Not a word about the other conversation about a ring. That could wait until the traveling players moved on to the next town.

After Garrett, more paperwork. Somebody's great-aunt had decided to make a donation instead of a tag sale…and honestly, everyone would have been better off if she'd stuck to the original plan. At least Lewis had made enough progress on his exhibit that he could take a break and help me sort boxes of tchotchkes.

We'd barely made a dent by the end of the day, and I sent Lewis home and wandered over to the theatre, where everyone was practically vibrating over the prospect of a real show. Some actors only come alive in front of a full house, and I suspected, or hoped, some of the people who'd been grudgingly sleepwalking through the last day of scene work might light up soon.

Couldn't prove it by the first half, which appeared to be an exercise in proving a bad rehearsal means a good show. I hoped the old saw was right, but if what this crew was bringing tonight was any indication, it was going to be a very long few days.

While I'm obviously not a fan of motivation by abuse, I was starting to understand it by intermission. I wasn't the only one.

Vic and Hitch—never mind Julia—all looked like they'd had more than enough.

"There's not even any point in giving notes," said Hitch, in a dull, despairing tone.

"He's right, ya mutts," Vic added. "Take a break, get something to eat, and do better. We're feedin' ya, which should give ya some motivation."

If anything was going to save this night, it would be the meal break, complete with a catered dinner from Malina's, Unity's favorite red-sauce spot. I was glad to see them getting the extra business, though it's not like they're ever anything other than busy.

The company descended on the big trays of chicken and/or eggplant parm, ziti, and garlic bread as if they'd never been fed. Since I was still getting used to the idea of being seen naked again, I just grabbed a big plate of salad and one slice of garlic bread. Alannah was the only other one who went big on rabbit food; everybody else, even our leading ladies, put a few token veggies beside the cheesy and rich parm and pasta.

For the hourlong break, the cast and crew ranged around the Green in knots of two or three or four, enjoying the food with the light, quiet conversation of people working intensely.

Before I ate, I took time to call Henry and Joe, who were in the midst of a grudge match on one of the racing games and brushed me off in less than a minute with assurances that everything was fine, and steak salads were on their dinner menu. I hung up with a rueful smile, and found an unoccupied bench, whipping out my phone to read a couple of articles I hadn't had time to read on my favorite newsmagazine site. Just before I dove into a think piece on a legendary TV show's long-running obsession with shoes, I heard a voice behind me.

"Article's overrated. So was the show."

I turned to see Vic, with a groaning plate of parm, walking my way.

"That's the sense I get," I agreed.

"Mind if I join you? Just need to be with an adult non-theatre person for a while."

I nodded, and he sat, the caftan—today fine turquoise cotton with a deep blue border print—billowing. I hoped there was something underneath. "How are you holding up?"

He stabbed an entire chicken parm cutlet with his plastic fork and took a bite that would have made sense from a saber-toothed tiger.

"Ahhh." As he chewed and swallowed, Vic let out a satisfied sigh. "Man, you people do not know how lucky you are. I haven't had real parm since we went to London to film that Tudor thing."

"You stayed after that?"

"Pretty much. Y'know, it got nominated, and we had more work than we could handle."

"I imagine you did." I took a much more restrained bite of my salad.

"You're too polite to say it, but you're wondering how a Jersey guy ended up with a twee British lord."

"I'm just impressed with a Jersey guy using the word 'twee.'"

"You're all right, doc." Vic gave a growly laugh as he took another huge bite of chicken. "We met on a production. Believe it or not, I was playing Mercutio in a Godfather-themed *Romeo and Juliet*."

Fortunately, I had just taken a bite of salad, so I could chew rather than say anything, because no matter what comment I made, it would be wrong.

"Let's just say opposites attracted, bigtime, and leave it at that."

"Works for me." If only because I don't have to put out my mind's eye.

"And since I have a master's in British Renaissance Drama, I was able to contribute."

"Definitely." I smiled to hide my surprise. "Rutgers?"

"Seton Hall for undergrad. Got into a grad program at this weird little Catholic college in London for the master's. Probably would have stayed forever if I hadn't met Jerry."

"Jerry."

"Yeah. He was so normal outside the theatre." Wistful smile. "You worked with him, so I know what you're thinking. But he really was."

"People aren't one thing," I said. "I've been alive long enough to know that any number of things can exist in space and time."

Vic chewed the last bite of his chicken cutlet, his features settling into a contemplative expression. "It's not that I thought he was perfect, you know."

"No."

"I knew he wasn't a good guy in a lot of ways. Knew there was something in his past he didn't want to talk about. And I suspected he'd done some shady things to get here."

"Shady how?"

"Well." Vic paused, clearly thinking about how much to say. "If you grow up in Jersey, you know a few families where you don't look too closely at where the money comes from, right?"

"Right. You don't think he was mob?"

"Oh, hell no." Vic laughed. "No way on God's earth. My family isn't, but I have pals who are, and trust me, that cutie wouldn't have lasted thirty seconds with the fellas. Just a comparison. I always knew there were things I didn't want to know."

"Don't ask questions you don't want answered?"

"Exactly. He was never anything but above-board while we were together, but I had a very strong feeling that his past was less than perfect."

"Money-wise? Work-wise?"

"The money, for sure. He was weird about the money. I joked once about him being the only non-impoverished British aristocrat, and he gave me this absolutely cold face."

"And you left it there."

"Wouldn't you?" He speared a new chicken cutlet and took another enormous bite.

"Absolutely," I agreed, nibbling on my garlic bread. "I don't like to talk about money on a good day."

"Must make consulting tough," Vic observed. "Don't you have to get people to pay your price?"

"Usually, we negotiate by email, which is less intimidating. And my rate's based on the prevailing market, so there's not a lot of negotiating, anyhow."

"Good to know. Assuming we all survive this, we'll send you some business, doc."

"Really?" I just barely avoided spilling lettuce as my jaw dropped.

"Really. You've been a good sport."

"Thanks." I blushed, knowing that from this guy, it was sky-writing my praises.

"Well, you know this business. There are a lot of jerks." He shrugged. "And I know Jerry was one of them, a lot of the time."

"To people who weren't you," I said. "Which makes a huge difference."

"It does." He took a big, heaving sigh. "I loved that sonofabitch."

Nothing to say. I patted his arm.

Yet another job for the Ambassador from Widowhood.

"Twenty minutes!" Hitch yelled from the dressing tent.

"Yikes!" I took one last bite of salad and jumped up. "I promised to help Alannah get everyone into their second-act costumes. "Gotta go."

Vic smiled. "Thanks, doc. Good talking to ya."

"Likewise."

I tossed my plates in a nearby trash can and hefted the prompt book. Back to work.

The next fifteen minutes were a whirlwind of lacing, buttoning, fluffing, and settling, as Alannah, her assistant, and I worked together...and we all once again cursed Sir Jeremy's obsession with literal authenticity.

As Alannah smoothed out layers of muslin—carefully and authentically starched earlier in the day, she looked up at me. "There are at least three easier ways to do this that look just as good."

"I'm sure. Did he make you boil the starch?"

"He talked about it," she replied with a dry brow flick. "I told him I'd boil him with it."

"I don't blame you. There's authentic, and there's nuts."

"And he was definitely nuts. Always has been. Same kind of thing on his other productions. I spent months searching online and at tag sales for

Tangee lipstick for the 1950s *Merchant of Venice.*"

"That's not even sanitary," I said.

"No kidding." Alannah smoothed the top layer of a supernumerary's skirt and turned back to me. "Didn't he ask you about doing homemade makeup for this one?"

As we moved on to another of the swings, I tried to think back through the emails. "He made reference to it. We were supposed to come back to it this week."

"Oh, you would have."

We started stacking and smoothing petticoats again, as the community-theatre actress winced at the sight of her hips.

"Last time we did a Victorian one, he had all the women make their own lip salve and lamp-black for their eyes." She shook her head. "It could have been a lot of fun, you know. Girls' day thing."

"Sure. I'd go for that."

"But not him. He stood over everybody, making sure each did it exactly the way he wanted. Made one older actress throw the stuff down and flounce out—and two of the younger girls cry."

"Ugh."

Alannah fastened the final petticoat. "That was him. It was going to be his way, and nothing else mattered. Nobody mattered."

"He seemed to like and respect you a lot," I reminded her as she knelt to check the woman's hems.

Suddenly and sharply, she looked up. "No, Christian. He didn't respect me. He just knew I would take it."

I wanted to ask her why, but just then, another woman came over to me with a handful of hairpins and a disintegrating bun.

No hairspray allowed, of course.

Honestly, in seven years of consulting, plus a couple of college summers in a costume shop, I'd never seen anything like this. Almost as if the degree of difficulty was an intentional part of the process for Sir Jeremy.

Probably not much help in finding his killer, but it definitely spoke to his personality.

With the hair disaster averted, I picked up the prompt book and started for the door.

"Can you give me a hand?" Caro called as she leaned away from the makeup mirror, struggling with the back of her gown. "Lita's still having trouble with that big sash."

"Sure." I put the book down on the table and started buttoning.

"Is that the prompt book?" she asked as I finished.

"Yeah. It's an unusually large and old one. I think originally from a 19th-century production."

"Could be," she agreed. "It looks like one of the really old ones we have in the collection at Yale. Like 18th-century or before."

"It could be. Apparently, Sir Jeremy guarded it like a hawk."

Caro ran her finger over the lettering. "He did. I've never been this close to it."

"You've studied the prompt books at Yale?" Alannah asked as she crossed from smoothing out yet another skirt.

"Yes. They've got quite a collection of playscripts and prompt books."

"Always been fascinated with playscripts," Alannah said. "The way people record what they did. It's a real window into the past."

"It's pretty neat," agreed Caro.

"I love being close to anything really old," I admitted.

"Did you ever see the ring Sir Jeremy wore?" Caro asked. "I did an internship at the Met, and it looked like something from the medieval collections."

I nodded and tried to keep my face and voice neutral. "It sure did."

"Wouldn't surprise me if somebody whacked him for that," Caro continued.

For an instant, Alannah froze. Then, she let out an awful, racking cough. "Sorry, swallowed my cough drop."

"You know," I said, "I have some peppermint tea over at the Society."

"I'm fine, Christian," Alannah said, in an aggressively brisk tone, as she focused on Caro. "And we need to get that fichu collar smoothed down."

"She's right—and much better at it than me," I said, picking up the book and heading out to my seat. The end of the day was in sight, I thought.

Yep. Irony alert.

Chapter Twenty-Seven

Yelling Fire at the Theatre

Later, we'd be very grateful that it didn't happen when we had a full house.

In the moment, though, none of us had the time for such cheerful thoughts because we were busy running for the exits.

We'd just finished the fourth act, and were in the scene change for the fifth, when I smelled smoke, coming from the dressing tents.

Any reasonable person finds fire in a tent frightening, but here in Connecticut, we have ingrained generational PTSD because of the Hartford Circus Fire, which left at least 167 people dead and more than 700 hurt in 1944. Or at least those of us with any knowledge of the state's history do.

Since the new scene hadn't started, I picked up my book and followed the scent.

"Oh, holy hell…FIRE!"

I only realized I'd yelled it when I heard a shriek and running footsteps behind me.

"Call 9-1-1!"

For the second time in a week, the usually calm Julia Henshaw was shouting in a shrill, terrified tone, the same as she had when she called me about Sir Jeremy's death. This time, though, she was entirely justified.

The front wall of the box office shed was fully engulfed, and the flames were spreading across the roof—toward the dressing room tent. Flameproofing is much better now than it used to be, but nobody wants to be anywhere near a burning tent.

"I'm calling!" I yelled as I hit the speed dial. "Get out!"

"9-1-1, what's your emergency?"

"Fire at the theatre on the Town Green in Unity," I said.

"Unity Town Green?" asked the operator.

"Yes," I said. "A shed is on fire next to a tent at the theatre space, and it's spreading."

"I'll send a truck. Get everybody out of the tent, okay?"

"We are. Thanks."

The line went dead, and I looked at the scene. Julia Henshaw had taken up a spot on the safe side of the tent, holding the flap open and waving people through. As they got out, they took a look at the shed and screamed. Since I was a little further away, I herded them across the gravel road and to the Society lawn beyond, out of range of the flames for now—and out of the way of the fire trucks that I sure hoped would arrive any second.

"Get out!" Hitch came blasting from backstage with a huge fire extinguisher in hand. He took a fighting stance and started spraying at the burning shed. It didn't make much of a dent, but that wasn't the point.

"I've got this!" Vic blasted out of the director's trailer seconds later, carrying another big extinguisher—thank the good Lord for building codes—and he took up a position opposite Hitch, spraying for all he was worth.

"I'VE GOT WATER!"

I heard the shout behind me and had just enough time to get out of the way before a wall of water flew toward the shed. As some of the splashes hit my arm and leg, I wrapped myself around the prompt book and backed away, moving toward the rest of the crowd of refugees on the Society lawn.

The sound of spraying water mixed with the odd, chewing noise of the fire, and the whoosh of the extinguishers, and I turned to see a truly impressive sight: Officer Colby, Raggedy Andy himself, was standing atop the big stone marker at the edge of the Green, garden hose in hand, shooting water at the top of the shed.

The leading ladies, one of the leading men, and at least a half-dozen supernumeraries were standing just out of range, staring at Colby. If I'd been a badge bunny—and even if I'd only leaned that way a little—I would have been, too. His hat was off, and his rusty hair formed a curly nimbus around his face, which looked a bit more chiseled in the flames. And of course, his uniform was wet, clinging to his muscular body.

"Kinda takes the edge off, doesn't it?" Julia Henshaw nodded to the scene as she crossed to me.

"Hard to miss, anyhow."

"I'm fighting despair with gratuitous lust," she said.

"How's that working out for you?"

"Well, it's either leer or weep, and I think leering is a healthier impulse." She let out a little snicker. "And there's too much male-gaze BS in the world, so why not?"

"Makes sense to me," I said. Enough said.

We watched for probably a minute or so, while Colby managed to knock down the worst of the flames, even as Hitch and Vic ran out of fire extinguisher propellant and backed off to check on their company.

By the time the sirens started blaring, it looked to me like everyone was safe, and the atmosphere had changed from terror to almost convivial, helped along by the fact that the flames were down to a dull sputter, thanks to Colby.

"What on earth?"

I turned to see Dina and Ben walking out of their house, well away from any direct danger from the fire, but not nearly far enough away for comfort, considering all the recent concerns.

"Hey." She nodded to me.

"What happened?" Ben asked.

Both had that very calm, careful expression people get when they're extremely concerned and don't want to say too much.

"I don't know," I said. "It looked like a fire in the box office shed. Could be something as simple as some kind of battery charger or a stray cigarette."

"Or not," Dina said.

"Or not," I admitted. "Probably know more in the morning after the fire marshal takes a look."

We watched for a few minutes as the fire crews quickly hosed down the shed, putting out the last of the flames. The Channel 14 SUV pulled up during the mop-up, and we got the fun of watching Lyman Damer squish through the damp grass of the Green in those ridiculous high heels. Good luck to her.

I had no intention of tuning into the eleven o'clock news for the latest developments.

Not that there really were any. As spectacular and horrible as this was, the shed was still standing, and it didn't look like there was even any damage to the dressing tents, so it probably would have very little real impact on tomorrow's opening night.

No concrete impact anyhow. Whether it would have any effect on everyone's focus on the show was an open question.

I was pondering that when my phone rang.

Joe.

"Hi."

"You're okay, right?" More than a little edge in his tone.

"Um, yeah." I realized why he was calling. "You heard about the fire on the Green?"

"At the theatre is what I heard."

"Shed outside."

He let out a long breath, and I realized he was more worried than angry. "Everyone all right?"

"Looks like it."

"Good. Can you get back here soon? I really need to go to the scene."

I glanced over at Dina, who was in jeans and a sweater, keyring laced through her fingers. "I think I can get a ride back."

"Thanks."

"Sure. See you-"

"And by the way, I love you."

Chapter Twenty-Eight

Curtain Up

The next twelve hours or so were simple logistics. Dina gave me a ride home in her spiffy powder-blue sedan, happy to have something to do. Joe and I exchanged a quick kiss and handoff, and I checked on Henry, drank a glass of wine large enough to get me to sleep, and collapsed.

It was only at the start of the next day, after a happily oblivious Henry left on the camp bus, as Lidia noted, but didn't comment on, my undereye circles, that there was any time to discuss and process what had happened.

I'd just started a pot of coffee and turned on my computer when Joe walked in, carrying a bakery box with distinctive red-white-and-blue string. To anyone who knows New Haven County goodies, it was unmistakable: Ersalesi's Bakery is the best around.

"Wow," I said,

"Had to go back into the office to talk to the Fire Marshal, so I figured I'd make it worth our while. Since it's a weekday, we get *cornetto marmalatta* instead of *sfogliatelle*—they only make those on the weekend."

"Still wonderful." I turned my face up to his. "Say it again."

"*Sfogliatelle?*" He said it close to my lips, then kissed me, pulling me close and whispering in my ear, "*Sfogliatelle, sfogliatelle—*"

"Have you heard anything yet..."

Dina trailed off in an embarrassed cough, as Joe and I pulled apart like teenagers caught in the den.

And then the sheer silliness of it all hit, and we started laughing together. Exactly what we all needed to break the tension of the last few hours.

"Well," I said, "I just made a pot of coffee, and if you'd like to stay, Dina, you're welcome."

"I brought a bunch of *cornettos*," Joe said. "You never know with this place."

"*Cornettos?*" Dina asked, her eyes lighting up. "The croissant-y things?"

"Yes. With orange marmalade."

"Sign me up."

"Me, too!" Lewis appeared in the doorway.

"Oh, you'll just do anything to avoid working on the exhibit," I teased.

"Not true. I'll do anything to avoid editing the catalogue notes." He gave us a proud smile. "I've finished everything else, and I just need to finalize the catalogue."

"Yay!"

Dina and I applauded. Joe offered a shake since he had only one hand free.

"Let's sit down and have *cornettos* and coffee in the workroom," I offered.

"And I'll bring you up to date on my visit to the fire marshal." Joe held up the box. "It's almost better than the *cornettos*."

"Hard to imagine that," Dina said.

Ten minutes later, though, properly fortified with a classic Italian breakfast of dark-roast coffee and pastry, even Dina was ready to concede the news might indeed be so good.

"So the summer intern running the box office is the one person on earth who has not heard of the dangers of lithium-ion batteries?" Lewis asked as he popped the last bite of his *cornetto*.

"That's what it looks like." Joe tore off another piece of pastry—he'd been talking too much to finish—with an annoyed scowl. "I know it's hard to believe in this day and age, but he really did plug his off-brand laptop in to charge during the rehearsal."

"And boom," Dina said as she nibbled the last curved bit of her pastry.

I took a sip of coffee. I'd left the part with the most marmalade until the end, and I was ready to enjoy it.

"Saving the best for last?" Joe asked as I picked it up.

"One of my favorite things," I replied.

Lewis and Dina exchanged glances but didn't comment.

"So," she began, making very serious eye contact with Joe, "you're really comfortable with the idea that this is an accident?"

"More comfortable than I am with a lot of other things here." He took a bite of pastry and thought about it. "Could someone with bad intentions have snuck in and set the fire near the laptop charger? Sure…but it seems like a lot of work."

"And if they wanted to damage either the temple or the production, there are a lot better places to set that fire," I said. "This may really be an accident."

"Or the target isn't what we think it is," Joe said. "I haven't had a chance to talk to Ms. Henshaw yet about what's kept there."

"I know one thing that was." I put down my last bite of *cornetto*. "The prompt book was locked there at night until I took over."

"Why?" Joe asked.

"Because it's a valuable nineteenth-century piece," I said. "But how would destroying it help anyone?"

"Was Sir Jeremy using it at the time of the murder?"

"He locked it up at the end of the day's work and then went to scheme in his trailer. That was his usual routine."

"Fingerprints?" asked Lewis.

"What do you mean?" I asked. "It's covered in them."

"But maybe there's somebody who should not have been handling it who left a print."

"And if they did, they might be afraid it would be found," Joe said. "Can I take it to the crime lab for a quick dusting? I know I can't seize it for evidence until the end of the run without tipping off our killer, but we can document its condition as of this place and time."

"Sure," I replied. "And I'll sign whatever affidavits you need to verify chain of custody from here."

He smiled. "You are a prosecutor's dream, Dr. Shaw."

Dina cleared her throat. Lewis snickered.

"Well," Joe said, shooting the last of his coffee and standing, "I'll take that book now, so I can get it back to you before the show."

"Thanks."

"I have to get back to editing," Lewis said, refilling his coffee cup with a beleaguered face.

"And I have to go get ready for the midday Torah study group. At least I'll be able to tell them we're not facing a new threat."

Dina and Lewis disappeared quickly, so I could walk Joe to the door.

"Thank you for the pastries." I handed him the book.

"Thank you for the evidence." He hefted it carefully. "I'll bring it back in a few hours. I'm going to try to get a nap before I pick up Henry."

"Tell you what. I'll move things around and pick him up if you can get to the house by five."

"Once again, Dr. Shaw, you are my hero."

Chapter Twenty-Nine

Another Opening, Another Show

When I left for the show, carefully dusted-off prompt book in hand, Henry, and a somewhat well-rested Joe, were making a chicken Caesar salad together, under Cookie's hopeful supervision. Cannoli was hiding under the computer desk.

Looked like a good evening for all.

Looked like my evening was going to be fun, too. Garrett texted me that he and Ed had tickets and would be happy to walk me home. Since they'd had to order the tickets months ago, there was definitely some real interest in Shakespeare…but it also coincided with an effort to protect me.

Whatever it was, they picked a good night for it.

Despite all the *sturm und drang* in the run-up to the opening, the weather was lovely—never guaranteed in Connecticut—and even better, everybody was on their game, ready to perform. I barely had any prompting to do and spent most of the show marveling at how well it all came together.

I sure hoped the rest of the run would be like this.

Afterwards, the curtain calls went on forever, followed by hugs and handshakes and a few bouquets—none for me, thankfully.

What a relief.

One show down and two to go.

And finally, it was time to meet my superannuated stage-door johnnies for the walk home.

Garrett and Ed were waiting for me at the edge of the performance space.

"Pretty good show," Garrett pronounced. "Leads were solid."

"You can dress it up any way you like," Ed said, "but I'm still not a fan of iambic pentameter."

I looked sharply at Ed. "Iambic…"

"Got sick of telling Garrett I didn't like that Shakespeare stuff. Figured I should be able to call it by the right name."

"Nice."

"Still don't like it much."

"Out of period dress is not my favorite," Garrett admitted. "But I still enjoy a good night of the Bard."

"You enjoy it more when there are men in tights." Ed grinned. "Come on, Christian, let's get you home."

"How are Joe and Henry doing?" asked Garrett.

"Only five texts tonight. Every half hour last night."

Both smiled, enjoying a chuckle at Joe's expense.

"No better than you two," I reminded them. "First time you watched him after he was diagnosed, you sent me pics every ten minutes."

They squirmed like embarrassed little boys.

"I'm not critiquing," I said. "I'm grateful you take it seriously. And that Joe does."

"He's a standup guy," Ed said, in a grudging tone. "He may not have enough time to take proper care of you two, but he's a standup guy."

Garret shot me a tiny glance and continued right past it, as I'm sure he intended me to do. "Anyhow, are you aware of what's being said about Sir Jeremy online?"

"When would I go online?"

"Most normal people these days check their feeds and such at least once a day."

"Even I look for grandbaby pics," Ed said. "Jana has us in a private group and puts up great stuff."

"Fine, fine. So I should be online more."

"You should just be online," Garrett said. "I keep telling you, a robust social media presence for the Society can only help bring in more support."

"Thank you." I managed a cool reply as we turned onto a quieter street, getting some distance from the Green. "What are you hearing about the late lamented?"

"There are entire threads devoted to speaking ill of him, and the awful way he treated his actors. Every once in a while, someone cuts in with how the final product was good, but it's horror story after horror story. Fat-shaming, screaming, name-calling, threats that would get you arrested or decked under any other circumstances."

"Yikes."

"A couple of people call him a thief, too. Unclear if it's creative ideas, or if they mean theft of actual goods."

I thought about the ring. "It might be actual goods. What platform has these threads?"

"Flutter and Weave both have some. I'll send you the links," Garrett said. "You're going to share them with Joe, aren't you?"

"Oh, yeah, at this point, any leads will do."

"It's not his fault if it goes cold, you know," Ed cut in. "That'll be on DiBiasi, and maybe whoever's catching at Major Crimes if they can manage to hand off."

"It won't matter, and you know it." We were passing under a streetlamp, and I shot Ed a glare. "Dropping this ball would create enough stink for everyone."

"You're right," Garrett said. "Maybe we need to nose around a little."

I didn't have to see Garrett to know his eyes were gleaming with interest.

"We don't need any amateur detective crap," Ed replied in his best command presence tone. "You can both stay in your lanes. This thing will be what it is."

"Fine." Garrett's tone suggested he was placating Ed, and Ed's growled reply suggested he knew it.

We were almost to my walk, and I hugged and thanked them both, and ran into the house, to find it as calm and quiet as if I'd been there, except for a glass of wine and a note. Henry was sweetly asleep in his room, with

Cookie at his feet. In the master bedroom, Joe was sprawled on my bed, with Cannoli sleeping on a couch pillow on the floor.

I went back to the kitchen and picked up the glass of wine. The note: "We'll leave you a better snack next time. Love you."

I smiled and drank.

After the last two days, the wine was more than sufficient for the purpose.

Chapter Thirty

Shalom in the Morning

I was sitting at my desk staring into my cup of coffee when Niamh walked into my office.

"Long opening night?" she asked.

"Could have been a lot worse." I blew on the hot liquid and took a sip. "Home before midnight."

Exhausted as I was, I couldn't help smiling a little at how wonderful and normal it had felt to come home to Joe.

"A little sleep is better than none," she said, her face tight. "I saw the police car at the temple. Has something else happened?"

"No, it's just for the morning minyan…they'll be there for Shabbat tonight, too."

"They have to have police for services?"

"They've been around all week."

"I guess I haven't seen them…I'm running unusually early today."

"Could be." If I'd been less tired, I would have thought more before I spoke, but her concern was so genuine, I didn't hold back. "It's because of the knife. Possible hate-crime involvement."

"The knife?" Niamh asked, sitting down in my guest chair. "What about the knife?"

"It was the one with the backwards swastika from the writing table. Remember? You saw it a couple weeks ago."

She nodded. I'd been showing her around the parlor and pulled open the drawer to reveal the desk set, then closed it quickly and, moving past with a very quick comment about 19th-century swastikas, because I didn't want to draw any more attention to it than absolutely necessary.

"You mean he was killed with that knife?"

"Yes. It wasn't in the media reports because it's an important clue."

"I had no idea." Her eyes widened, and her voice went soft and stunned.

"Authorities always hold a few things back in case they might be useful later. I've given it up now, at least with you." I shook my head, drank a bit more coffee. "But, yes, the dagger letter opener with the backwards swastika was the murder weapon. Somebody got it out of our drawer and went after Sir Jeremy."

"Oh, dear Lord, Christian. *Somebody* didn't get it out of the drawer. I did."

"You?" Despite my exhausted state, I shrank back, wondering if I had the energy to fight her off. Energy or not, if she came at me-

"I didn't do the murder!" she added, almost breathless.

"What—what *did* you do?"

"Oh, Lord. I'm so sorry." She ran her hands through her hair. "I went to church with police escort as a little girl in Ireland. It's horrible. So wrong. And those poor people thinking somebody was coming for them..."

"Somebody might have been. Somebody could always be."

"But not me," Niamh said. "I wasn't thinking about the swastika. It was the first weapon I could find after I saw him. After all these years..."

She broke off, put her head in her hands, and sobbed.

"What?" I stared, getting up and patting her arm. "You're safe."

"I wanted him dead."

"Why?"

"I recognized him. Jimmy O'Hearn. A friend of me brother's. Big brother. Seamus got arrested. He died in prison. Jimmy ran."

So much for Gerald O'Hara.

And Auntie Brig.

"I'm so sorry for your loss." It seemed like a good way to start. I stepped back and leaned on my desk. "What about your Auntie Brig?"

"She's real." Niamh wiped her eyes. "I was going to use her as my source for what I know."

"To let the police know what you know, while protecting yourself."

"Got it in one, Christian. I wanted to help."

"Did you?"

"Yes. Honestly, I did."

"So what really happened?"

"I recognized his face Friday morning," she said. "And when I got to work I looked up that man online. Traced him back to his first show, at a small college in Cornwall. No question it was him. And I bet he's the one who stole their priceless Shakespeare scripts, too."

"Scripts?"

"A couple of 17th-century playscripts disappeared shortly after he left. I'd bet anything he took them, nasty creep he was."

Which priceless plays? I wondered. But that wasn't the main issue at the moment.

"What did you do, Niamh?"

"I came back after lunch. I was going to march into his fancy trailer and bury that dagger where it would do the most good."

We'd all been upstairs with the tenth graders on their Regency tour. Even Lewis.

The building was open during the day. We would never have known.

"But Sir Jeremy didn't die until the evening."

"And not by my hand, Christian, I swear." She took a deep, ragged breath. "I stood there in your sweet little parlor for a good five minutes holding that knife and imagining myself stabbing that rotten Jimmy in the jewels."

"His throat was cut," I said quietly.

"And I promise on my children's lives, not by me." She swiped away tears, pushed back her hair. "I stood there thinking about the satisfaction of sending him to hell, and the idea of looking at my babies through bars for the rest of my life. And since you're a mother, you'll know what won. I finally put that knife down on the table and walked away. Stopped at Star of the Sea and lit a candle, begging forgiveness for the evil things I'd thought."

"Did it help?"

"Well," Niamh said with just a trace of a smile, "just a few hours after I left that spalpeen to God, the Good Lord removed him."

"Might be some karma there."

"No might about it, Christian." She gave a grim nod. "Somebody else with more of a thirst for justice and less of a concern for jail did what I couldn't make myself do."

"We know there's a long list of people who had cause to want him dead."

"I don't doubt it." Her eyes spilled over again. "The real problem here is that I left the knife sitting out on the table."

Lewis had seen it in the afternoon, so I knew she was telling the truth there. "Yeah, well."

"Anyone in the world could have come through."

"Most of the people in our immediate world did," I said.

"I know, and that's the truly horrible thing I did. I left it out for whoever might have grabbed it."

"A weapon of opportunity." I understood. "You didn't think about the swastika?"

"Not a bit, Christian. And that's terrible, too. I was thinking about it covered in blood, not about the design." She closed her eyes for a moment, calming herself. "All I knew was that it was a dagger and a convenient weapon."

"Really?" To me, the swastika stood out as if it were emblazoned in neon.

"It wasn't as obvious as you think. And I have to wonder if the person who used it noticed."

"So do I, now."

"Are there fingerprints on the knife?" she asked.

"None as far as I've heard."

"I didn't wipe it," she said. "I'll give the coppers my prints if it'll help."

"I'm not sure what will help." I sighed. "But your account definitely lowers the possibility that this was intended as a hate crime."

"Maybe you can tell Rabbi Aaron, then?"

"I will."

Niamh held my gaze. "I'm just sick about this."

"There's plenty of sick to go around, Niamh." I patted her hand. "You didn't actually *do* anything."

"But I made it easy for whoever did. And I might have terrified the rabbi and all those poor dear people at the temple."

"You didn't plan it as a hate crime," I reminded her. "And you truly didn't do anything except move an artifact out of place."

"With dreadful consequences." She looked at the clock. "This is awful, but I've got to go. Project due at close of business. Do you want me to call Mr. Poli?"

"Wouldn't hurt."

"I'll do it, then, when I have a lull in the action."

"Thanks. You'll talk to the rabbi?"

I took one last sip of my coffee. "I'll do it now...the morning minyan is just wrapping up."

"Thank you, Christian." She took my hand and squeezed it, holding my gaze. "I'm terribly sorry about this mess."

"We're here now. Let's just get through the run of the show and back to normal." Pretty much the last thing I wanted to do was chew on this with Niamh. Even the awkward and slippery conversation with Dina awaiting me was better.

"Sounds like a plan to me."

I stuck my head in the front room. "Lewis, keep an eye for a few, okay?"

He flicked a glance up from his diagram in acknowledgement, but didn't break concentration, and I saw Niamh to the door, stepping out into the muggy morning.

On the temple portico, Dina said goodbye to a few stragglers from the service, including Amy Taylor.

After greeting hugs, Amy looked me over. "You look awfully peaked for a woman with a cute new man."

"Up late, prompting at the show...Joe watched Henry."

Amy beamed and shot Dina a wink. "So it's like that."

"I'm not sure what it's like," I admitted. "But it's good."

"Good is all you need to know right now," Amy said.

"See?" Dina elbowed me. "Listen to the wisdom."

I shook my head. "I know I'm lucky. It's wonderful to see Henry and Joe together."

"You're coming to the Sisterhood Picnic in two weeks, right?" Amy asked.

"Um, sure." With everything else going on, I couldn't commit to two hours, never mind two weeks from now, but even in my frazzled state, I wasn't fool enough to say no to Amy.

"Excellent. We'll talk about what you're bringing later." As she turned to leave, her happy smile faded. "A—friend—and I have tickets for the show tonight. We're not entirely sure we should go after the director…"

"You definitely should," I said quickly. Not just because I wanted her to get a night out with her fella, either. "The company needs all the support it can get."

"And it's safe?"

"As safe as it's possible to be in this world," I assured her. "The place is crawling with cops, investigators, and plenty of alert civilians."

"Not to mention a stray Fed or two, since we have to tolerate them tonight."

"That'll do nicely. *Merde*, Christian!"

My eyes widened. The ballet world version of break a leg, a relatively mild French curse, didn't fit with anything I knew of Amy.

"Took ballet as a girl." She grinned. "I'd probably have been a terrible ballerina."

"You've turned out pretty well," Dina replied with a wink.

"Now I know why you're so graceful," I added.

Amy gave us a modest smile and headed toward the big old Lincoln sedan waiting on the Green drive. Dina and I exchanged glances, knowing it wasn't our place to acknowledge Amy's sweet little romance with Gerry Diamond.

I had something else to talk about, anyhow. "About those feds."

"What?" Dina's tone went brittle and metallic.

"You may not need them."

"Tell me."

As I did, her face went from relief to concern to annoyance.

"Well, I didn't have any of that on my bingo card," she said finally.

"I don't think any of us did."

"Have you told Joe?"

"He's next on my list."

For a moment, Dina looked at me, and then she pulled me in for a quick hug. "That's too kind."

"Nope. More important to ease your mind, at least as much as I can."

"Well, thank you. This certainly lowers the odds of a hate crime."

"It does."

"I think we'll probably go back to the usual Shabbat precautions." She nodded. "We'll have Tony DiBiasi anyhow."

"Has he started coming to shul?" I asked.

"His wife found out a couple of weeks ago that she's from a *converso* family, and she's exploring her heritage. So, he's exploring with her."

"Wow. You really never know." There was a lot more to that story, I was sure. Under the Spanish Inquisition, many families forcibly converted to Catholicism, and now, thanks to DNA tests and genealogical research, their descendants sometimes find their way back.

"Nope. When all this craziness settles down, maybe we'll have lunch with Mrs. DiBiasi and get the whole story."

"Sounds good to me. In the meantime-"

"You have a prosecutor to call."

"Yep."

I turned for the stairs.

"Christian?"

"Yeah?"

"You still need to do a real conversion course and get to the *mikvah*, but you've already got the right idea."

No higher praise.

Chapter Thirty-One

What Does the Internet Say?

Joe, who was sorting out financials, waiting to hear from the Irish authorities, and trying to collate Sir Jeremy's credits list with potential suspects, was glad to hear what I had to say about the knife, but didn't have time for the background. Part of the problem: he'd found out Sir Jeremy had programs from all his shows…but they were locked in a storage unit in London.

So much for that clue.

I hoped I'd have better for him tonight.

After a little happy domestic chat—and yes, a few lines of John Donne—it was back to the day's work at the Society: sorting sheet music and ephemera and helping Lewis work on the layout of his exhibit catalogue.

Late in the day, I headed back over to the dressing rooms to help Alannah and her assistant get everyone into costume. It was a bit less chaotic than the previous night, but still tough. Once again, Alannah and I cursed Sir Jeremy's obsession with authenticity. Most theatre productions made some invisible concessions to modern clothing changes, like hidden zippers instead of those benighted dress buttons.

As I hooked the two-dozen pale-yellow satin-covered ones on the back of Lita's Beatrice dress, I saw Alannah helping Caro out of her white bodice and re-adjusting the lacings on the corset and silently wished both luck. Nothing worse than spending the night laced too tight…unless it was the weird sensation of having your corset unevenly settled.

Nothing good.

Still, I reminded myself as I fastened the hooks-and-eyes on a swing's simpler light-gray dress, we only had one more night of this.

And then, having earned my fee, I could walk away from this and think about planning a getaway with Joe and Henry next week.

Well, as long as somebody caught the damn killer, of course.

Surely it would come together somehow.

After everyone was dressed, I stepped outside to get a little air during warmups. This was turning into one heck of a long haul.

A bark drew my attention, and I looked up to see Garrett and Norm at the corner before the Green, near the Society.

A few patrons had started filtering in, but it was still quiet enough that I didn't have to walk through a crowd to get to them.

"Hey," I said, drawing him into a greeting hug and giving Norm a pat.

"Hey. This isn't an entirely social call."

"What?"

"Finally got a free moment to do an image search on that ring."

"Image search?"

"Yes, Dr. Luddite." He dropped an exaggeratedly patronizing pat on my head. Norm gave him a disappointed look, and Garrett patted him, too. "Remember, I told you I'd run the photo of the signet and see if anything came up?"

"Run it how?"

"Please tell me you know what an image search is."

"That's the thing where you take a picture and send it through the internet to find similar ones, right?"

"Close enough."

I glared at him. "Does this involve AI?"

"Yes, some. But not the kind that takes away any writer or actors' jobs, I promise."

"Oh, fine." I sighed and patted Norm. "So what did you learn about Sir Jeremy's signet?"

"Well, it *was* a signet." Garrett gave me a dubious scowl. "And the husbands are right. It's worth plenty."

"Okay."

"But it never belonged to the alleged Sir Jeremy, which we suspected once you told me it wasn't the crest of the Hightower family."

I waited.

"It's the crest of an ancient noble clan from Northumbria."

"As in the people who were there before the Normans."

"Precisely. It could be more than a thousand years old."

"Holy hell. And he was just wandering around wearing it." I rubbed my face at the sheer clueless entitlement of it.

"He was. Hiding in plain sight."

"Are you sure?"

"As sure as I can be with the help of my little AI friend." Garrett allowed himself a lightly superior smile. "You took a good look at the photo. Doesn't the design suggest something extremely old?"

"Yes, it does. But I still have a hard time wrapping my brain around this. He was just wandering around in this incredibly ancient, breathtakingly valuable piece?"

"It sure looks like it."

"So, who did he steal it from?"

"So young and so cynical," Garrett replied with a wicked laugh.

"I know who we're dealing with."

"True. And you're right on the—no pun intended—money."

"So?"

"Until about thirty years ago, it was on display at an obscure manor house that had been turned over to the National Trust. Interestingly, it disappeared a few months before Sir Jeremy's first quarter at a college in Cornwall."

"Interesting indeed."

"Here's the kicker: the home was the ancestral seat of the family of a Northumbria Community College dean who was found dead at the bottom of a staircase after an entanglement with a young Irish protégé by the name of Gerald O'Hara."

"Who disappeared afterward?"

"Never seen since. I found an online article revisiting the cold case from about five years ago. As far as I can tell, there's no public record of Jeremy Hightower before that college year in Cornwall…and none of Gerald O'Hara after it."

"A-ha," I said. "With credit to Arthur Conan Doyle."

"I really don't think he ever said that. I know Holmes didn't."

"Your point is?" I asked. "So the ring came from his first reinvention, and he used it to back up his second."

"Exactly." Garrett's face turned very serious. "While apparently leaving at least one body."

"Yet more motive and potential suspects," I said. "So how much is this thing worth?"

"Priceless in every sense of the word." Garrett shrugged. "It's hard to nail down, because we would be talking about a black-market collector. But it's an ancient and exceedingly rare piece, and I'm sure there are some people out there on the dark web who would snap it up if they could."

"And who would not be too hung up on provenance?"

"Well, if you're buying medieval artifacts this way, you have, by definition, given up on legitimate tracking." He bent to pat Norm, as if wanting contact with the innocent animal. "As I understand it, art and artifact theft is a pretty rough world."

"Meaning, if somebody figured out what he had, he was a sitting duck." I met Garrett's concerned gaze. "And if there are serious art thieves in the mix…"

"We have a whole new kind of trouble in River City," Garrett finished for me.

"Because a murder with a swastika knife wasn't enough."

"Exactly."

A small honk from a big SUV, and a return blast of the horn from the sleek electric sedan in front of it reminded us this conversation wasn't taking place in a vacuum.

Showtime coming up fast.

"Good luck, Christian," Garrett said, putting a hand on my arm and leaving it there, holding my gaze. "Want me to send Ed to watch over you?"

"No. For heaven's sake, let the guy have a night off." I gave him a brave, and only partly fake, calm smile. "Only two shows to go. How bad can it be?"

And yet again, a question you should never ask the universe.

Chapter Thirty-Two

Goodnight, Hero

"Oh my God! She's dead!"

I'd been stretching in my seat, congratulating myself that the show was two-thirds over, when I heard the cry.

Like everyone else, I started running toward the sound.

Caro, the blonde actress playing Hero, was sprawled by the prop table, at least unconscious, if not worse. Her costar Lita was kneeling beside her, face contorted with fear.

Several other cast and crew members milled around.

"What happened?" I asked Lita as I bent down.

"I don't know. She left the dressing room a couple minutes before I did. I just found her."

"Call 9-1-1!" somebody yelled from behind Lita.

She wasn't breathing, and as far as I could tell, didn't have a pulse. "I'm starting CPR."

As I jumped in with the new hands-only kind I'd learned in my refresher class, a voice over my head yelled:

"Narcan!"

As I finished the first round, a burly stagehand joined me on the ground. "Hey—I was a medic in Iraq."

I pulled back, ceding to superior expertise.

"Here!" Vic shoved something into my hand. "It's Narcan."

I passed it on to the medic.

Within seconds, Caro was breathing again.

A minute or so later, Tiffany and one of her minions ran in.

"Some welcome back," I said as she blew past me.

She shot me an eyebrow, and a "talk later" look.

The stagehand medic pulled back for Tiffany and gave her a quick briefing. "Female, twenties, found unconscious, not breathing…responsive to Narcan…"

As the pros rolled Caro out, Lita started hyperventilating. The stagehand medic and I jumped in to help her.

For maybe five minutes, chaos swirled backstage as Lita slowly calmed down. While I grabbed her a water from the coffee table, it was pretty clear Lita was getting all the help she needed from the stagehand and likely a bit more. Nothing inappropriate, but there was definitely a vibe, and I didn't belong in the middle of it.

I stepped away, taking a breath.

"Is Lita okay?"

I turned to see Alannah, smoking in flagrant violation of backstage rules and basic safety. Not that I was going to argue right now.

"She is now. Looked like a mild panic attack to me, but I'm not a medic."

"What about Caro?"

"I really don't know. It's good that she responded to the Narcan, but who knows?" I'd never smoked, but I was suddenly tempted.

A thick hand with a bit of knuckle hair lifted the cig right from Alannah's fingers. "Good Lord, what a mess."

Vic, looking frazzled and furious, despite his festive purple and gold satin caftan, took a huge drag and handed it back. Alannah gave it a disgusted glance and held it loosely.

"What are we gonna do?" he asked.

"Do we call it?" Hitch wheezed the question as he ran up to us from the back of the house. "Half the audience was watching as she was taken out."

"How is she?"

At least two of us asked.

"She was talking when they loaded her," Hitch said. "She wasn't making sense, but she was talking."

"Well, that's good anyhow," I said.

"Poor kid," Vic said. "I still don't know what we do."

"The show must go on?" Hitch asked.

"I think we have to."

A new voice.

Julia Henshaw was crossing in from the dressing room.

"We do?" Vic asked.

"Well, I can see us having to refund the night's receipts, and…" Julia paused for a moment, then continued. "I don't want to be insensitive. I know that poor girl was just taken out of here in an ambulance, but she seems to be recovering. And we have an understudy, right?"

"Of course," Hitch said.

"We'd finish the show if she went home with food poisoning," Julia said, "so we'll finish the show now."

"Fair enough," Vic said. "I'll go talk to the understudy."

"Should I make an announcement?" Hitch asked.

Julia looked from one to the other, calculating the potential for a territorial battle, and calmly took charge. "I'll do it."

"Thanks." Hitch turned to Vic. "We need to get our understudy ready to go."

They headed for the dressing room, where they were about to give a community theatre swing the best news of her life. Vic looked back at me:

"Don't be surprised if you're needed more than usual."

"Of course. I'll be ready."

They trooped off.

Julia turned to me. "I'm not sure this is the right call, but I just don't think we can cancel."

"This show is keeping the Festival alive, isn't it?"

"We can't afford to lose anything this summer. I'm just praying the weather guys are wrong about tomorrow night." She sighed, clearly trying to balance financial need and concern for her players. "I really don't think it's insensitive."

"Broadway shows go on if someone goes home sick, don't they?"

"Sure."

"And you're the one who said…"

"I did." She straightened up. "Thank you, Christian."

"Don't mention it," I said, hefting my prompt book and heading back to my seat.

I understood, really I did, but I wasn't at all sure about this. There was just too much going on here. Even if Caro had "merely" accidentally overdosed on something, it spoke to the stress level of the company.

Despite everything, the rest of the show went well; our community theatre understudy stepped up and turned in a performance at least as good as the Yalie she replaced, and she knew her lines cold.

During a scene change toward the end, Hitch slipped in beside me and whispered, "She'll be fine."

At least something might end well.

Chapter Thirty-Three

Who's WHO?

After that night, I had no energy for arguing when Vic asked one of the stagehands to drop me off on his way home. Especially not when the stagehand was the medic.

"Thank you," I said as he clicked the locks on a well-kept but not new small SUV.

"Glad to. I'm Jordan, by the way, Dr. Shaw."

"Christian. I don't normally use the title."

Jordan, who probably wasn't all that much older than Officer Colby, but who had a gravity that suggested he'd seen an awful lot more, smiled as he climbed into his seat. "My mom taught me good manners."

"I can tell." I returned the smile. "And your first-aid instructors taught you well, too."

"Oh, this was an easy one."

I just nodded. No response that would be right.

Jordan started the car. "The Narcan worked, which means she didn't have a big overdose. Though I'm still trying to figure out how she got it."

"What do you mean?"

"My best guess is she thought she was taking some kind of anti-anxiety thing and it turned out to be something else." He turned onto the Green traffic circle.

"I read about that, but how often does it really happen?" I asked, knowing the question probably marked me as an 'old.'

"More than you'd think. Sure, you'd expect a Yalie would have health insurance and get her anti-anxiety meds above board…but the black-market stuff is everywhere."

"And much of it's contaminated."

"Let's just say I wouldn't put anything in my mouth that wasn't handed to me by a pharmacist."

"Neither would I, but I'm a boring old mom." I pointed. "Just take the right turn here—my house is two streets over. I could have walked home."

"Nah. Not a good idea, even here."

"Probably not with everything else going on."

"Lotta weird stuff in the company," he agreed. "Totally different vibe than last summer."

"You did last summer?"

"Yeah—it was just fun and happy and totally what I needed after…well, you know."

"I don't know…but, I know what you mean."

"Mm-hmm." He acknowledged my comment and kept going. "Good people having a great time. A lot of the same people as this year—the hands, the scene shop and the swings are mostly the same—but not nearly as fun."

"Murder will do that."

"It's more than the murder. Things felt off from the time I got here. I can't put my finger on it—I'm not a career theatre guy, you know. It just didn't feel right."

"Well, if it helps, I work on a lot of productions, and I had basically the same feeling. Also not sure why."

"Sir Jeremy was a real chaos agent," Jordan said. "He seemed to just enjoy upending everything whenever he walked into the room. Nothing was right, nobody could carry out his 'vision,' you know."

I did. "I got that. He was hard on pretty much everybody."

"He was. And I'm not surprised somebody decided to stop him."

"Turn here," I said as he stopped at the intersection near my house. "Can you get back to the main road okay?"

"Sure. Driven in a lot tougher than this, Dr. Christian."

I laughed. "That's what my—guy's—daughter calls me. My house is the small one, with the lights on."

"It's an easy compromise." Jordan smiled as he stopped the car. "Here you go."

"Thanks." I got out my house key, then opened the door. "How do you like your coffee?"

"Dark roast, black…is there any other way?"

"I'll bring you one from the Coffee Stop tomorrow."

"No need—"

"Least I can do. Good night."

Jordan waited until I got to the door and unlocked it.

Cookie was in the window, sitting guard, and he jumped down as I opened the door.

Inside, Joe was asleep on the couch with Cannoli on one side. The little dog looked up at me but stayed where he was because Cookie was already leading the way into the kitchen.

Joe opened one eye and smiled, half-asleep. "Hey."

"Hey, you."

Since Cookie was perfectly capable of howling the house down if he didn't get a treat, I tiptoed into the kitchen and put out a few more of his favorite tuna crunchies.

Then, of course, to my boy.

Henry stirred but didn't wake when I slipped in and kissed him.

Joe had fallen back to sleep on the couch. I sat down, and he reached for me, half waking as I snuggled in.

"Hey, *cara*."

"Hey. Good to be home."

"Glad you're here." He buried his face in my hair and pulled me close.

"That's nice."

"Henry lit candles with me,"

"Yeah?"

"Yeah. He told me I could just watch to be sure he was safe, but he was going to do it."

"That's Henry. Knows who and what he is."

"He's a great guy, *cara*."

"Preaching to the choir."

For a few breaths, we just sat there, enjoying the quiet and togetherness.

"We made you a snack," Joe said.

"Maybe later."

We probably would have fallen asleep right there on the couch if Joe's phone hadn't rung.

He picked up, snapping immediately into work mode, and this time, for good reason: I caught an Irish accent in the greeting.

Say howya to the Garda.

While he talked to his friend across the pond, I headed for the kitchen and that snack, stopping at the sideboard to make sure the Sabbath candles were out and cold. On the kitchen counter was a glass of wine, with a sticky note in Henry's printing on it: "In the fridge. Share with Cookie. We love you."

It was signed with an "H," two carefully-drawn paw prints...and a "J" clearly added by Joe.

In the refrigerator, I found a very artfully arranged plate of turkey slices, cheese cubes, and cherry tomatoes, with grapes in the middle, and a couple of pieces of flatbread stuck in at the sides. Henry had clearly given a good bit of thought to it, and equally clearly gotten some help from Joe.

We could get used to this.

All of us. Maybe even Cookie and Cannoli.

Wine and cheese in hand, I went back into the living room and took the other end of the couch, raising the glass and mouthing a thank-you to Joe, who shot me a smile.

Too tired to follow along, I took a sip of the wine and reflected once again that I was glad I'd started keeping good but not expensive Chianti in the house for Joe instead of the Box Mart red that had been my standard for years.

While the conversation was clearly animated and interesting, it wasn't long. Within a couple of minutes, Joe offered thanks and a promise to keep his new friend in the loop and rang off.

"It's more interesting than we thought," he said.

"Yeah?"

Joe reached for the glass of wine he'd fallen asleep on hours ago, barely touched and, like mine, probably improved by breathing for a while. He took a sip. "Yeah."

"We're not even a hundred-percent sure who he is—was."

"How's that?"

"There's no record of a Gerald O'Hara in Dublin at even close to the right time. There is, however, a death record for an infant by that name from 1959."

"A real one?"

"The Garda officer assured me it was. Apparently, she knows a little about American lit, too, and double-checked it."

"Wow." I took a sip of wine and held out the plate to Joe.

"No, that's for you."

"I'll never finish it all," I said, nudging him.

"And we can't leave evidence." He gave me a tired smile and took a couple cubes of cheese.

"Evidence indeed." I put the plate down between us and picked up a turkey slice. "Which brings us back to…"

"Yep." Joe swallowed and drank more wine. "No hard evidence for this guy's existence before—or after—that passport was issued in 1990. We know it's him because the fingerprints match. They also match the UK passport found in his things, so it looks like both are good fakes."

"Which would fit for a person who's reinvented himself at least twice," I said, thinking of all I'd learned today.

"How's that?"

"Well, I think I might be able to help you with the reinvention as well as the knife."

"How so?" He sat up straight. "All you told me was that your friend took out the knife and left it on the table…and that there was more to it."

"There sure is."

"Okay…"

"Well, she recognized Sir Jeremy as a guy who should have gotten arrested with her big brother, who was mixed up in the Troubles. The brother got arrested and died in jail—and the friend, one Jimmy O'Hearn, disappeared. Niamh didn't think of him until she saw him Friday."

"And she took out the knife." He held my gaze.

"She swears she set it down and walked away to go pray at Star of the Sea. There's a speed cam on that street, so you should be able to verify it."

"And how do you know that?"

"Got a ticket last year," I admitted.

Joe smiled. "Never figured you for a lead foot."

"Running late to pick up Henry."

"Nothing more dangerous than a mom rushing to her kid."

"Exactly." I took another sip of wine. "But in general, none of us are sterlingly rational when it comes to family, which brings us back to Niamh taking out the knife to avenge her late brother."

"How did no one see any of this?"

"It was her lunch hour, and we were taking the tenth-grade enrichment Regency romance class through the bedrooms and dressing room upstairs."

"And you think it's possible?" He held my gaze. "Both—her being there, and her deciding not to use the knife."

"It fits with everything else we know. Lewis remembers noticing the knife in the afternoon. And the theatre people were in and out all day getting coffee."

"We can check the Society door cam, right?"

"Yes. We can nail down comings and goings."

Joe looked into his glass. "Still. How credible is she?"

"I'm sure you'll want some corroborating evidence, I believe her."

"You do?"

"I was skeptical, but I really do."

"Okay." Joe's tone suggested he wasn't sold, but he toyed with a cube of cheese and contemplated. "So the knife was just sitting out there for anyone to come past and grab it?"

CHAPTER THIRTY-THREE

"Making it a true crime of opportunity."

"Right. Niamh says she didn't see the swastika on the knife…so it's at least possible that the killer didn't either."

"You told Dina?"

"Before I told you," I admitted. "Just enough to make her feel safe. She's carrying a lot, you know."

"I do. And I agree. She has a right to know."

I drank a little wine and picked up another turkey slice. "But there's more."

"Still more?"

"Yep. Niamh tells me there was some kind of rare book theft at a college where Sir Jeremy did his first high-profile production in Cornwall."

"Rare book theft?" Joe's eyes widened.

"This guy was apparently a rolling antiquities crime wave," I said. "And worse."

"Really?"

"His first stop in England was Northumbria Community College, where—Garrett has learned—his mentor ended up dead, and a priceless family signet ring disappeared from the old pile that was deeded to the National Trust."

"Priceless signet ring?"

"Sound familiar?"

"It does indeed." Joe took a bite of cheese.

"Garrett turned up the details on the death and the ring. I'm sure he'll be happy to send them to you in the morning."

"You told him to stick to online detecting, right?"

"Ed will take care of that." I took a piece of cheese. "But wait, there's more."

"Right—the book theft?"

"Niamh described them as priceless playscripts. I had time to check news archives in places Sir Jeremy directed, and I found something that might be it: the University of Cornwall reported the theft of two seventeenth-century Shakespeare playscripts."

"Like a prompt book?"

"Similar. Playscript usually implies something small used by an actor, often only with their lines. A prompt book is at least the entire show, often with notes. Tough to know what these were—except that they were valuable. I could only find one very brief item, with little detail—no word on the plays, or the exact age, or anything else."

"Guess they're on my list for calls tomorrow." He drank more wine. "Think anyone will be around on a Saturday?"

"No idea. Theatre departments are weird."

"Well, there's an understatement."

We both laughed.

"I needed that," I said.

"Rough night?"

"Rougher than you know. One of the leading ladies left in an ambulance."

"What?"

"Some kind of OD. She responded to Narcan."

"Well, that's good." He shook his head. "What do you think…"

"You know as well as I do that this sort of thing can happen. But it seems awfully coincidental that it happened today. One day before the end of the run, in the middle of a murder investigation."

"It does." He leaned back with his glass, wrapping his free arm around me.

"Thanks. I needed that." I moved the almost-empty plate out of the way, and snuggled in, hanging onto my half-full glass.

"Thought you might."

"Yeah. Poor kid—and her poor family."

"Hate overdose cases." Joe's arm tightened around me. "They happen so damn often, and they're always terrifying. A lot worse before Narcan was widely available, of course."

"Yeah."

He rested his head on mine, and we just stayed close for a moment, soothing each other.

"Is there anything about this girl that would make her a target?"

"She's one of the leading ladies, which, yeah, I suppose. But surely nobody's going to resort to violence over a summer theatre part."

"People will resort to violence for any reason, or none," Joe reminded me. "And it would be an awfully good way to sideline someone—temporarily or permanently—without much risk to the do-er."

"You think?"

"I know. There are so damn many tainted drugs out there, I'm amazed we don't lose more addicts. An awful lot of people end up in trouble taking what they think is some kind of relatively mild drug, like one of the anti-anxiety or ADD meds, and it turns out to have fentanyl in it."

"And it doesn't take much with that stuff."

"Barely any at all. I'm not a fan of the whole 'this is your brain on drugs' deal, but I have to tell you I've been warning Aly to take absolutely nothing that doesn't come straight from the hand of a medical professional."

"Makes sense to me. I think Henry is savvier because of the Type-1—"

"You can't assume anything, *cara.*" He pulled back to make eye contact. "Might want to use tonight's mess as a little teachable moment tomorrow. I'm going to when I pick up Aly in the morning."

"Good thought."

Our gaze held, and I smiled.

"What?" he asked.

"Just us, conspiring like a parenting team."

"We make a pretty good one."

"That we do." He picked up his wine glass. "How about I set a really good example about not drinking and driving and stay over?"

"Works for me."

Chapter Thirty-Four

To G-d and Humanity

Even though Joe and I were tired enough to sleep late, after everything that had happened, the Saturday morning service was not an option for me. And he had to drive more than an hour north to Kent to fetch Aly from band camp.

So, a luxurious lay-in wasn't an option. If parents ever get such a thing.

It didn't matter anyhow, since Henry bounced out of bed vibrating with excitement at the idea of watching Easton check the steeple in the afternoon.

The first thing I heard that morning was Henry telling Cookie about it and promising to bring back pics. With an eye to maintaining some minimal level of propriety, I carefully untangled myself from Joe and threw a sweater over my pajamas before tiptoeing past Cannoli on his couch pillow and heading into the kitchen to make coffee.

Smiled to myself at how glad I was to need to make coffee in a pot instead of a quick single mug from the BuzzMachine.

At the sound of running water, Cookie came blasting into the kitchen, followed more slowly by Henry.

While Cookie supervised my serving up his morning wet food and fresh water, Henry held forth on his exciting day, bouncing the way he had as a tiny kid.

"It's so cool, Ma. He's had Type-1 since he was in fourth grade, and he climbs buildings."

"Very cool indeed," I agreed, as I tried to get my eyes to focus.

"And remember, we're going to Kule's for slushies after. Easton likes lemon and AlysDad gets cherry—"

"What are you getting?"

"Cherry, too. They have blue in no-sugar, but…" He wrinkled his nose. He does not share his mother's appreciation for unnaturally colored summer treats.

"That'll work."

Cookie blasted between us, then, yowling and frantic, the way only a cat afraid of missing a treat could be.

We got him fed and settled, I made Henry his favorite cheese scramble, and by then, Joe was awake, joining us at the table and slowly sipping coffee. Cannoli was in a corner of the living room, which Joe had set up with water and kibble bowls out of Cookie's sight lines. It worked.

"Now what?" Henry asked as I loaded dishes in the washer. "It's still way early."

Joe yawned and drank more coffee. "Well, I've got to get Cannoli home, and then I have to clean up and head up to Kent. Aly's jazz band plays at eleven."

"We're meeting Mr. Easton at four, right?" asked Henry. "And going back to your house for dinner with Aly—and a sleepover?"

"Right." He yawned again.

It had clearly been a while since Joe had to deal with the early-morning energy of an excited medium-sized kid. Aly was probably nocturnal, like most teens.

"Want me to make you a cheese scramble, too?" I offered, as I made a mental note to pack Henry's bag for the sleepover.

"Oh, Lord, no." He drank the last of his coffee, then rubbed his face and tried to focus, looking at Henry, who'd started building a steeple of Legos in the living room.

"I haven't seen him this excited since we lit Hanukkah candles," I said.

"And why not? Easton is climbing a building." As he said it, Joe's eyes took on a boyish gleam like Henry's.

"You too?" I asked.

"Well, I don't get to light a menorah, but this is pretty darn cool."

"Stick around, and we'll let you help this year."

A suddenly serious smile as he stood. "Sign me up, *Dottore.*"

"Well, you've mastered Shabbat candles, so I think you'll do just fine."

For a moment, as our eyes held, we were back in the foyer a week ago. Before all the ugly stuff, with nothing to think about but us.

Maybe we could get back there after the killer was caught.

"Give my best to Aly," I said. "Tell her Henry and I will make her next concert if we possibly can."

Joe grinned. "She'll like that."

After Henry and I bid appropriate farewells to Cannoli and Joe—and Cookie glared from his window seat—Joe headed out for his busy morning.

Henry and I still had an hour and a half before temple.

"I'm going to do a yoga video." I clapped my hands and smiled brightly. "How about you join me?"

"Do I have to?"

"No," I said, "but it might feel good, and it'll eat up some time before the service."

Good enough. With only a little help from me, he followed along through some basic stretches and flow. He wasn't sold, honestly, but it was a good way to kill time, and I felt better, at least.

My yoga zen carried me right through the usually fraught process of getting Henry into appropriate attire (a collared shirt is *not* negotiable for services) and finding an outfit for myself that would work for both the temple and the prompter's seat if it came to that. I finally settled on a long, loose navy shadow-stripe shirtdress, comfortable for sitting or running around backstage. Not even remotely sexy, but Joe would know what I was going for—and that he'd get something saucy later.

Since we were going to the very place Henry would get to see Easton climb the roof, he was positively radiant with excitement as we walked over. Well, I walked. Henry skipped, bounced, and ran ahead until I asked him to pull it back a little.

At the Green, I heard my name, in an unmistakable cool, regal tone, and turned to see State's Attorney Amelia Porter, in a jewel purple linen suit and church hat. I'm sure it was her way of showing respect for the Shabbat service, but it was also straight-out, knock 'em down, elegant, which was definitely part of the point.

"Ms. State's Attorney." I turned and held out a hand to shake. "So good to see you."

"Just wanted to show a little support in the wake of last weekend's incident." She looked up at the temple. "And I love the warmth and community of the Jewish Sabbath service."

"Really."

"Oh, yes. Of course, I'm from an entirely different tradition, but the feeling of unity and God in the room hits in all the right places."

Henry squirmed a bit.

"Honey, you can go on ahead and find us a seat if you like," I said, then turned back to Porter as he scampered off. "You're so right about the service."

"Whatever traditions we come from, there are some universals."

Honesty time, I thought, and started with a sheepish little shrug. "I'm not official yet—Henry's father was Jewish, and I'm still working on converting, but we come to temple every week if at all possible."

"It's so important to give children a good religious grounding," she said, nodding. "The actual faith doesn't matter so much as the idea of a higher power and goodwill toward our fellow humans."

"You are absolutely right, Ms. State's Attorney."

Amy Taylor joined Porter and me on the temple walk. "It's so kind of you to come today. I'm sure Rabbi Aaron will be pleased to see you."

"Just important for you to know the local authorities are watching over you. We will not tolerate hate or intimidation of any kind."

Amy, whose family had been in the Netherlands when the Nazis arrived, gave Porter a small smile with a world of history in it and took her hand. "You'll just have to take my word for how much that means."

"I'm glad to help."

As I looked down at the two women holding hands, a beautiful gesture of support, I noticed Amy's cuffs. Her blouse was bright pink with button cufflinks—a different color but the same exact style as the lime-green one I'd found the morning after the murder.

Interesting.

"I'm not trying to change the subject to fluff, Amy," I said, "but I love the French cuffs on that blouse. They're so hard to find."

She laughed. "Trust you to notice, Christian. I know about you and your vintage oxfords."

"That's not an oxford, though."

"No, it's not. But it is vintage. B. Altman, I think. Don't ask me what decade—let's just say 20th century and leave it there."

"I could guess," I said, "but I won't."

Porter was watching the conversation. She had to know about the cufflink. "It's a wonderful color. I love the brightness…though I've always preferred green on myself."

"It's the funniest thing, dear," Amy said. "I remember it came in green—and white, too. And I could swear I've seen the green one lately. It's vintage fashion now, you know."

"It is indeed," I agreed. "If you think of where you saw it, let me know. I'd love to get that piece, if I can find someone willing to give it up."

"Would you and the State's Attorney care to sit with me? Gerry is standing outside being menacing again today."

"What about your son, Dr. Shaw?" Porter asked.

"If I give him the okay, he'll sit up in the balcony with some pals from Hebrew School, so that will be just fine."

Amy grinned. "Little boys never change, do they?"

"They do not," I agreed.

"Neither do big ones. My son is eighteen—freshman at UCONN—and he looks for any excuse to not sit with his boring mother."

"Well, we'll do just fine together," Amy said.

Porter and I dropped back a step as we reached the portico, partly to stand behind Amy for safety, but also to exchange a few words.

"Green cufflink?"

"Somebody in the company, I'm guessing."

"Keep your eyes open."

"Always do," I assured her.

We followed Amy into the vestibule, which was more crowded than usual on an August morning, probably because many other temple members wanted to show—or seek—support. I saw Henry huddling with the other kids, three boys and two girls from his class, and gave him a thumbs up.

One of the other mothers shot me a wave, and her daughter gave a nod, setting off a little flutter among the parents. As Amy led us into her favorite spot in the sanctuary, I saw the knot of kids head for the stairs. Everyone knew they were probably not paying as devoted attention as they might if we were sitting with them, but everyone also knew that they were enjoying the company of their friends, which had plenty of value on its own.

The rabbis of the Talmud probably weren't big fans of kids whispering in a corner of the balcony during services, but they *were* big fans of community.

Whatever ugliness was outside in the world, the congregation inside was determined to come together, and soak up the feeling of G-d in the room, and in each other, which may be the same thing (two Jews, three opinions again!). As it always did, the timeless pattern of the service took over, Dina's clarion voice calling us to prayer, and guiding us through the ancient words.

I don't pretend to know what other people feel during religious services, and it's none of my damn business anyway. But by the final prayer, it felt like we were all surrounded by some kind of invisible embrace, pulled together by our good intentions toward G-d and each other.

Exactly what we needed after this awful week.

At the end, the congregation milled about, talking and shaking hands, occasionally hugging. We're always a pretty social group, but this morning it seemed warmer, more connected.

"Well, what a lovely surprise." Dina, in prayer shawl over a smoky-blue dress with a subtle tone-on-tone floral print, had worked her way over to Porter, Amy, and me. "Ms. State's Attorney, it's so good to see you here."

"It's good to be here, Rabbi."

They exchanged a half-hug, half-handshake, and Dina shot me a glance. I took the hint, and Amy's arm.

"You haven't seen Henry recently, I don't think," I said. "He's growing like a weed."

"Really?" Amy smiled. "Well, let's go find him, and leave the rabbi and prosecutor to their pleasure."

"Thanks," I said. "I figured you'd get it."

"Christian, dear, the wonderful thing about being as old as I am is that I get almost everything."

Henry and his buddies were just outside, milling around the way medium-sized kids do, and Henry was clearly telling them what he'd be seeing in a few hours, because he was pointing up at the steeple.

"Ma!" he called when I saw me and Amy walking onto the portico.

"You're right." Amy beamed at Henry as he scampered toward us. "He's taller every time I see him."

"Hi, Mrs. Taylor!" Henry held out a hand to shake, just as his dad had taught him.

"Well, don't you have lovely manners." Amy took his hand and smiled. "You're growing into quite the young man, Henry."

"Thanks. Did Ma tell you I'm going to see AlysDad's friend Easton climb the steeple this afternoon?"

"Why don't you tell me while we walk over to see Mr. Diamond?"

Henry happily bounced along with her, warming to his topic, pointing to the steeple and diagramming the rigging with his hands. When they reached Gerry Diamond, Henry happily dove in for another round.

"Can I watch them climb the steeple, too?"

Officer Colby was behind me, watching the scene. His posture was neutral and his face open and friendly as usual, but I could tell he was ready to jump off and defend anyone who might need help.

In the wake of the fire, I was well aware our Raggedy Andy was no empty-headed doll. There was a brave man, and the makings of a good, smart cop under that curly hair. And also a boy who wanted to see something cool.

"Since it's taking place outdoors," I reminded him, "I don't think anyone will mind."

"And I should direct traffic."

"You should. Absolutely." I exchanged a grin with him and waded back through the crowd to Henry, who was enjoying his mutual admiration society with Amy and Gerry.

"C'mon, big guy," I said. "You need lunch—and so does Cookie."

Henry's eyes widened. "Oops. You're right. Let's go feed him."

Why did I have the feeling Cookie was going to have a much more relaxing lunch hour than me?

Chapter Thirty-Five

Boys (and Girl's) Day Out

Finally, after cat and kid-feeding, and what seemed like endless rounds of video games punctuated by more speculation about steeple climbing, and the possible menu for the dinner and sleepover at Joe's, it was a quarter to four, and Aly and Joe arrived at our door.

"Dr. Christian!" Aly, who was looking lightly sunburned and a bit tired in her red Jazz Band All-Star t-shirt and khaki shorts, gave me a quick hug. "I like that lipstick for you."

"No bright colors until you're at least sixteen," Joe cut in.

"I said I like it on her, Dad." Exasperated eye roll.

"How was band camp?" I asked, hoping for a subject change.

"Wonderful. I got to play tenor sax…and I'm thinking about switching."

From Joe's expression, I suspected a tenor sax did not come cheap. The concern, though, quickly gave way to a big smile. "What I can tell you is this girl can blow a horn. She was the star of the jazz band."

"Well, I wouldn't say that," Aly demurred.

"C'mon, AlysDad!" Henry said, grabbing his backpack. "We have to get there before he goes up. I want to see the rigging."

Aly rolled her eyes, but she didn't make the sort of sarcastic comment many teens would have. She might have been interested in watching Easton up on the steeple, too.

"The rigging?" Joe asked.

"Ma helped me find the rigging system maker online, and I want to see what he has."

"Top of the line, I'm sure," Joe replied, giving me the wide eyes that Henry can inspire at his most focused.

"I think so," Henry agreed.

"Well," I said, "have a great time. It's still warm, so keep a little eye on the meter and fluids, huh?"

"Don't we always, Ma?" Henry's exasperated tone drew a faint smile from Joe.

"You do. And so does AlysDad." I held Henry's gaze. "Remember, though, you're the pro. He's still getting used to your system. And you're a little excited right now."

Joe patted my arm. "I know all the equipment and such, but your mom's right. You live in your body, so you'll know first if there's any issue."

"There won't be." Henry slung the backpack over his shoulder.

I bent down and gave him a kiss.

"Have fun." As I straightened up, I smiled at Aly. "You're looking forward to this, too, aren't you?"

"Sure thing, Dr. Christian. I don't get to see people hang off buildings much. And Uncle Easton's super-cool."

"Super-cool," Joe echoed, drawing a little glare from his girl.

"Well, enjoy the coolness. If I get a chance to scoot over before showtime, I will."

"You really don't want to miss it, Ma." Henry urged. "Let's go!"

As they ran out, my phone dinged.

Hitch:

We have a corset situation, and I can't find Alannah. Please come quickly.

Considering all the things that can go wrong with modern people attempting to wear vintage underpinnings, I didn't need to be asked twice. I sent a quick "Leaving now," grabbed my bag, and started walking as fast as I could.

About an hour later, a very upset new Hero and an only marginally less shaken Beatrice had been rescued from the kind of mishap that happens when you try to get into costume on your own for a pic. There's a reason Victorian women had maids.

Our understudy, now leading lady, had laced her corset wrong and, in her efforts to fix it, gotten all tangled up. The real mistake was asking her co-star for help instead of sending for Alannah or the costume assistant. Between the two of them, the actresses had only managed to get the strings caught on the eyelets and pulled them tighter, until poor Hero was having trouble breathing, and her helper was running around the dressing room trying to cut the strings.

Fortunately, Hitch was checking the prop table, happened to hear the commotion, and sent for me. It took only a few moments for someone with a little know-how to free our new leading lady, and I showed both girls how to properly lace the corset and the fastest, safest way to undo the laces, too.

Hero returned to her original plan, to get some pics, only now, instead of a few amateur snaps from her stagehand boyfriend, she was going to get some really good art shots from costar Lita, who turned out to have a minor in photography. Everyone wins.

Only after they'd headed out to the empty stage for their photo shoot did I wonder where on earth Alannah was. The last time I'd done a show with her, she'd practically lived in the costume shop. Of course, that had been a college production, and she and her husband had been staying in the on-campus motel. Considering their current scenic accommodations, it wasn't really surprising that they might have lingered a bit at the beach ahead of the last show.

I supposed.

Hitch was waiting when I stepped out of the dressing room tent, his amiable face tight with concern. "All okay?"

"All just fine. Easy enough to fix."

"Whew." His face, and whole posture, relaxed. "That's the kind of thing no male person—no matter what their orientation—wants to deal with in this day and age."

"Absolutely," I agreed.

"Thank you for rescuing me, Dr. Shaw."

"You know, you could start calling me Christian. I think the roof has formed enough of an introduction, don't you?"

His handsome face cracked into a boyish grin. "Always liked that expression. My mother would say that if you went to the trouble of earning the PhD, you deserve to use it at all times."

"She had one, didn't she?"

"Yes—and is terribly disappointed that I don't."

"Never say never," I said. "Surely a graduate theatre program would scoop you right up if you were interested."

"Ah, that's the thing. If I'm actually studying instead of just mucking around, I'll have to get serious about it."

"I think you're pretty serious already-"

"STOP!"

The shout stopped our little conversation cold, and we immediately started running in the direction of the noise.

"Don't go up there!"

I'd thought I recognized the first voice as Joe's, and I was absolutely sure when I heard the second: Henry.

What on earth?

Outside, on the gravel in front of the temple portico, Joe and Henry were talking to Easton and his assistant. Concerned faces all around, as Henry pointed to the rigging, and everyone else stared.

"What's wrong?" I asked as I made it into earshot.

"Your boy may have just saved my life, Doc." Easton unclipped a carabiner at his belt and stepped over some rope to get over to Joe and Henry. Aly was snapping pictures of the rope with her phone.

"How?"

"The rope looked wrong, Ma," Henry said, pointing. "It's different than what I saw online. Aly's getting pics."

"Different how?" I asked

"Some of the rope's been replaced," Joe said.

"This piece is a different color." Aly pointed.

"Online, all the rope was the same," Henry explained. "It could be a different make, or strength, or something."

"Henry asked me if we'd replaced any of the rope in the rigging, and I told him we hadn't," Easton said. "I honestly would not have noticed. Black rope pretty much looks like black rope to me."

"But it's not." Henry reached for one of the coils, and Joe caught his hand, gently but firmly.

"There could be fingerprints," said Joe.

"Oh, that's right." Henry pulled his hands back and bent down. "Look. It's not just different, it's frayed."

"What?"

Joe and I followed Henry's gaze.

If I hadn't just spent the last twenty minutes untangling corset laces, I might have missed it. But the actors' struggles with the laces had left a few damaged spots, and it was clear to me that someone had partly frayed the rope.

"Do you have an evidence bag?" I asked.

"What?" Joe's eyes widened.

"This rope has been tampered with. It's not just different from the other rope in the rigging; it's been frayed."

"Somebody was trying to hurt Mr. Easton," pronounced Henry. His soft, horrified tone conveyed far more shock than a yell could have.

Aly looked up from her phone with wide, concerned eyes.

"But you stopped them, fella," I said quickly.

"You're my hero." Easton held out a hand for Henry to shake. "Nice catch."

"I'm calling DiBiasi," Joe said. "How long was the rigging sitting out there?"

"Not long," Easton said. "Maybe half an hour. My assistant laid it out and then went for a coffee before I got here."

"Enough time for someone to replace one of the ropes with that frayed one," I said, peering closely at the rope, which was uneven in color, unlike the smooth, flat black of the nylon rigging. "It's stage rope, hemp, dyed black."

"Someone connected to the show, then?" Joe said.

"I sure think so." I looked back at the theatre.

CHAPTER THIRTY-FIVE

"Good Lord."

The soft exclamation from Hitch was the first sign of life from him.

"What the hell is going on with this place?" he asked.

"I'd tell you if I knew," I said.

It took all of forty-five seconds for Colby to zip up on his moped. No surprise, he'd planned to start the shift by watching the steeple climb, so he was already on the way when he got the call.

For the next few minutes, we followed the far too familiar format of explaining what we'd seen, where we'd been, and how Colby could find us later. The rookie blocked off the pile of rope on his own, but Joe had to remind him to call in Crime Scene.

Still, Colby was doing a perfectly fine job of running the investigation, and he was wrapping up the initial phase when we heard a furious shriek:

"Holy Mother of Freaking God!"

Everyone turned to see Vic bearing down on us, this time in a holographic lamé caftan with silver sequin trim, obviously extra festive for the last night.

"Do we ever get a break from this horror?" he asked in full melodramatic tones as he rushed up to Colby.

Colby's big eyes widened, and his freckles suddenly stood out. But Raggedy Andy was no pushover. "I'd say the horror was averted, actually, since young Henry here found the tampered rope before Mr. Easton used the rigging."

Vic didn't exactly wilt, but the pushback definitely knocked some of the wind out of his sails. "Hmph."

"And honestly, Mr. Nero, I don't see any reason the show can't go on tonight." The young officer flipped his notebook closed. "I've gathered as much information as I can at the moment. I'd suggest Mr. Easton be extremely cautious about his safety while we sort this out, but there doesn't seem to be a threat to the show at large."

"No?" Vic folded his arms and gave Colby a dubious glare.

"No. You're already taking security precautions, and you'll keep up with those, right?"

"Of course," Hitch said.

"I'm supposed to be off tonight," Colby continued, "but I can swing by to provide some presence, too."

The rookie sounded only a tiny bit excited at the idea.

"Well, that's awfully kind of you, Officer Colby." Hitch held out his hand for a shake. "I'd appreciate it."

"Nice of ya, kid." Vic gave Colby a gruff head shake and grabbed Hitch's arm. "C'mon, co-director. We got work to do."

"You don't know the half of it."

As they headed off to the backstage area, I caught the word 'corset,' and a snort from Vic. I didn't need to hear that conversation.

"So are we good?" Joe asked Colby.

"As good as you're going to get right now. You're going to keep a good eye on Mr. Jeffries, right?"

"We sure are." Joe nodded to Henry. "Might call in a little backup, too."

I knew where he was going. "Ed was going to power-wash the deck today."

Joe and Easton exchanged glances. Deck maintenance is a consuming issue for almost all men here in suburbia, and most would do literally anything to avoid the power-wash, which was usually a spectacularly wet and messy job.

"I'll call him now," Joe said. "Before he gets started."

"Maybe you'll get some points for sparing him the deck wash," Easton suggested with a grin.

"Can't hurt, anyhow." Joe held his friend's gaze. "Sorry about this, buddy."

"You didn't send out somebody to tamper with my rigging," Easton reminded him. "And you did bring the guy who caught it."

Henry beamed.

"Y'know," Easton said, turning to my boy, "we're still going to need those slushies."

"Kule's is the best," Henry nodded.

"Nothing better." Aly, like Henry, looked much less troubled now that slushies were in play.

"You've got this, right?" I asked Joe.

"Absolutely."

"Good. Because I've already sorted out a corset situation, and I have to scoot over to the Society to check on the Empress before showtime—and more corsets."

Joe put a hand on my arm, the apparently casual gesture far more intimate than it looked, as the warmth from his fingers seeped through the thin fabric of my shirt, reminding me of much less neutral contacts.

"Better you than me," he said.

For a moment, we stood there, eyes locked. A week ago, we'd thought we would be enjoying a romantic new phase in our relationship. This was supposed to be our summer romance time, not an episode of some particularly messy police procedural.

Finally, I spoke: "I should go."

"Summer romance."

He'd read my mind.

"What?"

"Let's see if we can't find a way to sneak off for some summer romance. Walk on the beach, even just sit on the deck in the dark. Something."

"Works for me."

His hand slid down my arm, fingers twining with mine for a quick squeeze as he leaned in for a kiss on the cheek. "Just keep a good thought."

"All we can do."

Chapter Thirty-Six

B. Altman's Best

Only in my life would the answer to a murder case start with kitty litter.

While the fellows went for slushies, I had a much less pleasant task: cleaning out the Empress's box and setting up her food and water bowls to get her through to Monday morning.

Odds were good Lewis or one of the lead docents would come through Sunday and check on her, but when you're responsible for an animal, odds aren't good enough. And, anyway, I was the one in charge of the litter box. A board member with more money than sense and a soft spot for the Empress had bought her a top-of-the-line automated one, so it was pretty easy to clean up, once we figured out the technology.

I don't have to tell you that Cookie has a plain old-school box, with clay gravel, the only thing he recognizes as an appropriate bathroom because of his shelter history.

The Empress, though, had taken to the automated piece as her due, and it really was easy to clean. Most of the time, all I had to do was remove one bag of waste, put in a fresh collection bag, and wash my hands. Every once in a while, I had to replace the fine clay sand, but not that week.

Still, it was dealing with cat poop, and not exactly a party.

So, I left it for last, starting by cleaning up the Empress's food area under her watchful supervision and giving her a treat and a pet before getting into the dirty work.

Ultimately, though, nothing for it.

The job really isn't that bad—I kept telling myself, as I walked up from the basement with the bag in hand. The Empress chirped at me as I passed her, clearly wanting more treats.

"Sorry, sweetie. We don't put any more in until we deal with what came out."

She sniffed and ran off.

Out behind the building, our trash bin was waiting. Unless we're putting up or breaking down a big exhibit, or we get a large donation with a lot of packing material, we produce less trash than most private homes, so we have a standard residential bin, enabling us to save a few bucks on a dumpster.

As I reached the bin, I remembered I'd been so busy last week I hadn't even dragged it to the curb Monday night for the Tuesday morning pickup. Ugh, I thought. Last week's cat poo too.

When I lifted the lid, I saw something green sticking out.

I pulled it out and couldn't keep back a scream.

A green blouse, just like the pink one Amy had been wearing this morning, only covered in dried blood. The front was so soaked it was impossible to tell the direction of the spatter. The massive amount of blood you'd see, say, from a slashed carotid artery.

"Oh, holy hell." I dropped the blouse and grabbed my phone.

"Are you okay, Dr. Shaw?"

Colby, running over from the Green, a concerned look on his face.

"I'm fine…but I think I've just found something. This was in the Society trash can. It wasn't emptied last week, so it could be from the night of the murder."

"Do you think the killer was wearing it?"

"They certainly could have been." Trying to keep focus, I picked it back up and looked at the label. B. Altman's, just as Amy had said. Size 6, which would have been even tinier when it was made, probably sometime in the 1950s. And an extra ribbon tag sewn onto the Altman's tag: "Portia."

An actually useful clue.

"Do you want me to bag it up?" Colby asked. "It sure looks like evidence."

"Excellent idea, Officer. My fingerprints will be on it because I found it."

Colby produced an evidence bag from a compartment on his belt and took charge of the shirt. "I'm going to be at the show tonight, so if we need you—"

"Of course. You know where to find me."

So did everybody else, I thought.

Not the happiest thought.

Especially since that blouse had significantly narrowed the field.

Unfortunately, it was time to start buttoning those damn dresses, and I wouldn't have time to do anything about this until intermission.

The show must go on.

Chapter Thirty-Seven

Much Ado About Something

Finally, at intermission, I had time to pull the last pieces of the puzzle together. A little online research gave me the likely provenance of the green blouse, pointing clearly to the one person who could have worn it.

The stage hemp rope dyed black in Easton's rigging didn't hurt, either. I wasn't sure why Easton was a target, but I knew why the killer had chosen that weapon.

And a close look at the prompt book helped clean up motive.

I'd used the book, of course, and looked it over, but I'd never studied it with an eye to the possibility it was a seventeenth-century piece. Everything I'd taken for a hyper-authentic 19th-century copy was actually proof it was the real deal—from about two hundred years earlier. It did make sense; the ancient rag paper held up as well, or better, than the later stock.

The real issue was what I didn't find.

If it was a 19th-century replica, there would have been a page somewhere in the front or back matter to identify it as such. Or a sign that it had been ripped out. In these old sewn books, it's very hard to remove a page without leaving some evidence.

A careful look at the binding, with my knowledge of the old books at the Society, also strongly suggested the original book had been much older. Scientific tests would easily confirm everything.

But I might yet find something better. There should have been some kind of marker to identify the owner. It was probably taken before most institutions used an electronic tracking system, but there should be a label or stamp somewhere.

Nothing in the front matter. I turned the book over and carefully opened it. The last page was stuck to the endpapers. I teased it out, and there it was. Not a bookplate because Sir Jeremy, whatever his faults, was not a stupid criminal. But a square on the paper that was slightly different in color…and a bit sticky, which is why it stuck to the end page.

Confirmation.

Now, the only question was who knew—and who might act on it?

This was at least as valuable as the signet, if far less portable. And it was much more of an "if you know you know."

And only a limited number of people would know.

Had to be somebody who'd worked with Sir Jeremy more than once, which let out most of the company.

But not Alannah.

Who had walked over to Caro and me right when the actress was talking about the prompt book, reminding her of something she'd seen at Yale. And had startled as Caro mentioned that the signet ring looked very old and valuable.

Alannah, who'd laced Caro into her costume just before intermission, right before she collapsed.

Alannah, who'd winced when Easton asked her if she found what she was looking for when he saw her on his way to dinner at Dina's that night. Who really should not have been seen on the Green at that time.

Alannah, who was small, liked vintage clothing and the color green, and had been the costumer on Sir Jeremy's 1950s *Merchant of Venice*. She could easily have kept a blouse from Portia. Wearing the woman judge's blouse to kill Sir Jeremy might have felt appropriate.

But most importantly, I realized, as we reached a scene change: Alannah, who was even now backstage with Hitch, who had called Sir Jeremy a thief in that confrontation Sally Birdwell saw at Sunset Shoreline in Old Saybrook.

Hitch might know almost everything, even if he'd never put it together, and he was clueless enough he'd never see Alannah coming.

Time for the cavalry.

I walked back to Julia and handed her the prompt book. "Take over for me."

"What?"

"Just need to check on something."

"Now?" Her eyes widened in irritation,

"Right now."

I dug my phone out of my dress pocket, dialed Joe, and put it back in, figuring I'd leave the line open if nothing else.

Everything seemed pretty normal backstage, crew members setting up the next scene, actors waiting in the wings for their cue, Vic bustling around like the stage manager he used to be.

But no Hitch.

Without a good idea of where to look, I headed back toward the dressing rooms, thinking I'd ask if anyone had seen either him or Alannah.

Heard a crash from the men's side.

As I turned for the door, I realized I didn't have a weapon, and I grabbed the first thing that came to hand: a broom.

Bringing a broom to a knife fight, I thought.

"*Cara?*" Joe's voice from the phone in my pocket.

I pulled it out. "Backstage. Send the cops."

Another, louder, crash.

I stuffed the phone in my pocket and blasted through the tent flap, brandishing my broom.

"STOP!"

Seemed like a good opening line.

"Oh, thank God, Christian!" Alannah exclaimed. "Hitch just passed out-"

Hitch was sprawled on the floor, groaning.

"No, he didn't." I held her gaze. "I know you killed Sir Jeremy, and I know why."

"You don't know anything."

"Sure I do." I pulled the broom up and across so it made an effective block, then stepped between her and Hitch. "I know you saw the knife sitting out in the Historical Society parlor Friday and grabbed it. I don't know if you knew about the swastika, or if that was just a bonus—"

"My dad's Jewish, Christian. I'm not a monster."

"You might want to apologize to Rabbi Aaron later, then."

Alannah nodded. And then it hit her.

She slouched a bit. Gut punch.

"Yeah, you did just pretty much admit to murder," I said. "I figure you thought you'd steal the book from Sir Jeremy's trailer, and he surprised you. Which he really did, because the book was locked in the box office. So you grabbed the ring and ran."

"The book?" Alannah actually looked puzzled.

"Where's the ring?" I snapped. "Did you sell it already?"

"Where—what—" Hitch.

"You're okay, Hitch," I called. "We're going to have help soon."

"Not soon enough."

Enter Sean, with a gun.

Alannah's husband, the mild-mannered journeyman actor, was holding a very real-looking weapon on me.

"I'm sorry, Doc, I can't let you ruin her. She's already suffered more than enough on my account."

"Oh, Sean," Alannah breathed, in a tone more suited to an anniversary gift.

I'd like to live to have another anniversary, now that you mention it.

"I did it for you," Alannah said. "He ruined you."

"I wasn't that good to begin with, love. But you are, and you're not going down for that-"

"Aw, shuddup!"

Sean crumpled.

Alannah screamed.

Vic stood in the doorway, rubbing his elbow. "Rat bastard has a tough skull."

I used my broom to push the gun out of Sean's reach, and Vic picked it up, glaring at me. "Did you even think to call the cops?"

"She did better." Joe appeared right behind him. "I was on my way here. I finally finished cross-referencing the casts."

Alannah moved to Sean, throwing herself on him and sobbing.

"C'mon, ya mope, you're okay." Vic bent down to kneel beside Hitch, who was shaking his head and blinking hard, trying to figure out where he was.

A more than reasonable reaction.

"FREEZE, PEOPLE!"

DiBiasi, of course.

To a roaring round of applause.

It was just the end of the scene onstage, but it sure felt appropriate.

Chapter Thirty-Eight

Curtain Call

Within five minutes, Alannah was in cuffs, headed for the lockup on murder and grand larceny charges, the ring taken from a long chain around her neck, destined for a secure evidence locker in New Haven. Of course, Joe was off to write it up for arraignment. As for the rest of us, Sean was the property of the medics and Sergeant Ellis, headed to Yale New Haven under guard with what looked like a pretty serious concussion, Hitch was alert, and Vic had stolen his ice pack for his elbow.

And the show just kept going despite all the backstage activity—and even the ambulance speeding away quiet—no lights or sirens needed.

During all of this, I'd been happy to mostly be a bystander, helping Vic watch over Hitch, and exchanging a few significant glances with Joe. We'd have to sort it out later…and we would.

The secure knowledge was more than good enough,

Finally, Vic, Hitch, and I were standing in the once again quiet dressing room.

"Now what?" Hitch asked. "We still have to finish the show, and we have no Leonato."

"Hey, prompter chick." Vic turned to me. "You're tall enough, and you know enough Shakespeare to fake it."

"No way."

He nodded to Hitch, who reached for Leonato's bowler hat.

Vic picked up the long frock coat. "Come here, little girl. This won't hurt a bit..."

Talk about brush up on your Shakespeare.

I hadn't been in front of a big audience since I taught the European History Overview at Shoreline State a decade and a half ago. And I didn't like it any better in Victorian drag. The good news was, my voice still carried, and I could still reel off iambic pentameter. Probably a good thing Ed and Garrett were watching Henry instead of the show.

And really, Leonato wasn't very important. Mostly, I just had to stand up straight and look dignified.

When we reached the end, and the happy couples danced, to thunderous applause, I wanted to dance too. Until I looked into the pit and saw Julia holding her cellphone flashlight up to the prompt book.

She'd figured it out.

Whatever the thing was worth, it would keep the Festival going for a long while...or pay for Julia's escape to someplace she could spend her golden years living out her zero-zero motto.

Surely not.

Well, after this week, anything was possible. As soon as the curtain fell, I ran down to her and grabbed the book.

She kept her grip.

"Don't even think it," I hissed.

"What are you talking about?"

"There's a reward."

Julia's hands loosened but didn't release. "A good one?"

"I don't know pounds to dollars, but it was five figures, so..."

"Okay. But who gets it?"

"Only fair that it goes to the company, right? Since it was found during your production..."

Finally, she let go but held my gaze suspiciously. "We're going to get something out of this?"

"I'm sure."

"Shaw!" Vic yelled from the wings. "Get the hell up here and take your bow!"

And so I did, arms wrapped around the book, as Vic announced me as a last-minute understudy.

The applause went on for seemingly forever. Finally, the curtain dropped for the last time.

At long last, safe and done.

With the damn book.

I spotted Colby in the wings, flirting with Lita.

Realized she was a fascinating older woman to him.

"Hey! Officer Colby!" I called. "Can you take a piece of evidence for me?"

"Sorry, Lita, gotta go to work."

She gave him a naughty grin. "Meet me when your shift's over?"

Our Beatrice, a badge bunny? Colby *was* adorable, well, if you were into Raggedy Andy. And there was the night of the fire, after all.

He returned Lita's grin with a spark that would have concerned me if I were his mom, which, heaven help me, I was almost old enough to be.

"What's up, Doc?" he asked, then laughed and blushed. "Um, yeah."

"Please take this book to Mr. Poli," I said, loudly enough for Lita to hear. "It's a key piece of evidence in the case, and there's a very large reward on it."

Colby beamed. "Absolutely. He's still at the police station with the suspects. I'll be happy to voucher it and start the process."

"Thanks."

He sent Lita another adorable smile and got a wolfish look in return. I sure hoped Colby's parents had given him the talk. Well, I supposed Lita could figure it out.

"Brava!"

I turned to see Hitch, freshly patched up by Tiffany, and Vic applauding. Applauding me.

"Awww, thanks."

"Well, you caught the killer—and saved the show."

I bowed to them. "And the book will go back where it belongs."

"And so will we."

"We?" I stared at the men.

"Well, we seem to work well together," Hitch said.

Vic punched his arm lightly. "We're thinking of starting our own production company."

"After a decent interval, of course," added Hitch.

"The ex of my ex…" I started.

Vic laughed. "We may even call it that—X of X Productions."

"Good luck," I said.

"We'll probably need a good consultant for period projects occasionally," Hitch said.

"Top of the scale, of course, doc," added Vic.

"Call me anytime," I assured them.

"Want to come to the after-party at the cabins in Old Saybrook?" Hitch asked.

"No way. We're presuming on our babysitter's goodwill as it is. But if you're up at brunch time tomorrow, come to Malina's. We'll be on the patio."

"All of you?" asked Hitch.

"You get one, you get us all," I assured him. "You have no idea."

"But I think I'd like to build something like that," Vic said.

"I hope you do."

My phone rang. The sound made me jump.

I laughed, and so did the guys, because it was so silly to startle at something so small after everything.

Until I saw the screen.

Henry.

"Sweetheart, are you okay?" I asked, walking toward the exit.

"I'm fine, Ma. Aren't you supposed to be done?"

"Aren't you supposed to be asleep?"

"Aly and I are playing Dragon Race. She's kicking my butt."

"I bet she is." I sighed. Because she's a kid too. "Isn't it still past your bedtime?"

"That's what Aly said. I played her for it and lost."

"And now you want me to step in?" I asked.

"Would you?"

"Nope. She's the babysitter. You know the rules."

"Fine." He growled, and I held back a sigh of relief, glad that this, at least, was simple, and not dangerous.

"Everything's fine, fella."

"Did AlysDad get the bad guy?"

"It was a bad woman, and we all pulled together and got her."

"Nice." A pause, and then my very cool medium-sized guy came back sounding like a kid. "I think I want to come home with you, Ma."

"On my way."

Chapter Thirty-Nine

Sfogliatelle and Surprises

If Mr. Shakespeare had been New Haven Italian, he would have said: all's well that ends with brunch at Malina's.

Villains appropriately vanquished, the run successfully completed, and my stage career absolutely, positively, immovably over, it was indeed time to sort it all out in the best way possible. Unity's favorite family spot was trying out a "Bellini Brunch" on the patio for the summer, and it was darn near irresistible for the whole town.

Visitors, too. Lyman Damer was outside her giant SUV on the Green again, with a familiar-looking takeout bag beside her kit. Too bad it wasn't in the shot.

Malina's deserves all the praise we can give them.

This wasn't one of those overdone hotel-restaurant spectaculars, but rather a warm and wonderful little buffet of frittatas, breakfast meats, summer fruit, and pastries. *Sfogliatelle*, the shell-shaped, multilayered puffs filled with sweet cream, were the marquee treat, fresh from Ersalesi's Bakery, the premier Italian pastry shop in New Haven. Around here, everybody knows *sfogliatelle* are both wonderful and practically impossible to make outside a bakery, so Malina's drew nothing but praise for putting them out with an Ersalesi's card by the platter.

Since most of us had walked to the restaurant, and the bellinis weren't high-octane anyhow, we had a pitcher for the table, and the majority grown-ups had a taste, just enough to be happy and relaxed.

After an amiable trip through the buffet line, everybody reassembled at our table, the biggest one on the patio—with affiliated overflow in nearby seats: Lewis and his aunt, two Historical Society volunteers, and board chair Victoria Peters, plus Julia Henshaw from the Shakespeare Festival and a couple of sturdy young men who were her sons and/or nephews. Even Joe's parents were there, several tables away with the after-Mass group from Star of the Sea.

In short, just about everybody we knew except Vic and Hitch, who were probably sleeping off some serious drinking. Maybe alone, maybe together… none of my business.

Henry and Ava seemed to be busy with some new video app, and Aly was catching up on the band kid group chat—but the parental units didn't mind devices this one time, because we did have an awful lot of mess from the previous night to discuss.

Joe skipped the bellinis in favor of a double espresso because he'd been up hours later than I had, dropping off Alannah in the lockup before swinging back to his house to get some sleep. Aly, with all the imperious empowerment of a fifteen-year-old, had insisted on staying home alone, brushing off my offer to come back to my house.

I supposed I could have just crashed at Joe's and tried to rescue the sleepover, but by then, Henry and I were too tired to do anything other than go home to Cookie. A win for the cat, anyhow.

By morning, though, when Joe and Aly appeared at our house to walk with us to Molina's, having left Cannoli with the TV and plenty of treats, the awkward moment was long gone. Aly happily petted Cookie and teased Henry about beating him at Dragon Race. Which Henry loved. Since preschool, he's adored girls who push him around a little.

It occurred to me that yet another potential landmine seemed to have been defused.

With the amazing brunch, it was easy enough to follow our usual informal agreement to focus on greetings and food first, and move into serious matters once everyone was fed. Considering the high drama level, though, it wasn't really surprising that Ed only let Joe take a few sips and bites of his caprese frittata before he pounced:

"So, was it the ring, the book, or the husband?"

"All three."

Everyone turned to me, as I realized I'd answered for Joe.

Ed looked stunned. Joe laughed first, then Garrett, and everyone else joined in.

"She's right," Joe said, raising his espresso to me. "Want to start?"

"Thank you, Counselor," I said, taking a sip of bellini and clearing my throat. "It all started at a small British college in the 1990s."

"C'mon, Christian," Ed said, scowling over his coffee cup.

"Well, it did." You bet I was going to show off some of the research I'd done for Joe while he talked to the Brits. "The trail starts at Northumbria Community College. One Gerald O'Hara, who sure looks like our guy, taught literature and led the drama club for a couple of years."

"How did we get from Gerald O'Hara to Sir Jeremy Hightower?" Tiffany asked.

"Well, it seems Gerald was involved with the Dean of Arts, a sweet older fellow who was the last surviving member of an obscure border clan," I continued.

"Romantically?" asked Garrett.

"The local DCI seemed to think so," Joe said, glad to have something to contribute. "She described it as a romance scam, and I have no reason to doubt her take."

"Why's the local DCI involved?" asked Ed.

"Because one rainy day in May, the Dean of Arts was found dead at the bottom of a staircase in the family pile, a National Trust property. And several valuable pieces were missing." Joe took another sip of espresso. "Including a signet ring."

"With a bend, balls, and lozenges," I added. "Not the Hightower crest."

"And then he just shows up in London to direct?" asked Tiffany.

"First, the newly christened Sir Jeremy managed to get on with another small college, this time in Cornwall, about as far as it's possible to be from

Northumbria and still be in England. The book—and another one that was apparently sold on the black market—came from there," I explained. "There are news stories about the disappearance."

"Who is he at this point?" asked Ed.

"By now, he's Jeremy Hightower," Joe said. "Er, Sir Jeremy."

"People believed the title—in Britain?" Dina asked.

Ben looked puzzled, too. "Those don't grow on trees."

"Claimed it was a family legacy," I said. "And told people not to use it."

"So of course they did." Garrett nodded. "Brilliant."

"Slick, for sure." Tiffany broke off a corner of her first *sfogliatelle*. There would be at least one more—they're the only pastry she can't resist, other than her mom's *trés leches* cake.

"Soon enough, Sir Jeremy signs on with a regional theatre company and leaves. Because it's a small school, security was rather casual—and he was smart enough not to take them all, it was quite a while before they realized the two playscripts were gone."

"One of which was *Much Ado?*" Garrett asked.

"And another that disappeared into the black market?" I asked.

"It was a *Hamlet*," Joe said. "Probably got plenty for that."

"Somebody will pay a ton for anything," growled Ed, snapping the tip off a big strawberry.

"Looks that way." Joe nodded. "Now, Alannah worked with him in that first big production after Cornwall. A 1950s-set *Merchant of Venice*."

"Alannah and her husband," I reminded him. "Sean, at that point, was a rising actor."

"Or thought he was," Joe said. "Everybody I've talked to says he was good—but not lightning in a bottle."

"And you have to be to make it," Julia cut in from her table. "He had some anxiety issues, too."

"Alannah blamed Hightower for that," Joe said. "She kept saying he ruined her husband."

"He did apparently do something terrible to Sean's confidence," I explained. "He never had a lead role again after that show."

"All right," Ed said. "So he undercuts Sean to the point he's no good for anything but bits…but he likes Alannah's work enough that he keeps hiring her for costumes?"

"Seems that way," Joe agreed.

"Maybe he enjoyed seeing Sean suffer, too," Garrett said. "Seems like he was the kind of guy who'd go for that."

"Really?" asked Dina.

"Rabbi," Ed said, "this is one time that speaking ill of the dead is probably necessary."

"I guess so." She picked up her bellini. "I'll just follow along."

"So Sir Jeremy builds this amazing career on his ability to snow producers and bully actors—" I looked to Julia, who nodded. "And he decides to take a break from Vic and come over here for the summer."

"After the fight involving glitter and tequila," Tiffany reminded us with a snicker.

"Can't forget the glitter and tequila." Ben grinned as he looked up from his frittata.

"Which brings us to last week," Joe said. "Alannah decides she doesn't feel like going through another horrible run with this guy. She figures she'll take the ring and get out once and for all."

"Why now?"

"Sean," I said. "I didn't think much of it at the time, but the day before, I'd heard Sir Jeremy yelling at him. And that morning, he said something to me about being done with the two of them."

"How did she know about the book?" Dina asked.

"She worked with him right after Cornwall," I said. "She may have known all along and just bided her time. Until he pushed her over the edge."

"And then, it all happened pretty quickly." Joe took up the story. "They were the last two people at the theatre every night, so she figures she'll mug him as he goes back to his trailer. Whack him over the head, take the ring and book, and run. The timing—a week before opening—only added to the element of surprise."

"The knife was probably just insurance," I said. "I don't think she went out that night intending to kill him."

Though, admittedly, some of the facts might suggest otherwise. That was for the lawyers.

"Still first-degree murder," Joe said. "Murder in the line of another felony, namely theft."

"Whatever she planned," Dina cut in, "she did not have to kill him. And she did."

"True," Joe took a bit more coffee. "As best I can tell, from what little she's saying and the M.E.'s report, she whacked him over the head as he walked into the trailer…but he didn't lose consciousness."

"Attacking people is harder than it looks on stage," I said. "She panicked?"

"Apparently. Then she searched the trailer, looking for the playscript."

"But it was the prompt book, locked in the box office."

"Ah—here's the fun part," Joe said. "She didn't know it was the prompt book until I told her."

A chorus of "what's" rippled around the table.

"Apparently, she was looking for something smaller," he explained.

Julia nodded. "Some old prompt books are about the size of a paperback."

"Those are the ones actors used," I said. "The one used by the actual prompter or director would be larger. She was really looking for the wrong thing?"

"Apparently so. And you were using it in plain sight the whole time." Joe held my gaze for a moment.

"Yeah." I took a sip of bellini.

"All's well that ends well," Garrett said.

"Time wounds all heels, if we're doing old saws," Ed added.

"Anyhow, we've got her for murder, and that's all I care about," Joe said.

"I think we can drink to that," Tiffany agreed. "And we're done with the theatre people until the next summer."

"Hey!" Julia snapped.

"You're ours, so you're okay," Tiffany assured her. "Have some more bellini."

"Can't argue with that." Julia grabbed her pitcher and filled her glass.

"And a happy ending to all," Garrett said, holding out his glass to Tiffany, who topped it.

"Well, isn't this a great brunch!"

I recognized the voice and froze.

The Mad Knitters had landed.

My mother waved at me and grinned as her buddies trooped in behind her.

"Ersalesi's *sfogliatelle*! What could be better?" Suzanne cooed, beaming at the server.

"Talent pool looks pretty good, too," said Peg, her gaze landing on Ed.

Well, that would be easy enough to brush off, at least.

Thank goodness we'd just finished sorting out the murder. The last thing any of us needed was mystery fan Peg critiquing the solution.

"Aren't you looking lovely, Christian," Suzanne proclaimed. "And you must be Joe. Thank you for inviting us."

Joe blushed.

Inviting them? He deliberately did this to me?

Okay, then. Mr. State's Attorney might have to deal with another felony soon.

"Come see the buffet, Mom," I said, motioning to her and the ladies, and shooting a glare back to Joe.

My beloved beamed back at me.

It's probably felony murder to strangle a prosecutor.

No jury would convict me.

By the time I got the Knitters fed and settled, there was a pitcher of bellinis at their table, and fresh pitchers at ours.

"Everything good?" Joe asked with a maddening smile.

"All fine." I poured myself a very generous glass of bellini. "Why don't *you* go hang with the Knitters for a while?"

"Um, no. I have other things to do."

He poured himself a bit of bellini from the pitcher and shot it, then looked at Garrett and Ed.

They nodded.

Joe flicked his eyes to Mom.

Another nod.

That's when I got the hint.

Joe took a breath and glanced at Aly, who gave him a big smile.

When Joe stood, I was almost sure—but when he turned to Henry, I knew beyond a reasonable doubt, as my favorite prosecutor might say.

"What do you say, pal?" he asked.

"Go for it, AlysDad."

Joe grinned. "If Dr. Shaw would be so kind as to turn my way?"

I moved my chair.

"Thank you." He gave me a cute little bow, and then, as everyone in the restaurant turned to stare, he dropped down on one knee in front of me.

For a few seconds, I couldn't breathe.

Even though I'd seen it coming, the moment still hit hard.

My eyes filled.

Damn.

"*Dottore*, will you do me the honor of allowing me to step on the glass at a big Italian wedding?"

He pulled a small box out of his pocket. "The big Italian wedding isn't negotiable."

"Neither is the glass." I took off my wedding band and held it in my right hand.

"So?"

"Where's the John Donne?"

"*If our two loves be one, or thou and I*
Love so alike that none can slacken, none can die."

Last lines of "The Good Morrow," a perfect wedding poem.

For a moment, my throat choked with unshed tears. Then I managed a breath, as my eyes spilled over: "Yes."

"Sure you don't want to see the ring first?"

"No. But I want it now." I held out my hand.

He opened the box to reveal a tiny band of jeweled flowers.

"Not your usual engagement ring. Figured you'd want something with history." He settled the smooth little ring in place. "It's a reproduction of one a duke gave a diva at the turn of the 20th century. They had a long and happy marriage. And you can see, the design won't get in the way of your work."

"It's perfect. But how did you get this so fast?"

"Bought it weeks ago. I've known for a while."

I squeezed his fingers. "So have I."

"Gorgeous, Ma," said Henry.

"Henry, do you want to help me with this?" I motioned him over, as I threaded his father's ring onto my right hand, and he put his hand over mine as I pushed it the rest of the way.

My son's eyes, so like Frank's, held mine for a moment. No moving forward without remembering how we got here.

I pulled Henry close, and he snuggled in. "Nice, Ma."

"Love the ring, Dr. Christian." Aly piled on, and Joe wrapped us all in a big group hug.

And they all lived happily ever after.

Acknowledgments

Many thanks, as always, to my editor, Shawn Reilly Simmons, and agent, Mira Perrizo.

Special thanks to my best beta reader, Julie Von Wettberg, and neighbor Liliana Felix for their insight on life as the mother of a son with T1D, and how adults manage the condition.

And last, but never, ever least, to my family—of blood, work, and affection—I can't thank you enough for all your support and understanding. It doesn't happen without you.

With love, respect, and appreciation,
Kathleen Marple Kalb

About the Author

Kathleen Marple Kalb describes herself as an Author/Anchor/Mom... not in that order. An award-winning weekend anchor at New York's 1010 WINS Radio, she writes short stories and novels including the Old Stuff and Ella Shane series, both from Level Best Books. Her stories, under her own name, and as Nikki Knight, have been in *Alfred Hitchcock's Mystery Magazine, Black Cat Weekly, Mystery Magazine*, and others, and nominated for Agatha, Derringer and Black Orchid Novella Awards. Active in writer's groups, she's served as Vice President of the Short Mystery Fiction Society and Co-VP of the New York/Tri-State Sisters in Crime Chapter. She, her husband, and son live in a Connecticut house owned by their cat.

AUTHOR WEBSITE:
   https://kathleenmarplekalb.com/

SOCIAL MEDIA HANDLES:
   Facebook: https://www.facebook.com/Kathleen-Marple-Kalb-108294 9845220373/
   Instagram: https://www.instagram.com/kathleenmarplekalb/
   Threads: @kathleenmarplekalb

Bluesky: @mysterymarple.bsky.social

Also by Kathleen Marple Kalb

Old Stuff Mysteries:
The Stuff of Murder (2023)
The Stuff of Mayhem (2025)

Ella Shane Mysteries
A Fatal Finale (2020)
A Fatal First Night (2021)
A Fatal Overture (2022)
A Fatal Reception (2024)
A Fatal Honeymoon (novella, available free online, 2024)
A Fatal Waltz (2025)
A Fatal Flourish (forthcoming, 2026)

Vermont Radio Mysteries – As Nikki Knight
Live, Local and Dead (2022)
Live, Local, and LONG Dead (2024)

Grace the Hit Mom Mysteries – As Nikki Knight
Wrong Poison (2023)
Hound of the Bonnevilles (2025)
Murder on the Sea Otter Express (2026)

Short Stories in Magazines, Anthologies, and online, including:
"Other Voices Carry," in *Snakeberry:* Best New England Crime Stories, 2025

"All that Kissy Stuff," in *Crimeucopia: What the Butler Didn't See*, September 2025

"Boss Cat Rules," in Malice Domestic Anthology, *Mystery Most Humorous*, 2025

"Public Affairs Homicide," in *Devil's Snare*: Best New England Crime

Stories, 2024

"Mow Way Out," an Old Stuff Mystery, Black Cat Weekly, September 2024

"Things Look Different Up Here," in New York/TriState Sisters in Crime Anthology, *New York State of Crime*, September 2024

"Sorry Not Sorry," an Old Stuff mystery, M2D4, Mysteries to Die For Podcast and Anthology, Summer 2024 season

"A Fatal Saint Patrick's Day" (Ella Shane Mystery) in *Luck of the Irish* Anthology, March 2024

"No Angels Here," Black Cat Weekly, December 2023

"The New York Goodbye," Black Cat Weekly, September 2023

"The Telltale Request," *Mystery Magazine*, September 2023

"Second Chances are…Murder," *Malice, Matrimony, and Murder* Anthology, November 2023

"Pie a La Poison," in *The Perp Wore Pumpkin*, Misti Media, November 2023

"The Custodian of the Body," (Old Stuff Mystery), Black Cat Weekly, May 2023

"This Never Happened to Wolfman Jack," M2D4 Podcast August 2023, season anthology, November 2023

"Don't Mess with the Boss Cat," CatsCast Podcast by Escape Artists, June 2023

"The Annual Mud Season Homicide," *Alfred Hitchcock's Mystery Magazine*, May/June 2023

"Owl Be Damned," Mysteryrat's Maze Podcast, January 2023

"Blame it on the Blizzard," *Deadly Nightshade: Best New England Crime Stories 2022*